Praise for *To A Strange Somewhere Fled*

To open the pages of a historical novel written by D.M. Denton is to find that the past is no longer a foreign country.

In this beautifully realized sequel to *A House Near Luccoli*, the author once again effortlessly blends the vividly imagined fictional character Donatella with real-life historical figures and settings to create a world that is as beguiling as it is believable.

We are invited to follow Donatella's progress as she faces a very different future from the one she had begun to imagine for herself – without the quixotic musical genius who reawakened her passions and zest for life, the 17th century Italian composer, Alessandro Stradella.

This is a subtle, understated exploration of love and lost possibility and there are no easy answers or conventional happy endings. As Albert Schweitzer wrote, 'In everyone's life, at some time, our inner fire goes out. It is then burst into flame by an encounter with another human being'. There can be no better description of Donatella's encounter with Stradella in *A House Near Luccoli* – but now living in England, and haunted by vivid memories of her time with him in Italy, what can life hold for her?

The author's characterization of both her fictional and real-life characters is convincing and compelling. We find that those with exceptional, other-worldly gifts are also all too ordinary, standing in this world with feet of clay, while 'mere mortals' can become extraordinary in the depth of their passion and the stoicism of their self-reliance and restraint in the face of loss and disappointment. Donatella, her heart awoken and then broken, remains 'another man's secret'. She can perhaps reveal herself again, but surrender has many guises.

Scrupulously researched and historically accurate, the novel immerses the reader in its historical period. That we can meet Purcell within these pages and find him totally believable as a living, breathing human being is a mark of the author's imaginative powers and literary skill. There are, appropriately enough, no false notes to be found.

History is never cut and dried, and the author is careful to leave us with Donatella in a moment of time, her future rendered uncertain by a past she can't or won't relinquish.

~D. Bennison, bennisonbooks.com

In this tour-de-force book, D.M. Denton shows her command of a distinctive point of view and a writing style that enables her to communicate it. Her style breaks the rules, but it is just this breaking up and apart that reveals her character's experiences in new and unexpected ways. It allows for flourishes, nuances, changes in pace, and variations on themes, as music does. With delicacy and sureness, the author works with her themes of memory, love, and loss. Grief and love vibrate throughout.

Donatella is a spinster, young, but not too young, who captures the wayward musician/composer Alessandro Stradella's imagination, in *A House Near Luccoli*. In this sequel, Donatella has moved from her native Genoa to live with her father, now a retired sea captain, near the small town of Wroxton in the English countryside. She carries with her not only the memory of the extraordinary Stradella, who has been murdered, but some of his musical compositions as well. In this way she can keep a part of him with her, and protect his work from his enemies.

She is attuned to her rich interior life, as it is her most constant companion. This subliminal stream of images, emotions and thoughts, affords her a form of transcendence by overcoming time, as it links past, present and future.

Coming to a new and alien place, Donatella finds she has more freedom to explore the world. As she navigates the subtleties of unexpected relationships, she begins to open up, with the mature beauty of a late bloomer, made more enticing by her shyness and modesty. Her mother's overt and indiscriminate sexual flirtations offer a sharp contrast to Donatella's smoldering, deep-banked passion and careful sensuality. It is her virtue that attracts men. This is not the same as innocence; she is well aware of the human condition.

Donatella is intoxicated by her passion, which frightens her for what it might lead her to do. This is a story of a woman's passion, whether it is the bliss of a walk in the woods, or the transporting joy of music, or the recognition of loving and being loved by another. What an inspired and informed imagination to portray the young Henry Purcell. The composer is still finding his way, as are Donatella and another young man. Purcell appreciates the work of Stradella, and others who preceded him, even as he struggled to promote his own. The author's descriptions of music, particular musicians, and musical performances make this book a work of art itself. *To A Strange Somewhere Fled* is a virtuoso performance.

~ **Mary Clark, author of Tally: An Intuitive Life**

The music continues in *To A Strange Somewhere Fled*, D.M. Denton's lovely sequel to *A House Near Luccoli*. This story follows Donatella and her mother, Julianna, to England and to the home of Donatella's father, the Captain. The great musician, Alessandro Stradella, whom Donatella had loved, is gone now, but she has her memories in the form of copies of his never performed compositions. Those works are of great interest to the musicians in the novel, including the English composer, Henry Purcell and the Italian violinist, Carlo Ambrogio Lonati, both of whom play roles in Denton's story.

This plot is as much about music as Donatella's first story, which covered the time when she was a copyist for Stradella, but in this novel Donatella's role as a performer is emphasized, along with her relationship with Roger North, a neighbor and friend of her father's.

Denton writes with a lyrical style which swells, fades, and swells again, creating a perfect setting through its tone as much as its meticulous description. Her words pull her readers to 17th century England like music from that era.

In North Carolina driving from Asheville to Boone presents a choice. A driver can stick to the interstates or opt to take the Blue Ridge Parkway. The latter decision takes an extra hour or so, but along the way there are opportunities to stop at overlooks and enjoy scenes that are among the most magnificent in America. D.M. Denton's writing presents a similar choice. It takes a little longer to read than most books of a similar page length, but along the way there are breathtaking moments which make the choice a wise one.

~ **Steve Lindahl, author of** *White Horse Regressions* **and** *Motherless Soul*

Praise for *A House Near Luccoli*

Alessandro Stradella was a legend in his time, a celebrated composer who took Italy in the 17th century by storm; wrestled from fame to infamy, Stradella received accolades and evictions alike, finally coming to Genoa after being sent from Rome, Turin, and Venice. Despite his scandals, his seductive genius for Baroque music and his overwhelming charm reserved for him a place of esteem within the nobility of Genoa.

In D.M. Denton's languid new novel, *A House Near Luccoli*, the author examines the famed composer's time in Genoa through the lens of fiction, centering her story on the house near Luccoli Street where Stradella rented an apartment and filling it with her own brand of characters. Among them is the novel's protagonist, Donatella. Plain and a confirmed spinster, Donatella resides in and tends to the house near Luccoli along with her ailing grandmother and domineering aunt. When Stradella sweeps into the quiet house Donatella becomes enraptured with the world he offers, so much different than the life she planned to live with her bloom fading before even having the chance to fully blossom. After beginning work for Stradella as a copyist, his passionate realm of intrigue and music, artists and royalty, envelops Donatella's curiosity just as she begins to lose herself to the beguiling and reckless composer. But as her longings war with her own simple reality, she must find strength within to keep from being trampled among Stradella's many admirers and his own larger-than-life persona.

A House Near Luccoli is as charmingly crafted as Stradella's compositions, often mirroring their power, beauty, and delicate intricacy. It's a novel at once intimate and expansive, quickly ushering the reader into the vivid 17th century world of Stradella and exposing the history of a lesser-known genius while enfolding them in a fictitious story of romance, friendship, art, and intrigue.

Denton's narrative is complex and challenging, steeped in a richness that befits the grandeur of the time period. Her use of language and her inventive storytelling captured me from the first page; some passages of dialogue felt more abstractly constructed than others, lending me the enchanting image of an artist's story being told through an equally artistic medium. I enjoyed the freedom she displayed in writing. Her depiction of Stradella presented an absorbing study of a truly fascinating man, and left my interest piqued to discover more about himself and his music. In Donatella I found a protagonist I was keenly drawn to. She is perhaps a daring choice for a heroine, at times appearing melancholy in her situation at the house in Genoa, but I felt an understanding with Donatella, a timid woman with an artist's fiery spirit inside, who has somehow managed to lose her life to her own daydreams. Her interests have captivated her while her longings have been left dormant, only to be brought to surprising life by Stradella and all his colorful, vibrant artistry. The relationship forged between the duo, sometimes a friendship, sometimes a romance, sometimes a turbulent bundle of unknown feelings, is one I was loathe to let go of at the book's final pages.

Additional characters are ever on hand through Denton's story to create more intrigues and offer new dramatic surprises. It culminated into an ending that held me in rapt attention and made me want to immerse myself in the book all over again. Compelling, stimulating, and studiously researched, *A House Near Luccoli* is a beautiful representation of the boundlessness of historical fiction, and a story as sumptuous and engaging as the man at its center.

~ **Casee Marie Clow, literaryinklings.com**

A House Near Luccoli by D.M. Denton is a fictionalized account of the last year in the life of little-known Italian Baroque composer and performer Alessandro Stradella. Told through the eyes of one of his fellow lodgers, *A House Near Luccoli* is a portrait of the complex love Stradella inspired in others, as well as a celebration of his love for beauty and music. Meticulously researched, with great attention to historical detail, *A House Near Luccoli* is marked by poetic prose and literary flair, in a style very consistent with its subject matter. The trenchant and lovely dialogue is matched by passages of lyrical description that often leave the reader breathless. The book is a frequently beautiful, heady read by an author in firm control of the story, and possessed by a tireless ability to bedazzle. *A House Near Luccoli* inspires interest in the time period and culture of this under-appreciated composer. It is to this book and its author that I owe thanks for my introduction to Stradella's music, a source of inspiration that has become part of my daily ritual.

~**Matthew Peters, author of** *Conversations Among Ruins* **and** *The Brothers' Keepers*

Every facet of this book is wrapped in beautiful language. The plot and setting, characters and pace, all live within layers of poetry:

"…Nonna blamed a tendency to malinconia on her granddaughter's English side with too much rain in her blood. As if climate could be inherited…"

"She wanted to show ability beyond the ladylike diversion of scribbling thoughts or painting in a journal, obsessing over the responsibility for something greater than nothing better to do."

"She hoped they would be early or late to avoid scrutiny, but they were on time for her to be judged as an unescorted woman passing through a hall made for giants…"

I know very little about classical music or opera, and even less about 17th century Genoa, so the book unfolded for me as a lovely riddle. Musical terminology and Italian words added ambience, even as I stumbled over their strangeness. Scenes hid behind place names, ambled through unfamiliar streets and landmarks. But the story never failed me. I never felt forced out of the plot or detached from the characters.

The book's "Intimacy & Intrigue" are subtle, a veiled background of motive. The settings are lush, the characters complex, and the pace measured. It's an intricate portrait of loneliness, of the fragile passions that inspire music.

~Rae Spenser, raespencer.com

Imagine yourself a woman caring for a beloved grandmother and under the thumb of a domineering aunt. Imagine yourself in Genoa in the late seventeenth century, a woman circumscribed by being a woman in an era when women's single role was to get married and have children. One of the most reliable story plots begins like this: A stranger comes to town. And so begins Diane Denton's novel. The stranger is Stradella, famed Baroque composer, a roue driven from other towns and settling here, in a house with three women and a sexy young servant. Which one will bed him? Will he seduce rich women and make himself persona non grata here as well? Or has he come here to make, not mischief, but music? Will the sound of that music spill down into the grandmother's bedroom, a private concert, and will Stradella somehow come to know that Donatella, the thirtiesh spinster, is musically trained and could be of great help to him?

I love historical novels and any story that features a genius and the person who stands behind the genius: a muse, an amanuensis, a lover. Back in late seventeenth century Genoa, inevitably, that person would have been a woman. When Stradella, the feted Baroque composer, takes up residence in her house, Donatella is drawn to him as a moth to flame. The minuet of their attraction and our curiosity about whether the famous Stradella will recognize her gifts kept me reading from the first page to the last. The sentences in this poetic and evocative novel will echo long after you finish the story, but like poetry, you may find yourself slowing down to savor the whispers and stand, for just a minute, at the open window. If you like *Girl with the Pearl Earring* (book or movie), you will love this book.

~ **Marylee MacDonald, author of** *Montpelier Tomorrow*

A House Near Luccoli is a character-driven novel about the flamboyant Baroque composer, Alessandro Stradella. Recognized as a genius, he is wildly eccentric and irresistibly charming. His bold, gregarious personality, eccentric manner, and ungodly manners both endear and repel. When he flees Venice after a scandalous affair, he arrives in Genoa. He moves into an apartment in the same house where the unmarried, youthful spinster Donatella lives. She is thrilled when he hires her as his copyist. Donatella soon succumbs to this enigmatic man, his fascinating life and work. The more she is drawn into his life, the more she must struggle to maintain her own identity.

Author D.M. Denton writes with verve and great style. In Alessandro and Donatella she has recreated the romance between them with vivid believability. The 17th century is a period of extremes – lavish wealth and devastating poverty, lofty heights and dire circumstances. As the story unfolds and more of each character is revealed, I got a strong sense of the times, its foods, clothing, music, and art. Alessandro is a lovable rogue, a bad boy who never seems to learn from his mistakes. Ultimately, it all catches up to him in a tragic ending.

I always enjoy novels of unique historical settings with lesser known heros and heroines of the times. This is one such novel. Very well put together and researched. Highly recommended.

~**Mirella Patzer, author, historicalnovelreview.blogspot.ca**

A House Near Luccoli

A Novel of Musical Intimacy & Intrigue in 17th Century Genoa

DM Denton

CHAPTER ONE

She didn't fuss with her hair or use the vain clutter of the dressing table except to waste time rearranging it. Eventually she turned to what was behind her. Laid over a small unmade bed and the chair beside it were two fancy gowns, creased and dated, suiting a younger shape and needing somewhere to go. She was sure she wouldn't wear them again.

"Donatella? Are you in your room?"

The lace might be salvaged, for she couldn't be without lace, at least around her neck and, at most, edging her sleeves as well. Otherwise she dressed serviceably, invisibly, in gray or dark blue.

She no longer thought of being bolder or more submissive or, in a city on a bay-becoming-the-sea, swept away at last.

It was as if someone else recalled a ship, who sailed on it, and walking down a shady alley with a stranger. There was always the temptation of mixing imagination with reality, especially as the past was otherwise inalterable. Her reflection was plain in the mirror, her hair quickly pinned, her face flushed.

"Donatella, I need you!"

She moved to a corner table, begging light from a narrow window, cleaning brushes and closing colors yet to finish curled pictures of spring or begin the next season before it did. She had painted in brighter places, dreamed in them, too, and didn't care who saw her as a dreamer, until she committed herself to being withdrawn and forgotten like a lunatic huddled in a corner, hardly knowing the difference between a smile and a frown.

"You might answer me!"

She took the green dress off the bed and pretended to wear it for a small stroll around the room. Then she walked into the hall as if out into the city; her city, at least, as it was also born of land and sea, formed by highs and lows, ruled by outer constraint and inner abandon, safe and sorry in disguise. Of course *Genova* had a conceit she couldn't have, knowing its purpose and hiding or flaunting its features of beauty. Once she saw all its wonders and woes from the esplanade of *Castelletto*, the mountains closer and the *Lanterna* further away. Perhaps she made out her house; if not its signature portal of Saint George and the Dragon, then a signifying shine on its roof's slant. It was a prestigious place to live depending on how she looked at it, whether connected up to a parade of palaces, across divides or down crooked stairways to the port.

She was patron and prisoner of a gated entrance and more rooms than the closeness of the surrounding dwellings allowed, aspiring staircases growing them similarly into multiple stories. She could have done without so much unused furniture, mirrors, and silver to be cleaned but was greedily accustomed to a tenanted wealth of paintings, tapestries, frescos, and stained glass not created for outside views.

"There you are. What are you doing?"

Donatella had barely reached the doorway of her bedroom, throwing the dress in, not caring where it landed.

"Oh, it's so sudden."

Her aunt gave her a key and feather duster for gentler work than Nubesta carrying broom and bucket, hastening an end to the long vacancy of the third floor apartment, a little unnerving to step into its past. It offered another chore for the young maid complaining about wiping tall windows while Donatella removed furniture covers and thought of her mother sitting there, writing more letters than she ever received.

The girl opened a window and the room to the street below, a rag-waving hand jumping out. "Up here! Up here!"

Donatella felt a shiver that shouldn't have surprised her, the bumping and cursing of the movers fading into music and poetry from *La forza dell'amor paterno* as performed at the *Teatro Falcone* on Christmas Monday 1678. She had worn the green dress, agreeing to excessive curls and anticipation, Nonna encouraging her to fan away smoke from the chandeliers and smile although her shoes pinched. After the first act sonnets fell from garlanded boxes for those lucky enough to catch them; as much enthusiasm when the opera was finished. That was Donatella's last trembling in applause and first glimpse of its beneficiary too remarkable for humility as he accepted a gold tray of the taffeta wrapped accolades. He was as well presented in a long shimmering coat with flared skirt, accented with a looped and knotted cravat, an undressed wealth of hair changing the angles of his face as he bowed and then again. Obviously this was the legend of subterfuge, here and there, elegant and rakish, kissing the hand of *Centoventi*, goddess of the stage. He was clever and foolish not to worry she took exception at his as intimate approval of the contralto said to be the daughter of a cook, nothing but wisdom and faithfulness in his deepest bow and sincerest smile towards Genoa's Prince and Princess.

Even overlooked in the audience, Donatella felt he was a suitor offering the art of himself. So at least in the theater she could be chosen.

Nothing more intimate was expected, and shouldn't be. Not even when their landlord, one of the Falcone's managers, announced that *Signor Stradella would be moving into their quiet world.*

And unquiet hearts, resentment sounding in Signor Garibaldi's teasing. *Like offering the pigeons to the cat!* Aunt Despina couldn't resist.

It was assumed Signor Stradella would use the apartment for composing as well as sleep and light refreshments. Otherwise he would be out for tutoring and rehearsals during the day and church performances on Sundays, his evenings planned and unplanned with meals and diversions in more and less respectable settings.

Two large but struggling men maneuvered in a long walnut trunk with brass filigree corners and latch. They stood looking down the embossed hall to its sun-splashed end.

"Should we leave it here?" one of them asked.

"Why not?" Nubesta decided. "He'll put it where he wants."

"No." Donatella, not for the first time, had to correct her. "In the bedroom."

The men grumbled, did as they were told, then left, returning with musical instruments, a pair of trestles, square board, small stool, and a plainer case rattling with poorly packed contents. The apartment was already furnished, not with the Garibaldi finest, but bees-wax polishing gave console tables, armoire, credenza, and bed posts a higher shine. By the time citywide bells announced the vespers hour, Nubesta was done and resting on a frayed settee without any guilt for Donatella reaching over her to wipe the beveled mirror above.

The movers were less irritated as they brought in one crate dropping heavy and another floating to the floor, talking about where they would go drinking. Nubesta followed them out to be sure they were gone.

"Look." Donatella untied a note from around the handle of the fancier trunk.

"You know I can't read."

"To the most honorable ladies of this household, please make my bed with the hemp sheets, pillowcase and woolen blanket within. A.S."

"Not such a gentleman," Nubesta hoped.

The trunk's carved exterior was scarred and the latch almost fell off when Donatella popped it to fold back the top like a book she shouldn't read and hadn't any reason to beyond the first page, the noted bedding on top. She relied on Nubesta's willingness to go through Signor Stradella's things that were neatly layered and smelled of parchment and resin; no surprise that he owned the finest neckties, cuffs, shirts, jackets, breaches, dressing gown, ribbons, kerchiefs, gloves, stockings, belts, and buckles, and silver instrument strings unwrapped from a silk-velvet cloth.

Nubesta dug a little deeper, discovering two rosaries with gold medals, and a religiously embroidered runner with pointed ends and silk tassels.

"What is it?"

Donatella stretched it out, wondering, too. "A scapular, devoted to St. Dominic."

"Why would he have it?"

"Let's see to the bed."

It seemed a shame to strip already made wealth for grey hemp and brown wool, squeezing a plump pillow like the best sausage meat into a thin and tasteless casement. They pulled the sheets tight, laid out the yarn-hemmed blanket, finishing with a swollen brocade cover-up, the room ready or not for its distinguished if disreputable new occupant. It was the second adjective Nubesta seemed to know the most about, as servants often did, talk amongst themselves both informed and ignorant.

"Another note." The girl tugged at it.

Donatella was already fond of the forwardly fluid and looped handwriting. "Most honorable ladies, I imagine you hesitate. Please feel free to unpack and arrange my effects, like a puzzle, and see if you can know how I would like them. A.S."

"For a prize?" Nubesta squirmed, waiting for Donatella's next move.

"I don't think we should."

"You went through his clothes. What are a few knickknacks after that?"

"Take the cleaning things and tell my aunt we're done."

Nubesta obeyed sluggishly, the late afternoon warming the room's new belongings, the key Donatella tied around her arm under her sleeve too prominent to forget there.

***

She entered the dark room to soft meowing, both cats jumping down from her grandmother's bed.

Nonna stirred a little. "You could copy for him."

"I'm sure he has a copyist. I'm sure he has all he needs."

"He might think so." Nonna pulled her granddaughter's face so close to hers against the pillow Donatella almost laid down. "You shouldn't."

Donatella kissed her grandmother's dry cheek, combing her still thick gray hair, regretting more than that she wasn't a chaperone for the theater any longer. Nonna's hands had lost touch with the virginal, her trained voice weakened to whispers, her appetite merely for bread and broth.

"What's this?" A misshapen hand caught the bulge in Donatella's lower sleeve.

"Oh. The key to ... the ... linen closet."

"Well," Nonna's voice strengthened, "you might keep it, as you never take what isn't yours."

In the middle of the night Donatella rose to a dare and the third floor, bare steps as uncertain as candlelight on an unknown artist's commission of cherubs and festooned fruits and flowers in muted greens, grays, and sienna. The floor of the apartment didn't keep her entry quiet but it seemed only her carefulness was disturbed. The trestle table was set up in the salon, too close to the fireplace with its escalloped oak mantle and triangular copper hood illustrating Vulcan and Venus. Windows on both sides were almost hidden by red curtains with gold scrolling around the Garibaldi coat of arms, the moon somehow casting light on the secrecy of her endeavor. She unpacked Signor Stradella's clothes, carrying the pieces one at a time or in piles to the bedroom and shelves of the wardrobe that threatened to be too small. *He has more of what's necessary and unnecessary than a woman, a much indulged woman.* She opened another trunk holding the rewards of beautiful music, smiles and connivances, too, doubtful he carried the family heirlooms while by invitation or escape running around and hiding. Whatever explained the collection, he was aristocratic in everything but bedding and especially fortunate in moveable assets, even indifferent about some of them with silver candlesticks and snuffers, trays, bowls, spoons, toothpicks, and boxes as tarnished as his reputation.

Silver wasn't unusual in a city where even the lowest had the chore of it in their homes, while gold wasn't to be seen in any ordinary way, and she supposed he took pride in what he had of it, from buttons and medals to a locked tobacco caddy studded with diamonds.

She sensed some fraud, too, and quickly deposited a reliquary with the scapular in the chest at the foot of the bed. Otherwise she arranged with an eye for practical and creative importance, or just not knowing where else to put things without cluttering incidental surfaces and the narrow mantle. A candelabrum belonged on the trestle table as did a bookstand and bundle of folders with ribbons untied for a chance of revelation, placed next to a decorated writing slope for composing more than little notes to honorable ladies.

Three lutes huddled against the emptiness of a corner, stepsisters born separately of rosewood, maple, and ebony, sharing an inheritance of long necks, heads back, full bodies with rosettes like intricately set jewels on their breasts. Theirs was harmonious rivalry, recalling a master's touch and understanding. On the settee a leather case contained a violin resembling a dead man on the red velvet of his coffin, not mourned but celebrated by nymphs dancing through vines on the frieze high around the room.

As nearby *Santa Maria Maddalena* sounded for Lauds, the gold and diamonded box urgently invited investigation. She guessed where the key might be, pressing a button under the ink bottle section of the slope. A sudden drawer offered it, tiny, burnished, a promise of something special, not in that container but the one worth hundreds of *scudi* which instead of tobacco held more diamonds or a love note or pressed flower or curl of hair or ...

An accolade. She recognized the taffeta tied scroll at once, recalling applause that lingered, hearts melting for the music and man and impossibilities he left behind.

"You're in trouble." Nubesta startled Donatella, who could only hope she wasn't seen locking the rolled sonnet away again, placing its treasured box on the lower shelf of the nightstand. "She's looking for the key."

"Here. No." Donatella put a hand behind her back. "Where?"

Nubesta pulled it out of the door more for power than assistance.

"Give it to me."

Donatella waited for Nubesta to leave before returning one key to its almost private place, exiting the apartment herself as the other met Despina's outstretched hand. Her aunt might have wanted an explanation but didn't get one, Donatella escaping to her room to dress hurriedly, stuffing her hair under a cap, then on her way downstairs in time to welcome a man she had never met except as he inspired sonnets and forgetfulness.

To A Strange Somewhere Fled

Sequel to A House Near Luccoli

D.M. Denton

To A Strange Somewhere Fled
Copyright © 2015 by D.M. Denton

The events portrayed herein are the author's fictionalized account of a period of time in history. Certain historical figures are real; other characters are purely the products of the author's imagination. This work in no way purports to be other than fiction.

ISBN: 978-9907158-6-3

Library of Congress Control Number: 2015933861

Cover design by D.M. Denton

In memory of my father, Carmen,
who taught me the importance of
perseverance, purpose, and mathematics.

Acknowledgments

I must begin by expressing my appreciation to the readers of *A House Near Luccoli* who believed in my interpretation of the inimitable 17th century composer Alessandro Stradella, his world, music, associates, and the place of a fictional character like Donatella in a crucial part of his story. You encouraged me to continue with the sequel I had begun before *A House Near Luccoli's* publication in 2012.

Thank you to Deborah Bennison of Bennison Books, and authors Mary Clark and Steve Lindahl for their time and interest in reading and reviewing *To A Strange Somewhere Fled* before its publication.

And, once again, I must express my heartfelt gratitude to my mom, June, who has always practically, honestly and lovingly supported my writing aspirations, and to my excellent editor Deb Harris, who, along with Phil Harris, form my very special publisher All Things That Matter Press and have been so generous with their expertise and faith in my literary worth.

No comfort to my wounded sight,
In the Suns busie and imperti'nent light,
Then down I laid my head;
Down on cold earth; and for a while was dead,
And my freed soul to a strange somewhere fled.

~*The Despair* by Abraham Cowley, first published 1647

Settling

CHAPTER ONE

Wroxton, Oxfordshire, England, May 1682

There was music in the house, not entirely imagined. Mama was playing the spinet and singing a little like Nonna, but with less exclamation than anticipation. She stopped as the clock in the front hall chimed half-past six, and called her husband and daughter to supper.

For the second time that day she insisted on more fatty meats than soggy vegetables accompanied by glazed breads and followed by sharp cheeses as well as a fruit tart layered with thick cream or a pudding made with raisins, cloves and dates. Such a heavy meal for late in the day, but Mama believed, as many Genoese did, the digestive powers were stronger during sleep.

She usually shrugged off the Captain complaining they spent too much on food. On that particular evening she implied it wasn't enough. "Tomorrow we dine in style with the Baron."

Was it the confinement of English rain and consolation of English suppers that changed her from being a woman worried over losing her looks and lover and willing to sacrifice for both into one who wouldn't even give up a second and thicker slice of roast beef?

The Captain shook his head. "We're not invited for eating, Julianna, but dancing and other nonsense."

"Then I must satisfy myself beforehand." Mama laughed as she wiped her wide mouth. "Leftovers." Her hand waved over the table and landed on her daughter's arm. "It seems Donata won't have much."

"Little bread ... cheese," Donatella struggled with three words as if they were ten.

"You should have some meat," her mother spoke so it was just between them, "or your blood will thin."

Donatella's father raised another issue with his eyebrows.

"But, Edward, I must for my girl to understand me. She'll learn more English soon enough. Also, Lidia. Dear child. Why aren't you dining with us? Since we can't afford another servant, I won't have her treated like one."

The Captain didn't react to his wife, but vaguely smiled at the little maid who needed something to do.

In his company, Lidia was deaf and dumb and lowered her eyes, perhaps reminded of her own father, lost at sea although he still lived on it.

She did glance at Donatella, who was her confidant in feeling awkward and out of place. It wasn't long since they had disembarked the cutter bringing more mail sacks than passengers from Calais, and stumbled tired and dirty into a weeping sky and welcome by Donatella's mother. A friendly sailor was trusted with their trunks but not the cage purchased in Marseille, which Lidia carried until the Captain met them on the pier with a thin-wheeled wagon. He covered the cat cargo with his own coat, Mama's Italian chatter compensating for his silence as they walked to the inn where they would catch the coach to London. A snowy stag on The White Hart's whining sign encouraged him to finally say something, if only to quickly explain and wait for his wife to translate that 'hart' was an ancient term for a mature male deer. There wasn't time to explore the castle presiding in falling clouds behind the town, but at least it was more distinct than on its chalky pedestal in a foggy first view from the channel. A few hours were enough to have an early dinner under low-timbered ceilings and near a brass laden fireplace, Mama devouring half a roasted chicken and a glass of port wine, the Captain savoring a minced-meat pie and kegged ale. Donatella and Lidia shared a platter of steamed oysters with the cats and each other, as though they hadn't had enough of the sea.

If they had known how estranged they would soon be from it, the Captain wouldn't have seemed irresponsible insisting on one last look at Dover's harbor before the coach arrived with only ten minutes to spare for loading passengers inside, luggage on the back and hardier riders than they were on top.

Donatella and Lidia held the heavy carrier between them, Caprice and Bianchi quietly but pitifully complaining about their prolonged captivity. Mama sat next to Lidia and the Captain opposite her, a frail man and sizeable woman squeezing in to his side. Everyone was guarded, with limbs touching, body odors mixing, and coughs possibly infectious. It didn't help that Lidia, Mama, and Donatella saying anything to each other pronounced them foreigners.

Fortunately, Donatella was next to the window and set her sight on stretches of woods and clusters of cottages, spired churches, the approach of towns and the clutter and curiosities of their streets, and even a cathedral where the couple got off and no one got on. The vacancy they left was just wide enough to allow the caged cats their own seating, but not for long. Before leaving Canterbury, the coach made another stop to pick up two musk-scented men who didn't seem to notice the inconvenience they caused.

"Once we get to London, it will be easier," the Captain said and Mama brought unsympathetic attention to them again. "The North brothers have offered their personal vehicle and driver to take us the rest of the way."

They stayed overnight in Cheapside, the promised carriage arriving on time early the next morning. It made for a quicker and friendlier journey, and smoother, too. As the Captain pointed out, steel springs meant less bumps and jolts, while glass windows fogged but didn't leak.

A little over a week later the rain was still falling. Donatella lost track of the days since she had seen the sun.

***

"I can't wait to show you off."

"Must I go out?" Donatella continued to resist her mother's plans.

"Yes, you must."

Lidia began clearing the table.

"Oh, no. How to convince her, Edward, she's part of our family?"

"She's too young." The Captain turned to his daughter. "It's good you didn't travel alone, my dear, but now what to do with the poor thing?"

Mama made a noise between a moan and a scream before pulling Lidia into a maternally tight embrace. Donatella was as embarrassed as Lidia, but not surprised.

"Martha," Mama greeted a pear shaped woman wiping her hands on an already grimy apron, "you're still here."

"Ye knows I don't go home afore eight." The middle-aged servant pulled on the sides of her cap, noticing what Lidia was doing. "Hey."

Lidia offered a timid response.

"What? What did her say?"

"I think she wants to help." The Captain pushed back his chair.

"Oh, I give her summat to do."

The Captain stood up, straightening slowly to lean back against the long cluttered dresser behind him. "How's that? You can't even talk to her, Martha."

"I need only set a bucket in her hand."

Lidia made the sign of the cross and Mama moved towards the mystified girl again, just catching her hand this time.

"I don't let my Joseph know there be Catholics or he won't let me work here."

"Perhaps, Martha, it's even worse that a bad Protestant pays you." The Captain's face was redder than usual as he left the room.

Martha, folding her arms over her large stomach, was even more irritated as she could only guess what Mama was saying. "Dear, Lidia. There's something you can do. Bring the elderberry wine to the parlor and we'll also indulge in a Popish prayer and penitent song. Will you join us, Donata?"

***

Mama's regular after supper coughing fit meant there was no further playing, singing, or drinking that evening. Donatella was glad to retreat to the bedroom not much larger than the one she had in Genoa, the window wider and lower, the bed built for two and cave-like with its four posters and tasseled hangings. At its foot was a legless chest carved in arcaded designs, which she knelt in front of to open but didn't. Sloping walls rose to blackened beams where spider webs weren't out of place. Bianchi bunted her leg while Caprice begged the cheese unwrapped from an otherwise unused napkin. It seemed they had forgiven her. The first day they hid under the bed cleaning themselves constantly and throwing up frequently. By the second they peeked out for food, water, to use the dirt box, and slink around the room. Eventually, they considered where a door might lead, strange voices beyond, a few less stairs to tiptoe down, a dark hallway and cluttered rooms in a maze that held the rewards of a kitchen until Martha shooed them out the back door. Donatella found them huddling with each other in the rain, brought them in and rubbed them with her skirt. She thought they would be as unwelcome in the Captain's study and tried to push them by, but he recalled their mother, who had been his ship's favorite passenger. They didn't remember him, but it hardly mattered as they licked themselves dry in front of his crumbling fire.

They also made themselves at home on the softness of Donatella's bed, passively fighting over the mountain of pillows. When their mistress finally got in, they settled across her chest and legs, Caprice playing with her toes while Bianchi enjoyed a stroke through her fur up to the skin behind her ears so her eyes narrowed and her purring came from nowhere.

CHAPTER TWO

"You still haven't unpacked?" Mama finally noticed the following morning. "Everything so crumpled. It all smells of sea-salt and dust."

"Then I can't go." Donatella pushed the disheveled trunk aside to get to the window, a sunny glare emphasizing the dirtiness and imperfections of the glass. She reached over its deep sill to open it in disbelief the world could brighten overnight.

Mama left and was back by the time Donatella was half dressed—"Voilà"—a gown draped over her outstretched arms.

"How pretty." Lidia gave Donatella the jug she carried.

"I never wear red."

"Crimson. Like the azaleas behind the house in Genoa." Mama didn't otherwise argue. She took it away, and, before Donatella finished washing her face and Lidia straightened the bed, returned with another that shimmered blue and green.

"Like the Ligurian Sea," Lidia remembered.

"Stand straight." Mama held it up, a color Donatella would wear, but not such an enormously pleated skirt and so many bows.

"It's quite foolishly wonderful." Mama touched its short cuffed sleeves, front lacing, stomacher point and hips. She invaded the trunk again. "You must have a decent chemise under it. Here's one better than you have on. No time for laundering, but Lidia can hang it out for a few hours."

Lidia was as happy to obey as Donatella wasn't to witness her mother treating the girl like a servant after all.

"What will she wear?"

"Lidia?" Her mother forced a frown. "She won't be going." She noticed Bianchi considering a satiny nap. She lifted the dress off the bed and hung it on the wardrobe door.

"I won't be either, Mama."

"Why?"

"It's too soon."

Her mother pressed a hand to her breast. "Of course it was hard to lose Nonna. I've missed her longer than you."

Donatella couldn't argue with tears that weren't wiped away.

"Aren't you hungry? You haven't had any breakfast. I'm ready for dinner." Mama's arms actually lifted as she flew out of the room, Lidia ducking under one of them.

Donatella sat on the hard stool in front of a small table with two front drawers. She hadn't any intention of making use of silver and glass jars, ivory brushes, and tilting mirror, for she didn't want to go anywhere except into her unhappiness or face anyone who hadn't already seen her disappointed eyes and drawn cheeks. She was certain she would never again think about her hair beyond brushing and pulling it back in a knot.

Lidia had a different idea. "I saw ladies in France with ringlets all over, longer on the shoulders." She had already found clean rags and torn them into strips.

Later Donatella tried to be appreciative when Lidia arranged the curls to fall over her ears, but felt certain she looked ridiculous. Bending over to pull on her stockings, a tight-laced corset wasn't the only reason for her breathlessness. It was too soon to be dressing for attention.

Mama waited at the bottom of the stairs, her hair overly involved with ribbons, the crimson dress a few meals away from not fitting, her feet already dancing, and the Captain looking at her like something he wanted to resist but couldn't.

"I hope Roger is there," he said. He was the last to leave the house, a fresh breeze drawing Donatella out as she thought nothing could.

Mama wanted to walk arm and arm with her daughter. The sun was gone from the village; the short cape Donatella wore, on loan from her mother, was warm and disturbing, with speckled fur around its neck and bottom edge. They had to go single file through the arched opening of the privet hedge that fronted the cottage Donatella had yet to call home. Their hurried movement upset thirsty midges, Papa swatting at them violently and Mama laughing, as she meant to enjoy herself no matter what.

Donatella knew the pond was nearby ever since the Captain had told her why she heard ducks and frogs, the sound of children and splashing. As the evening silhouetted its lacy perimeter, it became the first thing she loved about the village.

"What is this scent, Papa?" Donatella slowly found the words to ask, then recognized the cascading vine of flowering honeysuckle almost completely covering the stone wall that rose up behind the pond and hid their piece of the village.

"Most intense early morning and evening." Her father put a hand on her arm to show his pleasure with their conversation.

Mama lost patience with their dallying and almost dragged Donatella to the tall ornate gates left open to what lay ahead.

The Captain greeted someone coming from the Abbey grounds who raised a lantern. "Good evening, Tobias. The devil's not afoot tonight, I trust?"

It was obvious he had upset the old man, who took the light away as quickly as he could.

Donatella felt her mother tugging at her. "He's of no consequence. Look ahead, then all around, inhale, and listen."

Donatella was glad she followed her mother's advice, captivated by the dusky enormity of trees, taste of frost, and rhythm of gravel as they made their way towards an apparently important destination.

"Are those lights the big house?"

Mama coughed with excitement. "Like stars in my eyes."

The Captain pulled them out of the way of a carriage in a greater hurry than they were.

Mama clapped. "We're not the last."

"Almost was our last." He wasn't joking.

"Like Genoa," Donatella recalled, so her mother did, too.

"Stretch out your arms and you crossed the street."

"Narrow in more ways than that."

"You don't think my sister is in there?" Mama joked.

Besides being far away in Genoa, Aunt Despina could never have dressed as affluently as the lady climbing out, or been so comfortable with a man hugging her waist or whispering in her ear.

The vehicle almost ran them over again as it departed, Papa waving his arms like he had for the flies, and swearing—well, a few words that sounded worse than impolite. The couple was startled into seeing something other than each other, Mama smiling so the gentleman bowed his head without hiding his eyes while the lady's opinion came with the back of her head, her pale hair capped with lace and, like her ears and neck, dripping pearls.

Donatella's anxiety found a practical cause in the comparison of her hair, even to her mother's, for she had insisted Lidia leave out any decoration.

Gravel turned to flagstone. Short pillars left and right offered smoky light, and with each step up skirts rose a little more, as did expectations.

Certainly, the Captain hoped for the best as Mama pinched at the chiffon disappearing into her bosom. "You look splendid, Julianna."

Donatella didn't hear her answer, just the roll of music on the most courteous of strings. Its performer was standing when he could have sat in one of the shell-shaped niches either side of the Abbey's elaborate entrance, although his long stiff jacket might have prevented him from doing so.

A lutenist plays best like a caterpillar curling into itself.

What Donatella heard came out of her heart with a pain she was glad to feel. An herbal fragrance interrupted the air as she and then her mother brushed the bay laurels in stone planters narrowing the central porch.

Donatella turned to the musician as he fumbled a few notes, his overstated cuffs not favoring the understated instrument any more than the times did.

Such subtlety is less and less what the public wants, for it means it has to choose to be still and listen. A violin commands attention, held high and, even as it falls, reaching higher, unapologetic for all those tricks up its sleeve.

It was not the young man who had spoken. Mama insisted Donatella move on, the Captain apologizing to the lutenist who had to wait for them to go into the Abbey before he could. The massive front door scraped closed, its latch clanked into place, and the floor dipped too steeply for slender heels. The Captain's seaworthiness made him a steadying escort between wife and daughter as they entered an oak-paneled hall to view a greater one crowded with small disconnected groups of guests whose dress and behavior in comparison to such a gathering of Genoese nobility was like the difference in style between a lute and violin.

Donatella stood behind her father and mother and one of four columns rising into capitals and shafts ridging the ceiling over their heads. It creaked with laughter and complaints as feet and chairs shuffled and instruments and voices prepared to entertain.

She stepped backwards to fully see the minstrel's gallery. Hooking his arm around hers, the Captain gave her no choice but to turn into the ancient baronial hall. Her sight revolved around suits of armor, crossed swords, blood-red carpets and upholsteries, wall tapestries, portraits, stag heads, and birdcage windows that glowed pink facing west.

"Welcome, Captain. And good mistresses."

The Captain extended his hand to a stiff-collared man with a prominent nose and darkly circled eyes.

"Sir Francis, you haven't met my daughter. She has lately come from Genoa."

Their host bowed his head. "Like her mother, not so lately."

"Yes, I'm quite at home here." Mama took a step closer to Sir Francis as she spoke.

"Wroxton allows for settling, Mistress." He put a proper but not insulting distance between them.

"Too far from the waves for me."

"Not meaning London, are you Captain?"

"No, never likely to stay there long."

"You're fortunate you haven't any reason to."

"Well, we thank you for your help in getting us quickly away this last time."

"It was Roger's idea, and one I was more than happy to endorse."

Donatella noticed how Sir Francis' smooth wig looked foolish with wisps of hair on his high forehead, but hardly realized him tilting towards her. She was surprised by what he said, but couldn't fault his Italian or generosity.

"Where's Roger?" The Captain moved out from under the minstrel's gallery. "Up there?"

"Are you implying my brother has a talent for music? Except for singing worse than I do?"

"Sometime you must allow us to judge." Mama lifted her chin in a way that made her look softer and slimmer.

"Perhaps." Sir Francis knew he was safer speaking to the Captain. "Roger isn't presently at Wroxton."

"Pity. I find him such interesting company."

"What I haven't taught him he's yet to learn." Sir Francis noticed Donatella left out of the conversation again. "Speaking of learning, I can arrange English lessons for your daughter."

Mama, unnecessarily, let Donatella know what he had said. "Yes. It's no good me trying to teach her anything."

Donatella stepped back and hung her head, afraid she couldn't hide her resistance to becoming less of a stranger, preferring to comprehend little of what was going on and remain in the land of broken English and dreams.

CHAPTER THREE

Donatella couldn't make out the performers in the candlelit gallery, but recognized their muse as if it was her own. A number of Purcell sonatas—announced as so new they were yet unpublished—came to life on harpsichord, violins, and bass viols. They connected her to pleasure and pain in the same measure, speaking without words, remembering without thoughts and realizing emotions that didn't need explanation. The best music came out of silence like love out of the impossible, made more beautiful because of loss and loneliness that never wanted company again. Only Sir Francis seemed to be listening as she was, standing at some distance but turning and nodding as though he sensed her empathy.

"Oh, Donata. Not here, not now."

Mama dabbed Donatella's eyes with one of the perfumed gloves she preferred to carry rather than wear, glancing around for witnesses.

"And look like you're going to stay." She slid the cape off her daughter's shoulders, handing it to a page, who didn't seem to know what to do with it.

The music changed pace and, as didn't surprise Donatella, achieved more attention than the sonatas had, composition for the soul never as popular as for the feet.

"I'll sit here." A bench of studded red leather between mirroring armor and a smoking fireplace offered to keep Donatella out of the way of the assembling dance formation.

"As if at a funeral," her mother noticed.

The Captain slumped beside his daughter. Somehow he knew his wife was about to ask Sir Francis to be her partner, and gestured his relief and consent to him.

There was tapping, counting out loud, and yet an abrupt start to a galliard that had a few of the dancers and even musicians trying to catch up. What would be the consequence, beyond that evening, for those couples discovering how well or ill matched they were kicking right-left-right-left into an uncertain cadence of jumping and posturing? The repetition was broken with a few lifts and spins by some of the more athletic and audacious pairs, and the Captain pointing out more than one stumble and foot or dress stepped on, another twirl that didn't quite happen as arms found a graceless way out of a tangle, and all those red faces caused by embarrassment and exertion.

Mama couldn't be faulted. She was voluptuous and engaging, giving herself to the dance as she did to every meal and expression, smiling at Sir Francis and anyone else as though irrelevant to her enjoyment. Perhaps the Captain observed his wife's self-sufficiency with relief, but to Donatella it seemed he was missing the woman who couldn't imagine belonging anywhere but in his sight and approval.

Frivolity soon gave way to poignancy, especially to those who listened for it. A galliard was often paired with a pavane, but usually as an overture, not conclusion. The dancers were sent into a column of slow curtseys and bows, their hesitant steps retreating and advancing as they lifted on the balls of their feet and swayed side to side. A few, like her mother and Sir Francis, justified it as the peacock dance, holding an arrogant posture and using the certainty of steps, fullness of skirts, and floating of sleeves to court dignity, hands barely touching arms or backs while nods agreed on discretion. Still, a wink over her shoulder as she and Sir Francis passed near Donatella proved Mama wouldn't allow choreography to suspend spontaneity altogether.

Donatella wondered about the Captain's reaction. A little boy sat in his place.

"I'm glad my father pretends to enjoy himself." He knew how to speak to her, saw Donatella's mother approaching and ran off.

Mama's cheeks were burning. She sat expansively, sweating, and exhaled noisily. Her head swayed, eyes tried not to close and upper torso fell sideways into Donatella's lap.

"Mama, Mama—"

"Mistress Hanley—"

"Julianna—"

Despite the perspiration on her mother's face, she seemed frozen in Donatella's arms before she was passed to the Captain's, his strength as miraculous as her mother's recovery while he carried her where Sir Francis led. Their stuttering host cautioned the step up onto the dais where a copper-banded table displayed more pottery and silver than food, which might have caused Mama to faint again if she had noticed. Instead, she was caught up in the attention of men, hanging onto the neck of one and following the urgency of another who pushed open an enormous door into a passageway also carved out of dark and heavy times.

"This way." Sir Francis turned left but Donatella glanced right and up at his young son sitting on the step of a staircase, its banister only partially constructed.

Quickly passing through what might have been a dining room, they entered a small parlor, Sir Francis pulling the fringed curtains closed and putting down the candle he carried before showing the Captain where he could do the same with his now wide-eyed wife. Donatella caught her mother's feet to slip off her shoes in time to help lower her onto a caned and cushioned daybed.

Sir Francis turned away, using the servant who had come into the room to disguise the reason he did.

The housemaid listened to her master's request, curtseyed, and was gone. He faced them to explain, "I thought something to drink and eat might help."

"It usually does." The Captain's sarcasm didn't lighten Sir Francis' thoughts.

"What's that, Mama?" Donatella was almost hugging her mother to hear her. "No. Papa jokes."

"Julianna," the Captain said as he went down to one knee, stroking his wife's arm, "you act without sense."

Sir Francis was obviously struggling with the scene. "My dearest lady would lie there before the severity of her illness confined her to bed."

The Captain also realized the strain his friend was under. "Please, sir. See to your party."

"Yes, yes. But stay, all of you, as long as you need. We could send for a doctor."

"No," Mama tried to sit up. "I just need to eat."

***

Donatella helped her mother down from the trap while its pubescent driver yawned and leaned on the equally sluggish horse that had saved them the walk from the large house. It wasn't Mama's fainting that spoiled the evening, but her argument with the wisdom of husband and host sending her home before half-past nine and the sack-posset had been served. Donatella felt the embarrassment of leaving by way of the Great Hall, ready to help restrain her mother's physical objection if the Captain was unable to do so by himself.

Such a contrast to the time spent quietly and privately in Sir Francis' parlor, so Mama could recover with a little soup and sleep. Donatella was occupied with sitting and watching her, and examining a book left on the window seat like a clue. She thought of her father and was surprised to feel curious as she read the inscription that presented it from one brother to another.

***

Within the hour, she was in a cottage kitchen with Lidia, who denied she had been crying. Donatella didn't know Lidia any better despite the intimacy of their journey together. Her companionship was almost invisible, yet consoling, perhaps because she had so little to say.

There was never a question of asking her to come. It was assumed so Donatella wouldn't have to travel alone, especially not in spirit, in memory, in any way that would leave behind the greatest secret of her life.

Once, Lidia had faith in every moment, but now doubt hollowed out her eyes. "Your curls held."

In her room, Donatella brushed them out even before she undressed, weeping at the mess that resulted. Bianchi and Caprice peeked from under the bed, light cast across it from the candle on the dressing table that singed a little of her hair and gave shape to the shadows around her. What could explain the music that broke her heart but not the silence? She rolled her stockings down to her ankles, removed her shoes and rubbed her feet, the large toes on each poking holes through her hose. She took one last look at herself, constricted by bone and made larger with frills and flounces in a dress colored and shining like a clear sky when clouds were all she wanted to wear.

Stripped to her chemise, she knelt down by the chest at the bottom of the bed and opened its drawer, lifted out quill and ink and her journal. *God waits for you to be like him.*

She wondered if Lidia had come into the room. No one was there, except whom she mournfully invited and didn't hope would appear. Until something was forming and even stirring, one line then two, black marks turning into graceful strokes, almost half-a-page filled before she knew it, pouring like blood from a deep wound. If only she could keep it flowing, instead of grief drying it up and making it hard and leaving a stain with no poetry about it.

She thought of Sir Francis facing and speaking of his loss and looked at her own flickering in and out of the life she had left. Of course, his was legitimate; nothing to confess but that he deeply mourned his wife, as he should.

Hopefully, it was a coincidence that her mother was coughing, the Captain's deep voice audible as he attended her.

It was the dampness. Donatella could feel it underfoot and wherever she touched. She could smell it and taste it, her throat always a little raspy and her hair never completely dry. She couldn't close her journal for hours; even with much powder and patience its pages would stick. There wasn't a fire that could get rid of it, fabric to repel it, window clear of it, or day without its threat. Yet she didn't hate it, for it was part of her nature; England's tears respectful of her own.

CHAPTER FOUR

Donatella didn't mind language lessons that came with the appearance of flowers sparkling in waves of yellow and blue and white. She soon found out why Martha sneered at her boots, nowhere as dry as the sky that morning. Even footwear made for traveling let her down as she ventured off slated paths onto turf that drank the rain without swallowing.

The Captain saved her from capsizing, lifting her a little as he showed her around.

She repeated after him: "Blue-bells, prim-roses, dan-de-lions, heart-ease."

Not all were strangers; not the little myosotis stars bursting unforgettably through dirt and grass.

"They always come up in legions, no matter how I thin them."

Somehow she knew what her father was saying, feeling a return of pleasure when he gave her the bouquet he had made with a few tiny daisies, too.

He proceeded to introduce her to the trees promising leaves or blossoms or both. "Haw-thorn, chest-nut, crab-apple, oak apple."

"Oak apple?"

"Yes." A reddish-brown growth blemished the branch he had lowered with his walking stick. "I haven't seen so many in years. We'll be popular in a few weeks."

She knew he was offering her something to look forward to. She didn't have to wait, violets spilling out of the shade and affecting her senses so she couldn't resist stealing one to almost taste.

"Sniff and sniff. You cannot get more out of it."

How could she mind that its appeal was in its reserve as it folded over a bright eye and seemed bluer than the forget-me-nots in her posy?

"They come up late here." Her father picked a few more for her. "The dampness of this corner feels like March, not May."

She stepped in deeper, crouching near a strong tree root, touching, even stroking what she had never seen before.

"Moss."

"Moss." She let the word curl in her lips and hiss over her tongue.

"Your mother hates it. No matter. It has its uses. Dried for animal bedding. Or kindling. Or kept damp for baskets of flowers and holly at Christmas. And to put out fire."

Donatella followed him to where he had begun turning over his famous raised garden. Mama had written about it in her letters, so Donatella couldn't help anticipating it in words of her own: A market outside the back door; herbs and flowers indistinguishable; beans running up their stakes like maypole ribbons twisting and untwisting to celebrate the scarlet as well as the green; cabbages and carrots also feeding the rabbits; radishes flavoring better than onions.

The Captain had begun digging again, mud splattering her. He leaned on his spade and wiped the back of his neck as Lidia delivered a message.

Mama was already dressed for going out, sitting in the kitchen eating a curd cake and missing fresh lemon to squeeze over it. Donatella took off her boots for Lidia to clean and went up to her room to change, wishing it was the last place on earth, Bianchi and Caprice opening their eyes and stretching their legs as if they were sure it was.

***

Donatella was impressed Sir Francis hadn't forgotten his promise and invited her and Mama to the Abbey again. His son's darkly-dressed tutor adjusted his silver wig as he came into the room that walls of books and sparse furnishings portrayed as a library. He immediately asked to be excused; Donatella and her mother were more relieved than offended.

He soon returned with the boy Donatella had already met.

"Remember me?" Mama stroked the cowlick in his hair.

"Yes. You like to dance."

"How you've grown. Are you ten?"

"Not quite."

"That's the best age to be."

The tutor put a hand over his smile and then some books on a rectangular table, pulling out two chairs adjacent to each other and wondering if Donatella's was too near the fire when it was only too close to him. He spoke Italian in a way that was painful to her, without a view of soft lips or twinkling eyes. She answered him and sat down self-consciously, soon realizing he wasn't expecting more than her halfhearted attention.

She should have been curious about what young Francis whispered to her mother that made them giggle and the tutor's face twitch. She would have rather gone to sleep, the fire warm on her back and, like words unnecessary, Mama's interruptions more irritating than the tutor's dry method. Donatella was glad her mother left to throw and catch a ball outside with the young master, until through the room's outreaching east window she witnessed her running up and down the sloping terrace. Finally Mama stopped, not in response to Donatella tapping on the window but because someone else had her attention, someone who might have been a gardener with wind burned cheeks despite his wide brimmed hat, who wiped the ball on his dusty breeches before he gave it back to the diminutive Francis.

"What's going on?" The tutor wasn't really interested, drawing the curtains but not completely when he realized they couldn't continue in darkness. "Please sit. And concentrate."

Another half an hour and the books were closed, one of the housemaids directing them into the dining room where Mama was indulging in a treat of tea, confections, and a life much grander than she knew what to do with. So it was quite normal for her to fill the tutor's cup and offer him the pick of a depleted selection of sweets.

"Nothing, sir? Oh, come on. Try an egg-white biscuit. So sugary and airy." Her mouth smacked with an indecency that made him look away and back again. "Oh, dear, I ate the last one."

"Mama." Donatella jumped at the sound of her own voice, turning to a caress of her neck coming from the window slightly propped open behind her. "No, stop." She gently wrestled the startled tutor away from closing it and leaned into a monastic outlook of tall trees and long shadows, the illusion of deer clustered at its height and sheep mowing down towards the disappearing roadway where daisied grass gleamed under an open sky.

The Captain looked small approaching the Abbey with a flat-footed and slowing stride.

"Papa comes."

"What?" Mama's annoyance was soon reconciled with how she could use his interference. "He means to check up on me."

The Captain stopped, raising his stick.

"You have a wife, sir?"

Donatella was drawn back into the room.

"Ah. Like Sir Francis, who still dances with his." Mama put out her hand, whether condescendingly or compassionately. "Comfort yourself, sir," she said, to feed his sorrow. "Ah, Banbury cakes. I've eaten too many over the years."

The tutor took one and so did Donatella, who felt strangely disloyal biting into flakey pastry, currents, spices, and something more deliberately intoxicating. Crumbs fell to the floor and she turned to the window to disown them.

"Can you still see him?"

"No, Mama."

"He wants to catch me like this. Be thankful, Donata. You can get old and fat without anyone minding."

The tutor ignored what she said but not how she said it. "English,

Mistress. Every word a lesson."

Donatella placated them both with a small smile that agreed to everything and nothing. She was as anxious to leave as Mama was to find out what the Captain was up to. Young Francis was bouncing a ball up and down the front steps and a cheerful conversation was going on behind a wall of yellow stone, dense holly, and feathery yews.

"Take the shortcut." Francis directed them through a canopied walkway that was soft and sticky underfoot, into a muddied cluttered yard where some building was well underway. No one was actually working, except the man she had seen earlier was talking to the Captain and probably pointing out what had been accomplished and was yet to be.

There was no doubt he was the architect of some improvement. He looked up more than once as if considering what to make of the sky.

Francis climbed over stone, timbers, and tools to disappear into a chance of mischief. The man in the sheltering hat bowed his head and folded his arms, not rude but reserved, barely acknowledging Donatella as she was introduced to him.

"What are you doing here?" Her mother saw the Captain's displeasure. "Oh, I didn't put that right."

"No, no. I understand. You refer to the addition of stabling. My first design had one through section, but then it was decided to divide by walls and doors for safety, privacy, and convenience."

"Of course." Mama sounded indifferent.

Donatella wished she knew why, especially as the Captain overcompensated for her. "Is there no end to your abilities, my friend?"

Roger touched the front of his hat, shading his eyes even more. "Perhaps my brother puts too much faith in my thinking I can build things. Or undertakes whatever I propose to show me how I may fail."

"Surely not." Mama should have also offered her smile in an artificial effort to redeem herself.

"I hardly mind, Mistress Hanley. It's his way of encouraging me to think in many directions and not settle for the inferior."

"You're forbearing, Roger."

"No, Edward, grateful. For a way to express my independent interests and find some competence and joy in dabbling."

The word joy perked Mama up a little.

"He seems older than he is." She spoke before they were far enough away not to offend Roger. "And doesn't stand straight or know how to look at a woman."

Whatever the Captain heard, he chose to ignore. She refused his arm as they walked back to the village.

"Not my idea of handsome. Clever but dull." Mama waved her comments at Donatella. "No doubt something will be arranged for him."

CHAPTER FIVE

Donatella couldn't say she'd ever had a lover. Yet, she might describe his glances and smile with or without the flash of his teeth. He was an artist, his hands designing music for the air as well as the page, and a vagabond who didn't need a place to stay. His voice was persuasive, his impulses outrageous, and his intentions something she could never be sure of. That was the tease of him: promising and not promising, rising and falling, an accident waiting to happen, a secret changing everything and nothing. In the wink of an eye, he dismissed her to never let her go, a trick that ensured she would feel the loss but also the return of him.

Thinking about him kept her awake, especially when she spent most of the night sitting by her window, the sky breaking open with stars and a slice of the May moon. She didn't cry but wanted to as Bianchi pawed her knees and Caprice didn't need an invitation to jump on her lap. They were so fully there and yet hardly present as she stroked them. When the wind moved clouds and trees to as affectionately touch her face, it was very possible she was living with ghosts.

Some were familiar, brought along in boxes of books, even pieces of clothing, and, of course, sheets of music. Some she didn't know, for the room had its own in furniture and dust, creaking floorboards, and a bed that was soft, deep, and dangerous.

She reached for the eiderdown to wrap herself in, Bianchi whimpering and darting under the bed, Caprice leaping onto it to catch the unseen. They were expected to be a little crazy, even magical, conjuring a great life out of a small one. When they slept, their whiskers and eyelids quivered for their wildest dreams. Were they back in Genoa, too, in Nonna's darkened room and big chair where falling asleep was required? Or wandering down to the kitchen so Cook would scold and then reward them? Or, as their legs extended, sneaking up towards what was off-limits but inviting, were their thoughts about how they escaped but never got away? Would they wake to the confusion of why bells weren't ringing from every direction and the sea wasn't close by? Did they miss not knowing what was beyond the window, the view of the street, or smell of the bay?

No, they just stretched and yawned and accepted that all they ever needed had come with them.

Donatella climbed back into bed to warm her feet and think in English, which was like trying to fit into clothes not made for her. Of course, she had done that. She struggled to form sentences she might use with her father or Martha or even teach Lidia. When there was enough dawning light, she referred to the book the tutor had loaned her, its pages turned into much more than she would ever need to say.

What an opportunity for a woman like you: another country, another life, another chance to be seen and heard, especially to talk about me.

It had been a nightmare after the murder. She was a stranger in the house where she had spent her life, silent about what had been taken, locked out of what was left, helpless as justice failed and rumors prospered. Eventually a spare key found under the mattress in her aunt's room let her in on Alessandro's legacy before others considered it their due. She went into his apartment only once, more familiar with his personal property than she had been the first time, letting go of it to whoever did or didn't have legal claim to it—except for those copies belonging to her steady hand as well as his faltering brilliance.

No one could care for them as she did. Yet she took the chance that, packing them with the books she sent ahead to England, regret, not relief, might be all she was left with. Fortunately, they had traveled as safely as she had. From then on, Donatella wanted to keep them close and private like Nonna's volumes piled on the unused side of her bed until her father got help to bring up a bookcase from his study.

The chest at the foot of the bed was the obvious option for the music copies and the special gift that had made the journey from Genoa with her. In only a few weeks, a gray-green wooliness threatened these treasures and brought Donatella to her knees.

"Look. Are they already ruined? Oh, I think they might be." Donatella handed her problem over to Lidia's consideration.

The young girl's calm was always more for others than herself. "Not all the sheets are affected. Only the ribbon and corners on this, a little." Lidia lifted the scrolled accolade with a curiosity Donatella had, previously, refused to satisfy.

"All right."

Lidia read to herself and then out loud, which Donatella hadn't given her permission to do. "Raising notes, sights and hopes, for to beguile."

Donatella gathered the music, took the sonnet back, and, as she rolled it, stopped Caprice from playing with its taffeta tie.

"There's a box in my room," Lidia offered.

"This chest, that box. There's nowhere safe from the damp in this house."

"Your chest is oak. The box is cedar, lined with silk, better to keep away the bugs, too."

"You opened it?"

"There was only an old quill inside."

"Is it large enough?"

"If the copies are folded."

Donatella wouldn't agree to such an injury. Alessandro always insisted his compositions be kept flat in leather folders. Also, he wouldn't have approved of Donatella hiding them like she did her writing and painting, great works needing great influence and especially great purses to promote them. Did he ever say such a thing, or was it her missing him that wanted to hear it?

"I shouldn't be caught moving it." Lidia left Donatella to decide what to do.

The crime was committed that very evening after Martha had gone home, Mama and the Captain hardly concerned if Donatella visited the tiny cluttered and windowless room at the end of the cottage's second floor that had been given to Lidia.

"You might ask your mama if you can have it." Lidia had put the box on the child's bed she was short enough to fit on if her feet hung off.

"No, no." Donatella knew she had seen the carved container before, full of unfinished needlework. Now, as Lidia had already revealed, there was nothing but an almost featherless quill inside. Donatella decided it could be salvaged and that she didn't have a choice but to crease and even crush the copies that, after all, weren't safer with her than anyone else.

***

"Where did you put it?" Lidia wondered the next morning.

"On the floor of my wardrobe. I used a dry paint brush to clean off as much of the mold as I could."

"Good. Take them out once in a while," Lidia still had the discipline of a nun about her, "on a dry day to air them, although not in direct sunlight."

"Of course."

"Your mama would love to see them."

"No. She'd ask too many questions."

"Well, you don't have to tell her everything."

Where was the nun in Lidia then, her eyes shining, her cheeks flushed?

Donatella was persuaded to be impulsive if not dishonest. "Will you go out with me?"

"To your lesson? Your mama likes to go with you."

"She's in bed with indigestion. Anyway, I'm not sure when I'll have another."

"Martha expects me to clean the larder."

"She can do it herself."

"Where will we go?"

"We can feed the ducks. And walk to the church. I hear it throughout the day and think about how I should go."

"It isn't ours."

"It can't be a sin just to take a look."

They didn't realize how warm a day it was until they were outside, Lidia running back to the cottage to return their cloaks to the hallway. A new brood of white ducklings on the pond could barely keep up with their mother swimming in circles. There were half a dozen other mature ducks floating and dipping and wagging their tails, large and snowy, some smaller streaked with brown or heads shining like emeralds.

Lidia skipped to the edge of the pool while Donatella unwrapped the loaf Martha would surely miss, immediately surrounded by a noisy onslaught of flapping beggars.

"I'll do it." Lidia uncovered and shook down her thick bronze hair.

She had never known such popularity and laughed as the ducks did no more harm than pulling at the ribbons on her cap that held the bread. Donatella waited for her where light and shadows and puddled avenues converged, almost consoled by whispering children playing on the gently-sloped village green, yellow-stoned cottages opening their windows to better days, and a dirty-faced little girl making a daisy chain into a crown for Lidia's hair.

CHAPTER SIX

The children led and followed Donatella and Lidia as church bells confirmed the morning's last hour. Most of the boys clambered up a thicketed embankment using their knees, elbows, and hands rather than take the gradually rising path. The girls called them idiots and stayed on the road below, hurrying to wait for the barking of dogs and women to expel the rowdy group from in front of a row of cottages. Lidia laughed at one in particular, taller than his years, better looking than behaved.

All Saints was literally situated on higher ground and seemed to lean against the mackerel sky, its three-storied tower embattled like one of Genoa's city gates with a small standard at its center inevitably catching the wind. Some of the youngsters were already in its graveyard, chasing each other around upright tombs and crosses and simple markers easily stumbled over.

"Me sister." The village girl who had crowned Lidia was as lost as her relative in prickly bushes. She responded to Lidia's approach and understanding. "Was yours younger or older?"

"You had a sister?" Donatella had overheard.

Lidia hesitated to make her sad, too. "Like you had a suitor."

The children, including both of Lidia's admirers, disappeared, but could be heard giggling and squabbling and then giggling again when a man scolded them. Donatella steadied Lidia who, as she concentrated on taking off her crown and twisting her hair under cover again, wasn't prepared for the irregular stoop in the church's porch.

The nave was comfortably silent, well-maintained rather than magnificent, with scrubbed floor and polished woodwork, white-washed walls, and smoothly columned arcades. It was a place for contemplation, not worship, offering the smell of beeswax rather than incense and a sense of solitude Donatella had never known in *Santa Maria Maddalena* or the Cathedral of *San Lorenzo*.

She turned to see what Lidia thought.

The girl was haloed by a doorway as she looked up and made the sign of the cross, her hastily positioned cap slipping off but spared a descent to the floor because it was loosely tied under her chin.

Donatella assumed Lidia believed the diffused light filling the morning side of the clerestory was effected by the rays of heaven rather than the sun. She was determined not to surrender to such desperate piety. She meant to study All Saints for its sparse architecture and ornamentation, the exactness in its rows of pews, the colorlessness of its lower windows, its accusing pulpit, and simply inscribed tablets, emblems, and banners. Its main oak-vaulted ceiling was like the overturned keel of a ship with foamy light flooding in, which, of course, made her think of her father and why he was a bad Protestant.

The church became less of a curiosity and more of an aberration without music or mystery. There wasn't one image of the Madonna, certainly not of her bleeding heart, and no representation of the crucifixion or sign of resurrection.

"Come see," Lidia called softly.

Donatella found her in the church's sanctuary kneeling before an altar slab that displayed a gold cross and white votive and was surrounded by cathedral windows illuminating suffering and salvation. With an almost motionless turn to the left, white alabaster and gray marble made a canopy for the sleeping effigies of a crowned man and veiled woman. Their eyes were open to paradise, their hands folded forever. At the head of that eternal bed two courtiers mirrored one another, each positioned down on a knee, holding a book and his heart. At its foot, a wide-sleeved, tightly-coiffed and bodiced young woman with the same pampered elegance of the dog companioning her held a Bible between her long praying fingers. All mourned for themselves, a family gone but not to be forgotten.

Lidia touched Donatella's arm, indicating the long brass markers on the floor: hallowed ground they were standing on. Donatella stepped down into the chancel after her, feeling the loss of such antiquity and grandeur, and relief that faith could be nearer and simpler—and sweeter and sadder, a small basket with blossomy branches and peonies left on the floor below a tablet. Lidia read some of its excessive Latin out loud. In turn, Donatella silently interpreted the wall memorial crested by an oblong semi-urn shelving a skull and bones for the form that could never return, an hourglass for the love that would never run out, and cherubim from a heaven that now only death could promise. She didn't need Lidia to understand it was all about the lady she had met in Sir Francis' eyes.

"Children, too," Lidia noticed. "Popio and Francisca."

Donatella slid into the north choir stall, Lidia sitting opposite and immediately closing her eyes and bowing her head before shriveling behind the modesty panel. Donatella admired the window above her that was divided into upstanding sections like an artichoke's petals. She meant to appreciate it in a methodically modern way, but, not for the first time, the mystery of painted glass not only captured light but also her imagination. She experienced it more than saw it in heavenly blue and earthly green, sunshine yellow and blood red, at its most reserved glowing from within, at its most brilliant shining like a jewel.

Lidia put up her head, having heard something. It came from where they had, or near enough, hesitant to speak but finding its voice, struggling and promising, familiar and not. Donatella huddled down in the stall, the violin music stopping and then starting again, in practice not performance, amateurish and yet haunting, especially in a slower movement, leaning on the notes in a minor but not insignificant attempt at lamenting what was lost. There was something so familiar about it. Yet it was too careful and apologetic, its sighs pretended rather than felt. It achieved a good deal of clarity, but couldn't quite find its inspiration.

Well, you never knew a master to play like that, did you?

The answer, like the question, must be inside her head, but Donatella only heard the awkward persistence of the unseen musician. Lidia had already stepped into the aisle, agreeing with Donatella, who put a finger to her lips. They tiptoed through the chancel arch and past the spiraling pulpit, into the nave and down to the vestibule. The music stopped, so they did, too. A little flourish of pages shuffled and strings tuned came from behind a screen just beyond the baptismal font. A chair scraped the floor, a nose was blown, bow and instrument met unintentionally, and the rehearsal continued.

Lidia was easily convinced to keep their eavesdropping secret. Donatella moved out of the church after her but looked back more than once. In the graveyard, deep shadows had grown out of the day's sunshine, few children left to bother a bent figure clipping grass. He turned to wave his shears at them and identify himself as Tobias, the old man the Captain had greeted at the Abbey gates the evening of the dance. Lidia was soon distracted by the village girl, who wondered why she wasn't wearing the flower circlet; Donatella by something only she seemed to notice along with the few and far between raindrops cooling her cheeks, one cloud seeming to hang over her alone.

There was nothing unusual about anonymous hands ringing the tower bells at noon. What could explain the sudden ability of the violinist to raise his voice over and beyond their resonance, finding his muse and virtuosity? He was amazing, coming from nowhere, better than he had ever been, having lost nothing of his passion for life, tempting the world into believing it was also of his making.

Donatella wanted to know if Lidia or anyone else heard what she did. The girl with the daisy chain atop her cap was sitting and gesturing with a newly made friend on the churchyard steps. A woman was shaking a rug across the street as her next door neighbor came out to chat with her. Tobias had slung a small sack over his shoulder; he looked distracted, even fearful. Roger North emerged from the church, his jacket concealing an object held under his arm. He nodded to Tobias and less obviously to Donatella before hurrying away in the opposite direction than she expected.

Making
Acquaintance

CHAPTER SEVEN

A year before, on her birthday, Donatella had worn a flower in her hair put there by the hand of a master. Now there wasn't any heat, just a fine breezy morning and afternoon showers clearing into an evening with full moonlight. To finish the day, her mother set out an overcooked sugar cake and the elderberry wine that made her too talkative and the Captain not mind that she was.

Mama's singing could still lure him back from his wanderings. There wasn't any sign of the cough that disturbed everyone's sleep and she was as nimble as ever on the spinet despite having to push back the bench and her arms rubbing the sides of her bosom. After three songs, her fatigue was evident and she fell into the high-backed chair the Captain gave up for one last inspection of the garden before dark.

Donatella took over and sat at the left-sided keyboard, tapping out a recollection, whispering its words until her mother revived and wasn't nearly as reserved.

"Beauty with her eye entices
"people into amorous dalliances,
"while Courtesy firmly guides their hearts
"while Courtesy firmly guides their hearts
"toward purer sentiments.
"while Courtesy firmly guides their hearts
"while Courtesy firmly guides their hearts
"toward purer sentiments."

Lidia had come into the room with the excuse of clearing up the dishes and crumbs, but joined in the impromptu recital. The result was the difference and agreement of three voices repeating the verse with its repetitions and ending with Mama musing, "Ah, those purer sentiments."

"Giving the world its spinsters." Donatella's hands fell to her lap.

"Perhaps less disappointed than the rest of us."

Donatella didn't disagree with her mother and not just because she was being respectful. Disappointment wasn't something she felt, not why she cried or kept so much to herself. If anything, it was gratefulness that made her sad.

"Nonna sang the part of Beauty, in Modena, I believe. Not with Signor Stradella, who hadn't come that way yet. She must've been thrilled when he moved in."

Donatella hesitated to speak of him, afraid of revealing what she didn't say.

"And you?" Her mother switching to English might have been so Lidia would only wonder what she meant or for Donatella to be less careful. "Oh, admit it. Despina said you were quite helpful, making copies, even taking care of him when he was sick."

"Yes, I ... copied ... him."

"For him."

"For him."

"Anything for him."

It was odd that it had taken so long for them to have this conversation.

"You shouldn't hide how you knew such a celebrity."

"Don't make it more than it was, Mama."

"Is that what my sister did? Yes, I suppose Despina would, welcoming the attention but not the possibilities. Well, at last I heard from her, after I wrote three times."

"She's well?"

"Would she have us believe otherwise? Do you want to read it?" She pulled a folded letter from under some music on the spinet.

Donatella refused and played a melody line that came into her head.

"That's pretty. But listen to this. She writes of rumors that Signor Stradella's music wasn't properly inventoried, dealings going on to exclude it and other things from his nieces' rightful inheritance."

"It was all there when I left," Donatella was quick to say.

"I can't believe it. No, my dear, I mean what Despina says next. Although considering Signor Garibaldi's own injury, who could blame him taking something for himself?"

"He lives. And so does his wife. That should be compensation enough."

"Ah, but the humiliation he suffered might need more."

"Julianna, you're not helping." The Captain returned quietly, as if to catch them breaking his rule that Donatella work at being more familiar than foreign to him.

"Some things don't translate, Edward," Mama teased.

"That's what I'm afraid of." He reclaimed the chair as Mama stood. She immediately attempted to sit in his lap, but Bianchi landed there first.

"See, Donata, how they refuse what they once wanted you for?"

Donatella sided with her father, not by saying so, but lowering her eyes and following the example of his understated repudiation.

A man who lived so much of his life on the sea, loving its ups and downs, unpredictability and endless ports, making money he hardly used and acquaintances he easily left, should never have had a wife and daughter. Yet that was the father Donatella had hoped to meet again:

gone ashore but not landed, retired but not removed from the spirit of adventure that connected her to him. She wasn't disappointed. She found him lost to the whims of the weather, charting a course with his garden, steering her mother from her fancies, sailing away for long absences in his study or garden or to circumnavigate the village. His thoughtful silences still impressed her. His eyes had lost their directness but not kindness; his hair was grayer but remained thick as did his accent.

***

Young Francis North's tutor soon departed to the continent for the summer, putting the obligation of Donatella's English lessons on conversations at home and slowing down her progress considerably.

She had just begun to feel relaxed at the big house, not as if she belonged there, but a little less intrusive each time she walked up its long crunching front road in sun and shade until the oaks had greened and dropped their catkins and the horse chestnuts lifted into candle flowers. It was odd, but quite helpful, that it never rained on those days. If her mother wasn't with her and the Captain hurried ahead in hopes of meeting Roger, Donatella would take little detours that didn't change her destination, although there was a sense of getting lost in the grazing sheep and naturalness around her. She felt her legs tighten as she went up the banks for she had walked so little in her life and run even less. Looping her sagging satchel of books and papers around her, she took off like a kitten moving faster than it knew how to. It felt good to leave the ground and swing her arms, to trip and even slide as she thought no one saw.

Once inside the Abbey, she couldn't hide the mess her boots were and made.

"Oh, Master Roger. I just cleaned the entryway." The housemaid hadn't yet seen the dwindling trail of mud through the Great Hall.

Roger positioned himself strategically so she wouldn't notice it. "What, Mary? Oh, dear. Perhaps young Francis did it."

"He's abed with a cold."

"I didn't know." Roger held his hat over his heart. "Well, I scraped my boots outside." He guessed Donatella was about to own up. "But not well enough." His hand behind his back waved her out of sight.

She was and wasn't surprised by his consideration. She could hardly say she knew him, except as her father spoke of his ideas and love of sailing. Otherwise, Roger was obviously serious, shy and more judicious than gallant in understanding a little dirt on the carpet was easier to sweep away than cross words.

She had seen his conciliation before on Oak Apple Day as a watchful yet indulgent guardian to his nephew Francis and a lad of similar age who didn't hesitate to climb the tree her father probably wished he hadn't advertised as having the best galls in the village.

"John Lely, be careful." Roger was ready to break the lad's fall before he seemed to calculate it wouldn't be in his own interest and stepped back. "You might, but I can't forget your well-being is entrusted to me."

Donatella imagined the Captain's garden trembled at the rowdiness in the village that day, and thought him wise to let in only the two boys under Roger's supervision. She was reminded of *Carnevale* with the streets full of people in ridiculous costumes rowdily singing, banging on pots and blowing horns, a squeaky fiddler here and there.

The celebrants called out anyone who didn't show agreement with their antics.

Her father made sure Donatella was wearing the oak as royally as she could, although the garden gate was as far as she would go to participate in the politics that seemed sillier and sillier, especially a chant that made no sense to her at all: "Grovely, grovely, and all grovely. The 29th of May is pinch bum day. Show loyalty to the king or it's your turn to run away."

Her mother waved a majestic branch over a wall to be seen from the street. A cheer acknowledged that, at least in spirit, she was on the right side. She approached Roger. "What about your park, all those fine oaks?"

"They're too tall to climb, Mistress."

"And the woods that stretch towards Banbury?"

"We try not to disturb what lives there."

She looked dissatisfied with Roger's quiet but unyielding answers.

"Come down now," he implored the boy in the tree.

John Lely climbed even higher and young Francis North seemed more upset than his uncle. Mama looked up, shielding her eyes from the daredevil leaning out of the glare of the sun.

The Captain was impressed. "He has the stuff for running up rigging."

"I won't have him on my vessel." Roger finally showed real annoyance.

"Of course, that's different." The Captain realized an opportunity. "When will you take her out again?"

"John. Come down."

"Damn. What a view. Hey, Francis. Don't be a sissy."

"Please, Johnny." Roger's nephew already preferred diplomacy to daring. "We're missing the parade."

"Piss off then. Perhaps I'll stay up here all day like our merry monarch at Boscobel."

"Well, as risky to your neck, I'll give you that." The Captain appealed more to Roger's predicament than the boy's cleverness. "I think he's bluffing."

John Lely dropped out of the tree, picked himself up, and dusted himself down.

Roger tried to ignore him. "You asked me something, Edward."

"Yes. Just wondering when you'll sail again?"

"I don't know. There's usually two yachting seasons, Lent and Michelmas. Down that way, summer is mostly too hot and calm, unless by accident we get a spell that's cool and windy."

"Uncle, we're missing the parade."

"Manners, Francis."

John Lely's were still in rebellion as he approached Mama. "My father should have painted you."

"I'll keep this one," Mama encouraged his insolence.

"You wouldn't want him for long." Roger seemed as displeased with his nephew, holding onto his collar as the other boy escaped his influence.

"The almanac forecasts a cool summer, for London, too."

"Is that so?" Roger inattentively answered the Captain. "All right." He released young Francis, who hesitated as if waiting for his uncle's counsel. "Go on, but remember yourself."

CHAPTER EIGHT

Donatella found it almost agreeable to get to know some of the customs and characters of the village, except when she tired of being amenable to anything but her bed, the cooing outside her window, and Caprice and Bianchi purring and kneading. She thought about sketching the bluebells her father had collected on one of his long walks, but they arranged themselves in a small cream pot too limply to motivate her. She had thoughts that once would have inspired poems or journal entries, and heard melodies as if they were her own inventions, which was absurd for she was nothing but an imitator when it came to music.

Even before she left Genoa, there were times she thought she was inventing it. She didn't attempt to write it down, so there wasn't any rational way to explain the few sheets of awkward music notation that appeared at the bottom of her trunk when she finally emptied it. As miraculously, folded neatly among her belongings brought from Genoa, she found the lace collar she thought she had negligently left hanging over the mirror in Nonna's room.

"How odd." Her mother couldn't help but notice the neckline accessory Donatella wore in contrast to the color and quality of her gray dress. "It looks like a man's cravat, a very fashionable one of ten years ago, such fine linen, and lace more Venetian than Genoese. Here, loosen it a little, as it's strangling you."

"Going out walking again?" The Captain exaggerated her taking exercise.

"I'd come along, but your papa doesn't trust my influence," Mama exclaimed and coughed.

"What was that, Julianna?"

"Oh, I told her to take Lidia and be back in an hour."

"Hmm."

Lidia was waiting outside, half-submerged in a wildly climbing shrub more effectively concealing the scullery porch. She probably hoped to avoid Martha's notice and nettled tongue, the servant teaching her more English than Donatella did.

The girl emerged and smiled. "I wondered if you'd ever wear it again."

Halfway up a back road overgrown with shadows, where unseen creatures shuffled about, branches whined, and bushes leapt out at them, Lidia finally revealed that before leaving the house near Luccoli she had retrieved the treasured collar and, once on the ship, waited until

Donatella was asleep to put it in her trunk.

It explained one stowaway but not another.

The way ahead was cocoon-like, lacking light and air while nourishing growth, giving the impression of protection except as a chill ran through it. The weather had been dry for almost a week, but overhanging trees, piney shrubs and ferns held onto the last rainfall as grief did its tears and with the same illusion of relief.

Lidia grabbed Donatella's hand as crows clamored in the trees and sky. The path they were on ended abruptly in bright light and a wider road with an untidy farmyard to the left and dry-stone walling to the right high enough to hide a competent whistler. There were also flowers: spikes of peacock-blue buds and sprays of silver filtering the breeze but not so many fragrances. Donatella inhaled all the scents that stood out and blended like the different colors, textures, and elevations from a plain iron gate down a cobbled path to a squat little cottage with its roof thatch wearing thin and front wall bulging slightly under some strain.

She propped herself on the gate and the whistling stopped, Tobias, aggressively waving a hoe, appearing in front of his home.

"Hello." Roger came out from the southwest sunshine in his familiar hat and sturdy leggings. "If I didn't know that strange fellow better, I'd say he created the Garden of Eden." He expressed wit, irreverence, and another competency: "The Captain would scold me, not addressing you in English."

Donatella could hardly mimic her father's familiarity with him, holding back a smile when she noticed the mud streaked from cheek to cheek over the long hump of Roger's nose. "You speak the Italian."

"You don't need 'the', but your English is improving."

"Well ... I want ... little words ...."

He pushed back his hat, showing short reddish-brown hair, embarrassed eyes, and a depression below his mouth. "So do I. Except when I write or am at the law."

"Have ye bin look'n down a rabbit hole, sir?" Tobias had come to the gate, Donatella soon discovering he hadn't any intention of opening it.

It was Roger who needed the remark interpreted. "What?"

Donatella supposed what the old man had said and came close to touching Roger's face, but instead wiped the air. He used his sleeve to remove most of the evidence of an unknown adventure.

Neither noticed what happened before squeaky hinges allowed Lidia into Tobias' yard, only that the white haired, short-legged, but surprisingly agile old man led her into his well-tended wilderness.

"Lidia?" Donatella panicked as they disappeared.

"Don't worry," Roger assured with a little tremor in his voice, too. Or perhaps it was that controlled irritation she had witnessed before, when something or someone disturbed his composure or wasted his time. "Tobias only cares to keep out demons."

She felt the chill of what Roger had said, even looked over her shoulder and tried to brush something off.

He pulled his hat forward again. "Must get back. My brother has important guests coming. I might wish to avoid them, but can't. Good day."

His abrupt departure should have been less surprising than his stopping and turning to add, "Is your father at home?"

She wondered about his hurrying away before she understood and answered, until she remembered the loss of Lidia. It was her turn to enter Tobias' world and she walked a narrow path between steeples rising in stained glass colors, bells mutely swinging and spicy incense claiming the same breeze, florid congregations rising and bowing to the sun as monk hoods led prayers for bleeding hearts shriveling into their fates. Her eyes followed a butterfly from flower to flower until it flew too high and went out of sight.

I might have liked to grow old. But not like you will with all those secrets and regrets.

She saw Martha passing by carrying the large basket Mama suspected accounted for missing food. The Captain blamed rabbits and rodents for disturbances among his lettuces, carrots, and early potatoes. Her mother tried to be forgiving because Martha lived on the shoddy side of the village. Finally, Donatella could give that consideration direction as she assumed the somehow well-fed woman was headed home.

Martha didn't notice either Donatella or Lidia, the latter hugging a bouquet of blooms with banner and wing petals bi-colored in velvety purple and maroon, yet as light as the organza Genoese princesses wore.

Lidia held them to her nose and then to Donatella's. "Pea flower." She was always proud to say something in English.

"He grew them?"

"Yes."

"Where is he now?"

The answer came with Lidia following Tobias to lose him in the gloomy interior of his cottage. The door slammed, opened and closed hard again and again, Tobias ranting, "Out. Out. Get out. Out."

Lidia was almost struck by his violence.

"Out. Can't stay. Out. Get out."

"It must be in his mind," Donatella reasoned and related, "Roger North said something—"

"There you are." The Captain was in the lane.

"What wrong with him?" Donatella was glad to see her father, even knowing why he was there.

He noticed the posy in Lidia's hands.

"Pea flowers." Donatella was suddenly convinced.

"He's crazy, but look at this paradise. No wonder he's desperate to keep the devil out."

"What?"

"Hey, Tobias," the Captain called to the old man now insistently sweeping his doorstep, "these aren't pea flowers like I've ever seen."

"Get out."

"So where did they come from? Not someone called Lucifer, eh?" The Captain should have resisted, a broom flying at him and Lidia begging for something no one could understand.

Tobias pushed her aside, pointing at Donatella, who felt very cold. "There. Behind ye."

CHAPTER NINE

Her father offered Donatella his jacket and idea of comfort. "Better the devil you know."

Donatella shouldered the weight of all the secrets she must keep from him.

Tobias continued to yell, the Captain motioning Lidia to come away from him. "You're a pretty thing. There are lads enough to pick you flowers."

Lidia lagged behind until she saw the boys hanging around the pond as they often did, the Captain's bulky arms urging her—and Donatella—safely homewards.

"This came." Mama met them as they rushed into the front hallway of the cottage. She showed off a communication and that its seal was broken before reluctantly giving it up. "An invitation to the Abbey. Tonight."

"What time?" The Captain kissed her cheek like Caprice licked Bianchi to coax her off the pillows on Donatella's bed. He read the note and wanted his daughter to do the same.

Donatella squinted and silently moved her lips.

"Out loud."

She understood his folding arms.

"Please for ... give ... the ... late ... um ... um ...."

"Notice—"

"Notice."

"Know what it means?"

"Yes."

"Hmm. Go on."

"We re ... re—"

"Request."

"Request?"

"Invite. Ask for," her mother's disobedient whisper ended Donatella's puzzlement.

The Captain hardly noticed. "I'll need to change. I think my wool. No, not for this occasion. Anyway, it's too warm. Then again, the Abbey is a drafty place."

"Trust me. I always make you look good. Lidia," Mama startled the pensive girl arranging the flowers Tobias had given her in a blue and white pot, "are they wild?"

"No. Rare specimens, not native, of course," the Captain answered. "I suspect Roger gave him the seeds."

"Well, your influential friend should give you some. A luscious scent. Imagine gowns in those colors."

Donatella always marveled how her mother's mind handled so many directions.

"Perfect for *Carnevale*. What a shame you never went, Donata. Or did you?" She saw the Captain wasn't watching and took the note from her daughter. "Well, there's no mention of us ladies. There would never be time to get ready. But you, Edward, you can easily manage a light supper and good conversation at the eight o'clock hour."

"English, Julianna. How will Donatella learn?"

"As she needs to."

Mama's hard coughing caused concern until Lidia and Donatella got her to bed and quieted with a cup of something hot and herbal. The Captain dressed in his warmest longest coat and vest after all, Donatella correcting him before he left with his wig a little crooked and a few wrinkles in his stockings. She re-tied his cravat so it didn't appear skimpy and mentioned as best she could that a recount of the evening, especially what was discussed, would be a good lesson.

"The words perhaps. Not the politics."

She saw him off in ignorance, loving him a little less than when the sea stole him away, nothing as attractive as not knowing when or even if he was coming back.

She hoped he wouldn't be late, having no excuse to stay up except that she was as in need of his adventures as when she was a girl and could count on one hand the times he shared any with her. She went downstairs just before midnight, silent enough in her slippers, giving the cats a little cream before they even whimpered for it. She left out oatmeal bread and cheese curds in case a light supper hadn't satisfied her father and he was stirred up and too restless to go directly to bed. Even if his body longed for it, his mind would want to hold on to the time he had just spent with Roger, who was slowly becoming a worthy acquaintance: resourceful if reserved, principled and pleasant without saying things he didn't mean, not afraid to have his hands dirty or ideas challenged. He seemed a noble fellow who took time out of his official life for more agreeable activities like sailing, which was something that might be discussed that evening.

It was a sultry night, too warm for waiting in the sitting room where the windows were kept closed to avoid the dust off the street, at least as her mother imagined it. The cottage was high and far back from Mills Lane, more likely to offer the pleasure of birdsong and welcome breezes than anything to irritate the lungs. Donatella slipped off her shawl, and, as she swung back her plait, noticed her nightgown was dampened with sweat. She was ready to cover herself up again, sitting on the bench in the front hall, putting her candle on the floor, counting the times it flickered but not on falling asleep.

Who was knocking? She woke in a panic as much for where she was as who would find her there slumped against the wall with a pain in her neck and confusion as to why the hallway was unlit and the ceiling so low. She realized soon enough that the candle had burned down and she wasn't in a tall chandeliered house in Genoa anymore. She felt for her shawl that had fallen behind the bench, stood stiffly, moved slowly and leaned against the front door.

"Papa?"

She went outside, her head brushing the bamboo chimes her mother loved to hear and her father was sorry he had taken from his ship to give her. She knew her way down uneven steps and kept close to yew bushes along the cottage's lengthy front to answer a dare that turned her into a prowler. Moonlight gave the night shape, trees a boundary to its clutter, honeysuckle and onions mixing sweet thoughts with sour, a low mist imagining the reason she was wandering to be more mysterious than mistaken.

If you were willing to follow me, it might be easier.

She realized she was crying, in a way that hurt physically as it was hard to breathe.

"Who's there? What are you doing?" a man's voice bellowed.

She took her cue from a rabbit standing upright a few feet away.

"If you're stealing from my garden, there'll be hell to pay."

Such a threatening tone was all she needed to make a run for it, too. She hoped the scullery door would save her, except her father used the same shortcut into the cottage.

"Oh, dear girl. Did I wake you? I thought I saw someone in the garden."

"I ... yes ... also ...."

"I need to repair that break in the wall."

It was only as he moved towards the larder that she realized he was tipsy.

"Let me."

"Were you waiting up?" He sat heavily at the table used more for kneading bread than eating it. She brushed it with her hand before setting down the plate she had prepared earlier. "No reason for you to."

She settled across from him as though ignorant of his dismissal.

"What do you want to know?" He chuckled. "I know that look. You're not much like your mother, but I know that look."

He must have laughed a lot at sea and that evening as she rarely saw him do, using all his face and both shoulders.

"Who was there? Great company, or so they obviously think of themselves. Near thirty gentlemen, among them Lord Northampton, a mayor and aldermen along with the council of Banbury. I'm sure they all expected Sir Francis to conduct the evening from start to finish, but once he received them, conversed a little and drank to them, he retired and left the rest to his poor brother. Roger is so ill-equipped for entertaining such a number, especially when sack is the business and drunkenness the end. I'm sure that's why he sent my invitation last minute."

Donatella pinched off a little bread, those emotions she thought she swallowed stuck in her throat.

"I have to say it loosened me and put us all on the same footing. What we talked about at first was too dry to recall and eventually not for your ears in any language. It shows the little difference between men when they are attended with glasses and bottles, and apt to find their lodgings in ditches on the way home."

Donatella suspected it wasn't appropriate to smile.

"Still that look. For I haven't told you anything that makes sense, have I?"

She shrugged and lifted her hands.

"I feel how alike we are. But, dammit, I can't talk to you. And I can't teach you. I'm no good at that sort of thing. And your mother lets you cheat. I asked Roger if he could help."

She felt some embarrassment.

"By then he was like a wounded deer, saying he was on fire and needed some shady moist place to lie down, certain he would be sick for days." The Captain chewed slower and slower, bracing his elbows on the table, rubbing his hands together, his head swaying and eyes closing as he continued, "There isn't much time. Roger expects an appointment to King's Council in the fall. I just hope we can get in that sail before he's lost to us."

Donatella didn't quite touch her father's arm.

"You should've got married, my dear." His hand covered hers. "That's what every woman should do. I suppose it's too late."

"Yes, Papa." She knew what he wanted her to say.

CHAPTER TEN

She was anxious because Roger didn't smile or sit or know where to stand. He moved around the room, as pious as the paneling depicting Christ and the Apostles, and looked up at book-crammed shelves for deliverance, all the while listening. If Donatella stumbled over her reading, he came closer, touched the page, his face as flushed as she hoped hers wasn't. He continued to circle the library while she struggled with the words and stuffiness and, especially, his glances at the clock on the otherwise empty mantle.

She couldn't fault him cranking open a few lower panes of the bay window with a morning bright view of the estate's back terracing. His shoulders relaxed.

The sound of whistling was unmistakable.

"Another warm one. Take off your jacket, Tobias," Roger called.

Donatella closed her book with a pressed leaf she had found in it keeping her place. Lidia got up to see, her hands folded in front of her as she walked to the window. When Roger commented softly and simply in Italian, she might have been his sister or cousin or a niece shyly smiling and tilting her head.

"He won't do it." Roger meant to check the time again, Donatella's self-conscious approach obstructing him. "The man will roast rather than be seen without a coat."

"Don't bother over him," offered the servant sitting in the room with them, a constantly sighing woman who wasn't very good at embroidery.

Lidia must have understood her tone, glancing at her before leaving a space alongside Roger that Donatella felt obliged to fill.

"Oh. What happens to the ... parterres?"

"We're taking them out. I should be getting stuck in, too, for it has to be done quicker than is possible." His eyes could hardly seem more apologetic than they naturally did. "I mean, I don't mind sparing this time. I understand the Captain's concern for your—"

"But why the parterres?"

"Well," he hesitated, "I'm on a mission. To do away with much of the formality. At least, the appearance of it."

"Yes."

"You understand?"

She nodded, looking straight ahead, feeling a breeze and that she had pleased him.

His demeanor opened like a peacock's tail. No doubt he was proud of his plan as he revealed it in well-chosen words and gestures that, if nothing else, told her he was a writer. "We'll reuse the box yew for serpentine walks hedged like straight ones, through little forests of flowering trees and shrubs, cherries and Laburnums and in some sheltered spot a Judas, with places for losing sight of the house or one's grievances and to enjoy the scent of honeysuckle or barely the sound of water, to sit a while and then walk on without knowing where one path or other leads, coming upon a sundial circled by lavender and finally the sight of a ladies pond floating with lilies and framed by willows with barks of bright yellow.

"Of course, I'm probably a fool to think informality can be accomplished by design."

"Yes."

"Yes?"

"No? Oh." Donatella had another reason to panic. "Lidia?"

"She left." The servant was pulling out stitches again. "You might guess where to."

Raising his arm to direct Donatella's eyes, Roger's hand brushed the edging lace on her sleeve. He had her attention by accident and as intended when she looked out the window and down to where Tobias seemed as shocked when Lidia crouched by him to wrap the roots of one of the shrubs he had dug up.

"Lidia," Donatella was embarrassed to raise her voice, "you spoil yourself."

The girl stood and lifted her skirt to see her shoes.

Tobias must have thought she was leaving and caught her hand, but let it go when somehow she convinced him to.

Roger conspired, too. "We could use the help. She's small, but there are things she can do."

Donatella knew she was losing, not only Lidia, but the battle to remain impassive.

"I'm sorry," Roger meant one thing and then another, "that your lesson was interrupted. Shall we continue?"

Donatella's few steps to the table were slower than his towards the servant with her head slumped and needlework hanging from her hands.

"Mary," his soft entreaty didn't wake her, his insistence not much louder. "Mary."

"What ... oh ... sir. I can't sit so long without doz'n off."

"Never mind. I need you to go find some clothes. For the girl who came with Mistress Cavanna-Hanley."

"She seemed dressed fitting to me, sir."

"Not for gardening, Mary."

"I might find her a large apron, sir."

"Yes, that would do."

"Now, sir?"

"Please."

Her eyes rolled around the room to Donatella.

"Have you ever heard of me behaving improperly with a woman, Mary?"

"You don't have much to do with women at all, sir."

Roger opened the door to Lidia, who curtsied and avoided Mary by setting her sights on Donatella, who didn't know where to look until the girl sat down, her fingernails dirty, eyes reddening, and her cap and even hair caught by a few small but stubborn stickseeds Donatella tried to pick off.

By the time Mary came back with a hugely pocketed apron, Donatella had exhausted her concentration, and Roger, if his distraction at the window was anything to go by, didn't mind.

He asked if Donatella would stay for dinner, relaxing his shoulders again as she declined.

"Mary, tell the kitchen to put together a basket of bread, cheese, hard-yolked eggs, and cider for my sharing with Tobias. Also, butter, jam, and lemonade for Lidia if she joins us."

Hearing Tobias' name along with her own was enough for Lidia to assume what Roger was talking about. She turned to Donatella with a gentle hold on her arm. "Can't you stay? Just another hour or two? Not to work, but you might watch."

Roger understood enough of Lidia's entreaty to support it. "You could have some refreshment after all, on the terrace behind the chapel, and study more. Take these books." He picked up two from the table, then replaced one with another, thinking to give them to Donatella but hesitating until with a slight smile she accepted them and whatever else he was suggesting.

***

Donatella wasn't certain what language she was thinking in as the high sun warmed her face, throat, and lower arms. A soft slice of bread carried salty cheese to her mouth, some of the cider she drank strayed sourly up her nose, but she managed to swallow and then muffled a sneeze into her hands. Determined flies couldn't spoil the significance of her sitting there in a strange place that begged to be familiar, pasturage rolling to the left and right and rising and lowering into diversely deciduous woods. She might be anyone more fortunate than she was, basking in the glow of golden stone and acquaintances she should be entirely out of place with.

Lidia's labors were invisible since Tobias' wheelbarrow led her voluntarily into the shadows. Roger instructed them in low uncertain terms, much as he had Donatella earlier.

"Take these, as well. You'd rather write than speak, I think."

Her stomach had jumped, Roger's perception affecting her like a deaf person suddenly able to hear. She had felt there wasn't any choice but to accept the writing materials and what he assumed she would do with them.

On the bamboo cart rolled out with her lunch, her arm resting on the books Roger had lent her to shield a blank sheet of paper from the wind, she wielded a well-sharpened quill with good intentions, but couldn't help clinging to her mother tongue and every sinking feeling. After a little while, Sir Francis approached along the ivy draped wall that overlooked a sunken courtyard of vines and ferns, clipped conifers, creeping sedums, and basins of shriveling azaleas encircled by marigolds. His heels hit the slate walkway with an authority his brother didn't have.

He lifted one of the books she was afraid he might ask her about. "Ah, Marvell. 'Society is all but rude, to this delicious solitude.' We may admire his lyrical gift despite his politics."

Again, she was surprised by how much she was suddenly hearing, more than pronunciations or translation word by word, as if listening to a musical phrase or seeing a painting for all its strokes. She wanted to think English should only to be used for practical expression so she might need it without ever really loving it, but it was inevitable that a writer in one language would be unable to resist the poetry of another.

"'Such was that happy garden-state, while Man there walk'd without a mate.'"

Roger appeared with the wheelbarrow and raised his hand when he saw his much older brother.

"'How well the skillful gard'ner drew of flow'rs and herbs this dial new. Where from above the milder sun does through a fragrant Zodiac run. And, as it works, th'industrious bee computes its time as well as we. How could such sweet and wholesome hours be reckon'd but with herbs and flow'rs.'"

Sir Francis laid the volume on the cart, examining the other one there. "Botany. Some fine plates. I hear you paint well yourself." He closed the book and consideration of her artistic abilities. "Oh, your neck and arms are burned."

"Yes," she answered as she thought might satisfy him.

"It might not be as hot as you're used to, but this time of year the pavement and midday sun can soon cook anything in-between. Perhaps they have something in the kitchen."

"Cucumber." Roger was coming up the hill, taking off his gloves and hat. "Prevents blistering."

"That's right. Lady Frances was always so careful, except once at a fete when the sun caught the back of her neck. We used cucumber slices to soothe her."

"Yes, I remember. She had a true English complexion." Roger was attentive to his brother walking away with his head bowed. He looked back to Donatella and his face reddened more than her arms. "Yours has an Englishness about it, too."

"It does?" She couldn't help but be playful.

"What's this?" He looked for and almost immediately found something else to talk about, "You've been writing music."

She couldn't remember what she had done. The composition he held wasn't really hers, although she wanted it back to keep a secret that was.

He wouldn't give it up. "I see you've just begun a comfortable soprano line. One you could sing yourself? Don't get carried away with flourishes. So far, just a few notes of basso continuo. Make sure it has regular movement.

"Above all, the text must be considered. 'Courtesy cost me your devotion.'" He paused, his head angled upwards. "It must be heard. 'To speak of the heart's secrets is to give away their endurance.' How aptly an unfulfilled passion is pictured in the key of F flat."

She was glad Lidia was finally there, taking off the apron somehow as clean as when it was loaned to her.

"Yes. Time to go."

"Time to go," Lidia echoed.

"I hope you'll finish it and perform it sometime. Do you play an instrument? Not the lute, I hope. I always think the spinet or harpsichord keeps a lady's posture better, while a lute or guitar tends to make her crooked."

If Donatella understood anything of Roger's opinion, it was that she shouldn't seem too receptive, even as he returned what he thought was hers, his bow and admiration just one more thing she must be imagining.

CHAPTER ELEVEN

Roger was away from Wroxton more often than not, frustrating plans for the estate gardens, sailing excursions, and English lessons. Donatella had one more class with him at the big house, which was also about testing young Francis and John Lely's Italian before they returned south to school. Lidia was only interested in knowing where Tobias was working that day, an uncertain answer leaving the girl to look out the window without another word to say in any language. It was the end of August but as chilly as Genoa in November, and barely half an hour after they arrived, it began to rain hard.

Due to the weather or because of a sufficient number of encounters, Roger was more sociable, to the point of sitting across from Donatella and leaning forward even when she didn't need to be corrected. He kept to the strategy that allegorical poetry and botanical pictures were the way to teach her what she needed to know. At least she would be well versed in English conceits and paradoxes and imageries overusing buds and blossoms. She didn't fault his approach because that would have been ungrateful and disingenuous while lyrical phrases translated into more about the evolution of her writing than speaking.

Just after two in the afternoon, Roger suggested showing her more of the house. He realized his nephew, John Lely, and Lidia were all he had for chaperones and organized them in the library hallway without much hope they would stay in line. Donatella resisted smiling at Roger's tenaciousness one moment and faltering the next, which seemed to be annoyance that he ever had to order anything but his own mind. She didn't doubt it was safe to be with him and even alone with him, a younger man so dedicated to reasoning that only actions well thought out were for doing. If there was any impulse in him, surely it would never manifest until examined and cross-examined and found to be innocent enough.

"Follow me."

Her skirt lacked the fullness to sweep up the main stairs, which in any case would have been impossible behind Roger stopping and stooping to inspect the spiraling balusters and unvarnished paneling piled perpendicularly for the first half-a-dozen stairs.

"Please, watch your step."

Donatella heard his frustration and saw it was with himself, until he noticed Lidia trying to avoid the tussling of two boys acting as one.

"Lads. Watch your step."

Roger frowned on John Lely ribbing Francis, who stood straight with his hands at his side. His dealings with them gave Donatella a chance to linger on the golden portraits checkering the high walls: prominently positioned ladies and gentlemen staring down on her interest in paintings that convincingly captured the pursed mouths, peculiar hairstyles, requisite jewels, rouged flesh, and folded fabric of long lost lives. The rainy day dulled colored windows and a hanging tapestry. A servant, hardly older than Lidia and wearing a mop hat a size too small, stepped past Donatella with a pungent taper, its flame flapping like a flag, wax dripping on her hands. She gave it to Roger, who was on the first landing and only had to stretch a little to open and light a six-sided lantern suspended almost two stories from the stairwell's domed ceiling.

He returned the candle to the compliant maid with a softly worded command that wouldn't let her escape, perhaps for Lidia's sake as much as his own.

"Through here is another of my projects."

Donatella assumed from the shuffling steps behind her that otherwise quiet girls and boys were coming along.

"Again, I'm asking you to perceive with the imagination as well as the eye."

In contrast to the ochre and oaken corridor, there was brightness around him. He stepped aside so Donatella might see the cause of it on entering an unfurnished room that was large and lofty with walls that angled in and out. Its competently tongue and groove floor was coated with plaster dust and its bare views east and south, far and wide, magnified the dreary afternoon into a remembrance of sunshine.

She should have been embarrassed by Roger studying her reaction.

"It looks as if it doesn't know what it wants to be, don't you think?"

"No. It wants to be ... splendid." She was hopeful she had found a real word.

"Yes. It can't help but be so. That's the problem."

She found translating easier if she followed his expression, in this case the lowering of his eyes. "Oh, I see. A cruel beauty who craves nothing but worship."

"That's it." His clap condoned, even appreciated, a slip into the music of her past. "This room insists on elegance and extravagantly displaying itself, shown off for grander folk than Francis and I care to deal with. Something I fear will only become harder to avoid."

Roger reminded Donatella of a turtle, poking his head out of his shell to swing it around with a little curiosity and even ambition, only to pull it back in rather than face the prospect of going somewhere. When he did move he was slow and faltering, as if suspicious of his own intentions, let alone anyone else's, although he might be quick enough to escape harm.

"Well, what's begun must be finished."

Donatella walked around his predicament of needing but not wanting to dress and adorn that shapely space at the expense of a quiet life. It might have seemed barren without furniture and drapes and other complements, but instead had the glow of expectancy its architect had given it and now couldn't abandon. She touched chalky walls and corner flutings and imagined what more could be made of the ceiling between crown moldings, counting her steps one end to another, pressing her nose to windows cold with condensation and curtained outside with mist. Roger had sat on a low ladder rung, hugging his knees, watching her every move except when she looked to see if he was.

"How to say? I see ... gold."

Flossed wallpaper, brocade curtains and, yes, golden mirrors and light fixtures.

He shook his head, not necessarily in disagreement. "You sound nostalgic. Some place in Rome?"

"Rome? I no been."

"Have not been." He got up. "As I have not been to Genoa. Do you miss it?"

Just another city to love and hate.

"What?" She pivoted to question the space behind her.

"I'm sorry. Of course, it's not my business."

Why not? Ask if there will be music.

She didn't have to.

"Over there, in front of the south window, space for a small ensemble, including a harpsichord if called for. Music while dining."

Nothing a musician hates more.

"The dining table is ordered. Larger but lighter than downstairs."

Remember the one that burst through the doors? Ha. These unimaginative English couldn't pull off something like that.

"Perhaps, if there's time, I'll show you samples for draperies and —"

"Lidia?"

If Lidia's face wasn't red from crying, then her embarrassment was for something other than finding Roger and Donatella half a room apart.

"Where are they? What are they up to?" Roger rushed off, a great deal of noise culminating in a scream as Donatella and Lidia completed the ascent of the staircase. They entered what must be the bedroom passageway.

"What's happened?" Roger confronted John Lely at the far end of the hallway. "Where's Francis?"

"He fell. Only to the first landing."

Roger disappeared and John Lely turned away, leaning over. "Can I help?"

"Out of the way," Roger raised his voice, the top of his head, and side of his face, until he emerged cradling his nephew. Then, "Come here, Johnny. Pull back the bedclothes."

"Hey, he lives."

"Lucky for you, too. Did you push him?"

"Would I do that?"

"Quite likely." Roger noticed Donatella crossing the threshold of the room.

Francis was laid on a heavily posted bed, its brocade quilt and other fine covers almost all on the floor. He whined like an infant as his uncle stroked his hair.

Lidia was also there, murmuring a prayer.

"It is bad?"

Roger put up his hand as Donatella began to approach. "I'm sorry for this."

"No, no. Can we give help?"

"The doctor is being sent for. It seems he landed on his side, not back, and bumped his head. I hope I was right to move him."

"Yes," She wished it was easier to speak to Roger, not only in English but also the most appropriate manner. "I think ... see how he—"

"There she goes." John Lely had opened the only window, calling, "Quickly, quickly now, lass."

"Close that. Francis shivers, as Mistress Cavanna-Hanley observed."

"All right. I like that little maid. She has eyes like a sheep. Still she'll probably grow up to be a dog."

Roger's face was flushed as he covered his nephew, whispering close to the boy's cheek.

"I guess I was a little rough." John Lely shrugged and walked towards Lidia who hadn't moved out of the doorway. "Well, I'm not the first guest here to lose his head."

John Lely would soon enough be unsuitably attractive with an extravagant wig to frame fleshy dark eyes and lips, highly defined cheeks and defiance chiseling his nose so it didn't matter if it was a little larger than handsome usually required. He had one foot in roguishness, rarely smiled but was often amused, and always seemed tired yet never wearied of being impossible. Lidia looked at him once and again, the curl of his chin certain she had forgiven him.

Within moments, Roger had his hand on John Lely's shoulder and then escorted Donatella and Lidia down the narrow staircase of Francis' fall, obviously the shortest and least formal route to the front hallway. He ordered their cloaks and hoped it had stopped raining, but, whether it had or not, Donatella's fumbled words relieved him of responsibility for their walk home and left him unaware of her ambivalence over glimpses of sunshine that hardly promised its full return.

***

A few days later Roger was at the cottage, as apologetic as its occupants should have been for letting him stand too long on the front stoop. Martha offered an excuse of being surprised to see him there and suspecting he wouldn't come in even if she had asked him to. Who he was might suggest so but not how he looked, more at home in a county cottage than Whitehall. His wig needed curling, his coat pressing, his shoes cleaning; his ringless hands held a simple package the Captain didn't seem to notice. Roger took the few steps into the sitting room with the posture of a self-conscious giant, which made the taller Captain laugh and forget there was a serious question to be asked.

"How is Francis?" Donatella carefully pronounced her concern.

Roger sat, as directed, in the large armchair still shaped to the Captain's afternoon nap. "His right arm is broken."

Donatella understood "broken" poetically, as what happened to a heart.

"Could've been worse, eh?" The Captain poured but Roger refused a large tankard of ale.

"You wouldn't think so, if you saw his moping."

"Will it keep him out of school?"

"No. That's why he mopes."

"I don't blame him." The Captain brought the drink over to him.

Beyond a sip or two, it was consciously ignored like the brown paper bundle on Roger's lap. "Well, he has to go. It seems his father and I will be stuck in London for a while. Myself to take the silk, and my brother for—"

Mama was suddenly in the room, wrapped in a shawl that almost hid her dressing gown and Bianchi, who loved to be carried around.

Roger stood and the parcel dropped.

"Julianna, should you be out of bed?"

"We have a visitor. When do we ever have visitors?"

"My apologies, Mistress." It was obvious Roger wasn't going to sit again or drink more. "It's just that I wanted to—"

"Bring a gift."

"Well, only a few books I promised to let your daughter borrow and forgot, in all the upset, to send her off with."

"A generosity, all the same." Her mother was pushing Donatella forward, unnecessary in such a small room.

Donatella had read that the turtle's carapace was covered in nerve endings—touch it and the seemingly sheltered creature would feel it. She reached out and it was possible Roger wasn't as protected as he appeared.

CHAPTER TWELVE

The wind blew from all directions up on the Banbury road. Donatella wrapped her arms around her mother to also warm herself. There shouldn't be such a chill in mid-September, the leaves just beginning to turn, days still long enough to grow weary of, and her father's garden not completely harvested. A gust lifted the Captain's wig and his high spirits almost let it blow off his head. The small sack he carried seemed insulting to his stature, but was more than enough for the journey he was about to make. It would be easily set on his lap for the ride by road and stowed on the vessel Roger claimed had room for a man and boy, one servant and himself.

The coach was late and yet again the Captain told them to go home. In another few moments, it was heard before it appeared and threatened to keep going, so the drama of goodbyes was avoided as he chased and cursed it and convinced it to stop.

He had a quick word with the driver, his boots the last thing seen of him, the cabin door closing, his escape also jolting the couple huddling their baskets and each other on top, and the luggage well-strapped into the box at the back. Donatella thought she heard her mother sigh as the vehicle sailed away, listing a little as it disappeared around a corner.

"So what will we do he wouldn't want us to? Oh. I've just done it!"

"But, Mama, I need speak English."

"Yes, of course." Her mother embraced Donatella's waist. "But there must be something, some way to take advantage of your father's absence."

The quickest way home was down Mills Lane, as steep, narrow, and medieval as any of the *carruggi* in Genoa. Walking so close to the privacy of others, it was impossible not to look in windows, listen to some disagreement, and almost run into a woman turning from a door shutting and then opening a crack.

Dark, dirty, and beautiful, she was peddling something more than the apples in her basket.

"Dare we?"

"What, Mama?"

"Yes. I think we might," her mother actually answered the wandering woman who was only slightly less handsome when she smiled and showed the gaps in her teeth.

***

Their lives seemed a little dangerous with the Captain gone. Mama ate in the kitchen between meals and sat on the front steps in the same draft that blew wildly through the porch chimes. Italian was spoken most of the time and sung as unapologetically when she performed on the spinet any time she pleased. She had Martha prepare more sweets than savories and light the parlor fire in the morning as soon as the grate was cleaned, Donatella not adverse to any offense that helped them warm to each other again. Bianchi and Caprice raced up and down the stairs as suddenly even their age didn't prevent, scratched furniture, and discovered other beds than Donatella's to curl up on. Martha was caught sleeping in the Captain's chair.

Only Lidia seemed unaffected, her quiet eyes watching over them, her life yet to be decided, rosary beads hidden in her sleeve, any fears in her faith. The night of the reading she willingly went to her room before Martha was, without explanation, ordered out of the house even though supper hadn't been cleared away.

The timing wasn't quite perfect, and, hopefully, Martha didn't see who was let in through the front door. The visitor was garlanded with ragged scarves of once bright colors, wore heavy earrings that caught in her loose black hair, smelled of sage and rain, and carried a basket without apples this time. She immediately insisted on sitting at a table not in the kitchen. Ushered into the dining room, she eyed the food on the sideboard and didn't hesitate when Mama told her to help herself. The strange woman was uncomfortable because she was watched, but not enough to refuse more than she could eat by wrapping meat, bread, and cheese in a large napkin she would never return. Obeying her persistent, and perhaps rude, gesture, Donatella extinguished all the candles but one.

The gypsy's skirt was even shorter when she sat, her shoes held together with string, her lower legs bare, her fringed shoulders leaning into smoothing out a black cloth where she laid a tattered Tarot deck.

Her lips moved before she said anything aloud, "What you want to know?"

"Everything you can tell me." Mama was sitting across from her, Donatella standing behind her mother.

"Begin. With the cards."

"Yes, oh yes." Mama reached out to the grimy but graceful hand covering them.

"Shuffle first."

Mama was very good at sliding the cards in and out of each other, at different angles and speeds as if in control of her fortune, moving her arms like a juggler and her head like she was dancing. She became breathless with the exercise and lost her grip on what she was doing, one card popping out and landing unrevealed.

She immediately gave up the rest, too, and, despite their curled edges, they flowed out of their owner's hands into a fan across the table. It wasn't Donatella's first experience of divination, but it felt more forbidden without her grandmother's acumen and aunt's surly skepticism.

"Why you stand there?"

"Oh." Donatella sidestepped one way and the other. "Should I leave?"

"I might say so." The woman glanced towards one end of the table. "He is distracting."

"How many?" Her mother only heard her own impatience for the reading.

"No. Don't touch them."

Mama's hands hadn't moved from her lap.

"Not you. Go on. Pick ten."

"I think they pick me."

Donatella was wandering the room, not knowing why she was there or looking for a way out—like Saint Catherine of Genoa's vision of a soul in purgatory.

"Don't turn them, or they turn on you."

Mama let go of the chosen cards. The gypsy flipped and arranged them in a puzzling pattern, holding back the spare one, looking to her left again.

"Ah. He gone."

"My husband? Yes, but only for a week."

The woman gasped, brought back from the dead. "Husband. Yes, I see that."

"What else? Any trouble for us?"

"Mama. Do not ... prompt her."

"Here. And here." The woman tapped one card then another. "A quarrel between your heads."

"He always thinks he's right."

"But not your hearts."

Mama nodded reluctantly.

"I see you not always glad of his love. Like a trap. A door closed on you. Something missing you not free for finding."

"I am fortunate," Mama tried to argue, reaching out to Donatella coming closer.

The rogue card was shown. "Not for long."

"Her cough?" Donatella ignored her own advice.

"Not good. You need a lease."

Mama tried to smile. "A lease?"

"A little longer for a little more."

"You can do that?"

"Illumined from above."

"Donata. Get the box."

Donatella panicked and then realized her mother was referring to a pin-cushioned container that rattled with spools and buttons and, as she found out, coins. It was by Mama's chair in the parlor where the fire burned as if someone had just built it up. The curtains were closed without their folds smoothed and songs sheets littered the floor beside the spinet. Donatella put the sewing box down to pick them up, a cold sensation at her back that ran up her arms and tore the sheets of scattered music in half, a whisper in her ear that asked why, an answer in her heart that tried but couldn't put them back together again. She sat down, almost forgetting what she was there for.

"She needs her money." Lidia made her jump.

"Were you in here before?"

"Not since this morning."

The music was in her head. That's what Donatella told herself and the fortune teller and seeker who had no qualms about pocketing Mama's money and wondering who was showing off on the keyboard in a room she wouldn't mind having a look in. Donatella escorted her out and all the way to the street, watching her fade up Mill's Lane and then the light in her mother's bedroom window until it went out. The music wasn't merely in Donatella's head, but also tingling at her fingertips and quickening in her breast, making her sad and hopeful all at once. It was in the soft staccato of the rain and silence of it stopping abruptly, the moon peeking through but not enough to clear her muddled thoughts and feelings. Lidia echoed Caprice and Bianchi's cries for Donatella to come in, all three surrounding her when she did, rubbing her legs and shoulders and hair. The cats followed her into the parlor where she put the sewing box back on the pedestal table. The fire was smoldering ashes, the curtains were open, and a small stool was pushed under the spinet with a few sheets of Italian songs intact on its closed top.

By Association

CHAPTER THIRTEEN

"I told the driver to take it easy," Roger began a discussion with the Captain regarding the weather and how it affected the roads. "There's no mud but more bumps when a freeze hits hard, and, of course, a great danger of sliding."

Donatella wouldn't have minded if the excursion had been called off or she had to stay behind with her mother who shouldn't be out on such a blustery day and was like an ailing child beneath the blanket that covered them both.

"I must be there for the Italians," Mama stressed as she had all day, her eyes large and watery.

"Pity we have to go so far. Could you have them at Wroxton, Roger?"

"I don't know, Edward. Everything is upside down with the renovations."

"Which, my friend, I think you mean to never finish."

It was too late to change Mama's mind once she was climbing into the carriage with a fringed handkerchief to shield her cough, the Captain unfolding the warm cover neither he nor Roger would admit to wishing there were two of. At first it enforced the cold, but soon drew warmth up from the foot warmer Lidia had insisted they bring along.

"Good thinking," Roger recognized.

With a gesture Donatella offered to share it.

"No, not necessary." He dropped his eyes and tucked his plainly gloved hands under his legs.

The Captain's were immediately on display, their covering a prize from some exotic port, thick fingered with long embroidered cuffs. He reached out to pat his wife's concealed knees. "Julianna needs it most."

"Don't worry so, Edward. I have a lease."

Roger looked up, the Captain about to say something through a scowl.

Mama was saved by another's secrecy. "Where's Lidia going?"

Donatella knew without saying as they rolled past the pond and gained momentum up the western end of the village, on and off the top road to turn south for further discourse between the men that tested Donatella and bored her mother. The carriage's innovations were a topic that used up some time, Roger assessing every sway and rattle. He was, at least, content with how the window to his left slid up.

A blast of snow blew in before he could close it, his face reddening as he considered but decided against brushing off the ladies' laps.

The Captain stretched across his friend to pull the tasseled shade down. "To make us feel warmer."

"No," Donatella raised her voice and hand.

She had just realized what she was missing, even limited by a small one-sided view. The Oxfordshire landscape sparkled with winter: the sky bright between stretching clouds, roadside hedges hunched as they were frozen but moving past, trees near and far barren yet dressed in lacy frills. She noticed a hawk following and swooping lower and lower before disappearing into a coppice sculpted in ice like blue-veined marble, and a fox stepping further and further away from her knowing for sure what it was.

The glass fogged with her face pressed against it, and then as she rubbed it squeaked like a violin playing to amuse, not impress.

The journey stopped at a sign post for Shutford right and North Newton left, the carriage choosing the latter and rolling along slowly until it was standing still again. Children, dressed more for August than December, played in the streets of a village the Captain observed as less pleasantly arranged than Wroxton. Roger agreed while expressing an interest in the structure of the buildings, his study interrupted by red hands and faces wondering who they were. The driver shouted a warning for a few of the boys to get away from the horses without giving them time to do so before he threatened them with his whip.

This time Roger was more solicitor than engineer as he opened the window. "Steady, my man."

"Well, it worked, didn't it?" the driver retorted.

"Wait." Her mother's generosity emerged with a handful of boiled candies she passed under Donatella's chin to throw out of the coach.

There was no knowing whether Mama's sacrifice was widely received, greedily hoarded, or if it just rolled into wastefulness. The light went out of the afternoon as they left North Newton, closing them into thoughts and more conversations and even dozing off. The talk between the Captain and Roger didn't anticipate how soon their destination would welcome them with bells ringing, water coldly mirrored, the clack of a bridge, tunneling blindness, a curtain wall with battlements and the opening of the sky that gave an orange cast to the almost shabby exterior of Broughton Castle.

The Captain helped his wife down from the carriage and every step of the way indoors. Donatella refused Roger's hand as she suspected he hoped she would, but did agree to going ahead of him to catch up with her father and mother. They were still waiting to be acknowledged, Mama making a disapproving noise with her tongue until someone took their cloaks, asked their names, and passed them on to a white-washed hall where they were introduced to Christmas colors and smells, and anyone in its well-dressed crowd who would listen.

A young woman with unadorned dark hair pulled away from her long face came forward to take Roger's hand and congratulate him. He squirmed but was composed enough to announce her as Lady Celia Fiennes from Wiltshire, granddaughter of Old Subtlety whose likeness hung in that very room and for whom all had been forgiven.

Donatella wondered what needed to be, but hesitated to find the right words and enough nerve, which allowed her mother to ask her own question first.

"The Italians?" Lady Celia seemed glad of a distraction. "Do I detect an accent, Mistress?"

"Oh, I still have one?" Mama held her bosom as she laughed.

"Well, anyway," Lady Celia's thick eyebrows were suddenly all of her face," your countrymen are here and preparing for the performance. So you can enjoy them as, I'm sure, we all will."

"Lady Celia, a word?" Roger urgently led the young woman away, a respectful detachment between them until they stopped and assumed the posture of a proposal intently made and more naturally accepted.

"Now, there's one for him." Mama showed some unexplained disappointment. "What is she, twenty? And not so pretty there could be much competition."

"I've heard she's quite the equestrian," the Captain tried to improve the conversation.

"So he competes with horses," Mama was even louder. "That might be a problem."

Donatella was surprised her mother was so ungracious towards someone whose influence gained them access to the kind of society she longed for, and even front seats for the concert.

"Ah. They are here." Mama held up her handkerchief like a mask that didn't disguise her anticipation.

Donatella squeezed her hand as much to steady her own. A frantic chatter, in one language and another, came from behind evergreen garlands in an open gallery about eight feet off the main floor where, on closer observation, a group of men were agreeing and arguing as if there wasn't any difference.

The Captain stood off to one side. Roger had reluctantly abandoned him for a group of well-nourished men giving him cause to slump his shoulders and, as Donatella knew him a little, plan his escape.

"Please, everyone sit." One of the musicians was bowing before them, rolling his English pronunciation. "I am Albrici the younger. We must begin. Ah, Carlo," he reached for the drink handed to him, decorations and shadows preventing a good look at the donor, "else we forget what we're here for."

There was a mix of chairs, some elegant, even gilded, while a few in the rear row might have come out of the scullery. They finally began to fill until only the seats either side of Donatella and her mother were available. Lady Celia took one and Roger the other, which he soon jumped out of to assist Albrici turning the harpsichord to the maestro's advantage.

"Good of you to come, Bartholomew. Winter journeys aren't easy."

"Well, I stayed a night in Oxford with Reggio."

"Good plan. Is he here?"

"Like a whimpering pup, I must bring along."

Roger fought a smile but not the desire to return to his seat. He remained upright as Lady Celia also stood to formally and familiarly greet a brocade-coated man whose curl-curtained face bore some resemblance to hers.

"Now, William, will you sit?" Celia offered without knowing where he could.

"Viscount," Roger offered his chair.

"No, no. I will hover. Like that gentleman over there, although I'll try not to look so unimpressed."

Mama rose, curtsied, and gestured for Donatella to do the same, forgetting what was appropriate when she blew a kiss towards the Captain who quickly sidestepped as if it was a rock.

"I hope, Mistress, someone you know."

"Of course, sir. Someone I know is easy to embarrass."

"Yes, now I recognize the red-faced Captain from Wroxton."

"His wife and daughter," Roger offered the vaguest of introductions.

"I believe I've met one not the other of the Genoese ladies you asked be invited, who likely wish they were home by the fire on such a bone chilling day."

"Not to miss the Italians," Donatella stole her mother's refrain and gained the Viscount's smile.

"Your brother is much older than you," Mama commented to Lady Celia once he was gone.

"We're step-siblings. Actually, my home is in Wiltshire with my mother and sister."

Mama pretended to listen while enjoying another glance from Maestro Albrici as he flipped out the back of his coat to position himself at the harpsichord.

"Albrici. What's the delay?"

Albrici grunted and his head fell forward, his fingers immediately finding their tension and touch, rolling an introduction into a breathless pulse.

Smeared arpeggios gave pause as a singer carrying a lute and lovely tune came into the light and performance. The lyrics were in English but his intonation was not, his voice giving him a beauty he didn't have and a youthfulness that contradicted his graying face. His eyes were downcast, his mouth wet and a little whiskered, his wandering back and forth courting romantic notions he probably never pursued.

Music also came down from the gallery in long shimmering phrases from viols, treble and bass. It was sublime and subdued, individual but uncompetitive in contrast and counterpoint, necessary for life like inhaling and exhaling. Certainly, Donatella breathed easier, unfolding her hands and closing her eyes, almost unconscious of where she was as she heard her mother humming a harmony all her own.

The viols were slowly persuasive, the audience surrendering to their calm and melancholy, even Albrici joining their passive resistance to more sound than expression. It seemed their victory was imminent, that they had conquered the field and could hold on unguarded.

However, without more power, they were unable to stave off the invasion of a single violin.

It irrevocably broke the consort, twisting and turning and working itself into a manic mastery, its bow slashing so every listening heart bled. Sudden remorse was just part of the act but affecting all the same, nothing but pretension wrong with its accomplishment, not a sound that wasn't beautiful despite its arrogance, such difficulty created and brilliantly overcome. The applause seemed to wait for the maestro at the harpsichord to offer a toast to a shadowy figure hunched over the gallery and taking up his arms again to declare superiority as a performer in Italian words as well as music.

"Albrici, drink deep of my talent, too!"

CHAPTER FOURTEEN

Roger was on his feet. "The staccatos, tremolos, divisions, indeed the whole manner, every stroke delicious. It must be. Matteis. That masterful musician and all that he plays his own composition. By what I've known of him and other music of Italy, he isn't even second to Corelli."

"It isn't Matteis." Albrici stood stiffly.

"No? He's not in royal service, is he? Unless—"

"Neither is this one.

"Reggio," snarled the voice that wasn't Matteis', "don't cower like a child. You're not quite as ugly as I am."

"Ah. Here he is." Albrici waved his hands and made someone appear. "Carlo, must you outplay us all?"

"Who is it?" Roger responded to Donatella's gasp.

Donatella tried to speak louder, but it felt like a bone was caught in her throat, her mother even slapping her back.

"Not a name I'm familiar with," Roger had his answer directly from the hunched man hugging a violin on his hip, whose scowl hardly encouraged a compliment, "but one to be remembered."

"No one knows I'm here," Lonati directed his explanation towards Donatella. "I've been on the move since last winter."

Roger's reach suggested an interest in Lonati's violin. "A beautiful instrument. Some say England has depopulated Italy of violins."

Albrici laughed. "And violinists. Can we convince this one to stay? Do we want to? After all, he's prettier in the shadows."

Carlo Ambrogio Lonati was still conceited and defensive, holding up his talent as he couldn't his head, unforgiving of ridicule, reacting against his limitations but never admitting them, a man constantly on the run without anything significant chasing him. His music was even bolder and more effortless. Like a stutterer who sings as confidently as the angels, his deformity disappeared into his talent.

"You must introduce us," Mama pleaded with Donatella.

"How do you know him? Through Stradella?" Roger was more curious than Donatella was comfortable with.

"Very little." She looked at her mother instead. "Why did you tell him?"

"You're too modest with what could make you more interesting and even attractive."

***

Lonati had never found it easy to play down his skill and sat with his violin on his lap as the concert continued. Mama's sighs hoped Reggio hadn't entirely forgotten why music was made, his simple chords cascading into singing discomfited with so many consonants and intellectual melancholy. Donatella was accommodated perfectly as harmonics soothed histrionics, and harpsichord and viols agreed to appeal to the mind as well as the senses.

She wasn't so content when Reggio's performance seemed specific to her loss and his eyes fixed on hers.

"Tis well, 'tis well, with them I say

"Whose short-liv'd passions with themselves can die ..."

The music defined the words and the words defined the moment as poignant and providential.

"Whatever parts of me remain,

"Those parts will still the love of thee retain ..."

Yes, she might have written such lyrical expression herself. At least, she owned it with her grief.

"For 'twas not only in my Heart,

"But like a God by pow'rful Art,

"'Twas all in all in every part."

She should have looked away. What pleased a singer more than hypnotizing a heart into believing it was revealed to him?

***

"Pietro Reggio, Genoese. Here is someone you should meet." Lonati brought him forward. "Donatella Cavanna, Genoese. A lover of music, as you can see."

"Maestro Lonati. Magnificent playing," Roger couldn't resist demonstrating his facility in Italian. "I thought at first it was Matteis, who taught me a little violin."

"A little is none at all."

"Of course. I'd never attempt to play anything of yours."

"Glad to hear it."

"He doesn't let anyone." Albrici put a hand on Reggio's shoulder. "He won't publish."

"I know you're talking about me." Lonati grinned and then bowed a little more than was already enforced on him.

"I told them you won't publish."

"Explain why, Albrici. Explain I don't want my music subject to the scrutiny of those who can't even tell the time."

"Unlike Pietro, who shares his talent like a blushing whore."

Mama had been deliberately quiet and didn't make a move that might give her plan away. It was obvious to Donatella that her mother had noticed the reason for Reggio's lingering.

He looked Donatella up and down, bit his lip and cleared his throat. "You are ... from Genoa?" He spoke with the same consoling resonance of his singing.

"We are." Mama hooked Donatella's arm. "I'm long gone. My daughter is still there."

Reggio shakily smiled, forgetting the gaps in his front teeth. "My birthplace, so I'm told."

"Excuse us." Mama swayed an arm in the air. "Is there food? Will there be anything left if I'm last in line?"

Reggio moved closer to Donatella. "I hope we may speak more. I mean, we haven't really at all. But we should. If you like."

The Captain appeared to save his daughter as much as his wife, and ushered them away from Reggio and anything else that wasn't supposed to happen. He broke through the waves of people he wouldn't let set him off course, holding up his wide-sleeved arm like a mast.

His voice rose in a plea he must have made many times to Neptune, "Let us through. Let us through. We must get through."

Surprised ladies and gentlemen obliged with left and right surges of rich fabrics, ribbons and lace, curls and chatter, the Captain and his wife sailing through with Donatella following but somehow losing them. There was nothing she could do but hold her breath with her arms folded, bobbing side-to-side as the final swell of guests moved past her, leaving her vulnerable to sharks in those waters.

"Here you are." Lonati made sure Reggio saw him taking Donatella out of everyone's sight.

He offered her one of the cloaks piled on a bench behind a screen. "That's not mine."

Lonati cocked his head and tapped his nose. "You may borrow."

"We're not going outside?"

"No. But I suggest you put it on. The higher we go, the colder it gets."

"We can't ... shouldn't."

Lonati dropped his insistence with her hand.

"It was a shock to see you, Carlo." Donatella was trembling, not because Lonati had surprised or touched or frightened her, or even compromised her reputation. She felt relief that no matter how far away and impossible, the past could come into the present.

She refused the vermillion cloak with gold trim—"This is mine"—was calmer as she straightened and turned, draped in dark blue with simple ruffles around her neck.

"Ah, *Signora*. I'm surprised how well you look."

Lonati took her down a dark passage vaulted with corbel heads and slate-flooring that prepared her for more of the same and not an ascent into the brightness of a long gallery presenting bay windows and pink walls hung with the portraits of those who had exercised a privilege to it. The sky might have been the limit of a series of narrow stairs, Lonati's hobbled walk and heavy breathing drawing her, against her better judgment, to the top and a room too small and out of the way for a castle to have except as it didn't.

"You've been here before?"

"We were given a tour last night." Lonati seemed to rest his forehead against the stone surround of a mantle-less fireplace that was intensely scorched, its grate too clean. "The Viscount had no intention to. His sister brought us up."

"It hardly seems worth showing off, except for the view." Donatella tried to move past her mistrust of Lonati to each of three mullioned windows blinded by frost and fading light.

She was surprised by him closing the door, rush matting muffling his steps to it.

"Oh."

"Do you know what happened here? Within these casemated walls? Commerce concealing politics. Plotting against a king."

He began circling an oval gate-legged table and three mismatched ladderback chairs, while rubbing his hands. "A room that hath no ears. That's what she called it."

Donatella knew she didn't have to stay.

"A place for confidentialities, for speaking as nowhere else." Lonati moved faster, around the table but also pacing. He shook his head and faced the ground, so she could only imagine the insanity in his eyes. "For taking a risk, let the devil be dammed, I cannot deny, I cannot pretend," he interrupted himself by pounding the table so hard its strange centerpiece of five musket balls rattled.

His anger disintegrated into a sobbing heap. "I loved him. I loved him. Oh, how I loved him."

CHAPTER FIFTEEN

"I could never tell him." Lonati massaged the musket balls like dice he was about to roll. "For the same reason I won't publish my music."

He raised his head the little he could. Once Donatella wiped her eyes, she noticed his wig had shifted halfway down his forehead.

"Not about to throw myself into the mix."

They sat across from each other, already estranged from the impulsive marriage of their grief, the table creaking with their elbows pressing on it, the wind whirling in the chimney flue.

"He haunts my conscience."

"It wasn't your fault."

Lonati smiled with some guilt which even that room wouldn't allow him to reveal.

Donatella hoped it was as innocent as hers. "He took his chances."

Lonati's chin was wobbling again. "And you?"

Did he really care? Or was he still too unpredictable to confide in? "It must have been a blow to your career," she tried to sound unkind.

"On the contrary, it rid me of my only competition." He couldn't fool her, either, as his sleeve slid under his broad nose.

"Where did you go?"

"Milan. Then Mantua. Then, in October, London."

"How did you travel?"

"By land, except for crossing the channel of course. The sea is for inspiration not negotiating. What's the choice? Boats or carriages, one rocks as nauseatingly as the other and neither could guarantee arrival with my life."

"But you are here and have it."

"'Hunchback, you were born to misfortune, yet you are the lucky one.'" Lonati pushed back his chair and almost fell off. "His fate continues to be more in the hands of his enemies than friends."

"Oh, no."

"Unless you've been a little dishonest."

"What?"

"Remember, these walls can't hear you."

It might have been the treacherous atmosphere in that room, but she believed her crime was as unavoidable as a starving person stealing a little bread. "I've done nothing wrong."

Without a candle, they were almost in darkness. She was startled by Lonati pulling her down to spit in her ear, "Seems you've done something right."

"Wait." She caught up to him on the stairs.

He resumed his descent, his fingernails scraping the railing.

"*Signora* Cavanna? *Signora* Cavanna?"

"That's Reggio."

"Oh, dear."

"Mistress Cavanna Hanley?"

"Who's that?"

Donatella thought she knew, but didn't say. She followed Lonati down to but not through a molded and crested doorway to the left of the gallery that was losing its light and length. She looked into a room largely indistinct except for the faint flicker of its ceiling like an upside down cake with meringue peaks.

"*Signora* Cavanna? *Signora* Cavanna?"

She could just make out Lonati collapsing on a chair.

"Goodbye." She removed her cloak, crumpling it as small as she could under one arm, using the expanse and polish of the west staircase to dignify her return.

"*Signora* Cavanna, where are you?"

"In here." Lonati was suddenly pushing her until she was turning around to marvel at the interior porch he had forced her through. It was a grander entrance than she deserved, decoratively crowned by obelisks and a centered panel, its whiteness chipped off here and there to reveal oaken origins.

"Read the inscription."

"Where?"

"The cartouche on top."

"It's Latin. I only know a little, from Mass."

"'*Quod olim fuit meminisse minime iuvat*'," Roger recited from memory, stepping in between her and Lonati as if he knew she hoped someone would. "Are you all right?"

"Why shouldn't I be?" she really answered Lonati's smirk and dry eyes.

"'There is no pleasure in the memory of the past'."

She didn't know whether to feel flattered or dismissed by Roger's insight.

"The inscription. Its translation is 'There is no pleasure in the memory of the past'."

"Oh, but, I feel—"

"A play on '*Forsam et haec olim meminisse iuvabit*' by Plato, which loosely translates into 'One day perhaps even this will seem pleasant to remember'. Though the perversion—"

"I prefer that," Donatella decided.

Roger wasn't deterred and moved further into the room. "—the perversion suited a purpose, an expedient one for the eighth Baron Saye and Sele upon the Restoration in 1660. Most likely he intended to show gratitude to our present King for pardoning his family's support of Parliament during the Civil War. For the same reason he had the exquisite, one can only imagine, Tudor paneling in this room painted white. Even as monarchist, I think that was going too far."

"I'm glad I don't know what he's talking about." Lonati left the room but was still heard, "Ah, Reggio. Looking for love in all the wrong places."

Donatella backed away from the nervously determined little man shuffling out of the porch and almost comically opening his arms. "*Signora* Cavanna. Here you are. Ah, Master North, you found her."

"Safe and sound, Maestro Reggio. Mistress Cavanna-Hanley is very interested in the manner and history of the place." Roger meant to rescue her from further interrogation, but the slightly plump and slovenly Reggio wasn't satisfied until he was before her like a confessor who would only hear the truth.

"Why were you crying, my dear?"

"Lonati," she immediately regretted saying.

Roger approached attentively. "Lonati made you cry?"

"He's a cold-blooded fellow." Reggio went a step further, bowing his head, bending his knees and groaning when she refused him her hand.

"I don't know him." Roger was examining one of the places on the porch where the paint was peeling. "He did play the violin rather violently, but usually that shows too much heat in a musician rather than too little."

"Ah. Here you all are." Lady Celia strutted into the room and lightly slapped Roger's investigative hand. "Even the missing *Signora* Cavanna, who's quite flushed."

Donatella's impulse to curtsey was thwarted by Lady Celia immediately reacting to stop her.

"You're fine. Of course, you are. I believe you already know that what they think they've saved they will never treasure."

***

Relief was also disappointment; Lonati nowhere to be seen when it was time to leave. Mama was certain someone had taken her cloak, but the Captain soon found it. They weren't the first to be ready to go and had to step aside for those who bid them good evening and those who didn't. A great door opened and closed more than a dozen times before they went out into the cold where the torch light made it seem later than it was, a parade of carriages rolling cautiously away towards the towering gate through low mist.

Roger's carriage waited for them impatiently, its horses snorting and shifting.

"It's still slippery as you walk." The Captain, relaxed by drink, fondled his wife as he held her up.

"You're too independent, Donata," her mother noticed Roger's awkward offer of gentlemanly support.

Donatella didn't need to be reminded of the risk of falling if she let her guard down. She balanced herself with her arms and paced herself with knees a little bent and toes landing first. There was some comfort in knowing Roger was behind her as an advocate for continuing upright and climbing very slowly.

Her mother, already blanketed in the carriage, begged her to hurry, "Else I freeze to death."

"Why you shouldn't have come out today, Julianna."

"Don't start that again, Edward."

"Mama, move over a little."

"Oh, you are warm, Donata. Too warm."

"Hope you aren't sickening." Roger brushed Donatella's knees as he took his seat and again as he reached to close the door.

"You should let the driver do that," the Captain looked pained to criticize his friend.

"He slams it so hard."

Mama's hand was ice melting down Donatella's face. "Oh, dear. You never know what comes with Londoners."

"Just the excitement," Donatella admitted before she thought how it might be misconstrued.

"What excitement?" Mama swayed her head and rolled her eyes as if about to pass out.

The Captain grinned. "Didn't your Italians provide enough?"

Roger frowned. "I wonder why we're not on our way?"

Donatella groggily looked out the window, mainly to rest her face against it. She was about to close her eyes when she saw Pietro Reggio slipping and sliding towards what must have seemed a hesitation to leave him behind.

There was no doubt Donatella was feverish, aching to disavow his approach. "Go. Please, go," she alerted her companions and pulled the curtain on the chance of them knowing why she panicked, the innovation of glass and fortuity of escape almost soundproofing the carriage to an excellence of lute and voice she might not otherwise resist.

"No. You never know what is brought with Londoners," Mama repeated as she rubbed her own throat and finally offered Donatella a share of the blanket.

"It played well," the Captain said strangely, "until it hardly seemed worth the bother."

The journey home was confined to looking inward, and shaky enough to prevent anyone falling asleep. Roger seemed the most uncomfortable, holding onto and staring at his knees with a concentration that might have been exemplary if it hadn't seemed evasive. Donatella couldn't remember if he said anything as they left the carriage, only that the wind was harsh, the church bells rang more than the six times she counted, and the walk up to the cottage from the street made her feel even weaker.

"Lidia? Lidia?" Mama called when the Captain announced that there wasn't a fire lit, not even in the kitchen.

"No Martha, either?" He had forgotten it was her day off.

Donatella was desperate to crawl into her bed where Bianchi and Caprice had created the only warm place on earth. Within moments, they were nuzzling under the coverlet again, discovering their mistress fully clothed and restless. Still, they weren't deterred from lying near her, their purring like a polyphonic prayer to soothe them all. So it did, until Donatella was disturbed by a dream of Lonati holding up his violin like a dagger and who, by association, insisted she was as culpable for what had happened to the man they both had loved. She knew she wasn't and yet struggled with her inability to save him, pushing everything away, aware of one small thud and then another, shaking and weeping until she was curving into the cloud of a shirt and experienced caresses, her hair loosening and skirt riding up, the nakedness of Chinese silk and Genoese lace bringing her some relief, losing her virtue as her worth a remedy that broke her heart but not her fever.

CHAPTER SIXTEEN

Donatella pulled up the blankets when Lidia said something she refused to hear.

Mama, fully dressed so soon after she got up, came into the room. "You won't believe who was here before your papa had his breakfast."

Donatella hesitated. "You, Lidia?"

"No. She appeared in the kitchen just after Martha did." Mama filled the doorway again to prevent the girl's escape. "Wherever were you? Never mind. Tighten my laces." She turned her back on Lidia.

"Who, Mama?"

"Maestros Albrici, Reggio, and Lonati."

"You sent them away?"

"Of course not. They're having ale and sausages. They took a detour in order to call before returning to Oxford."

"I won't see them."

"Are you still sick?" Mama felt her forehead. "It doesn't help having a cat lying on your chest. You must've had a fitful night. Get out so Lidia can straighten your bed. Well, then, later. Lidia, fetch her something to drink. I'd better go, for the Captain hasn't much to say to them. Not like he does with Roger, though God knows they talk too much.

"Of course, we're grateful to him for our evening with the Italians. And now they're in my house. Probably something to do with him, too." She laughed and preened herself. "Which, of course, you don't thank him for."

Donatella did get up as soon as her mother and Lidia were gone. Cross and crumpled, she followed Caprice to the top of the stairs despite a stronger inclination to behave more like the cautious Bianchi. It was soon obvious the risk of being seen wasn't worth it, anything overheard muffled except for Martha's earthy remarks. Lidia didn't seem to notice anything but how tired she was coming upstairs carrying a tray with a cup and plate of biscuits, lifting each leg with similar strain. Caprice bounced past her and Lonati hardly startled her, either, as he put a finger to his lips.

Donatella sidestepped into her room, sat on her bed and then at her dressing table, smoothed up her stockings, let down her hair, rubbed the corners of her eyes, and noticed Bianchi's tail twitching from under the bed.

"I didn't think the poor girl would make it up. I'm surprised you brought her with you."

Lonati didn't wait to be invited in with the platter that rattled him, too, cursing under his breath as he looked for somewhere to place it.

Donatella was immediately tricked into becoming his servant and took it from him.

"Well, Cinderella," his voice was convincingly soft and pursuant, "have you found another prince yet?"

She decided not to explain why she was still dressed as he had last seen her.

"I'm being ill-mannered and am sorry to upset you."

She couldn't believe Lonati cared for her feelings. He almost disappeared as he became more agreeably present.

"You know Reggio is downstairs?"

"I won't see him again."

"That's not what he thinks."

"Why? I didn't encourage him. Why would I?"

"He's old.

"Is he?"

"Ah. Sandro was right. You're too courteous. Reggio's fifty. And looks it."

"That's not why I won't see him."

"And he's not why I'm here."

"You must leave." She anticipated that any moment her father would wonder what was going on.

"I could've sent you a note, but you might've ignored it, as you will Pietro's."

There was an elaborately folded and sealed missive on the tray she finally put down on the chest at the bottom of her bed. She drank something lukewarm and honey-sweet.

"I'm here to implore and employ you to make some copies."

The milk she had swallowed was coming back up.

"Well?"

She cleared her throat that felt on fire. "Of your compositions?"

"No, Sandro's. Except for what I can less and less remember, they're lost to me."

She silently questioned the intention of his request.

"Well, I didn't think you would give up your copies. Where do you keep them? In there?" His eyes squinted towards the trunk.

"No."

"Ah. Somewhere in this room. I would like to see them. Are there any originals? Well, it's possible you might've taken some. Otherwise, what would you have of him?" Lonati looked around until he focused on the half-open wardrobe.

Donatella thought she heard something happening downstairs at the same time she did a tapping at the window that must have been the ice clad ivy that smothered the east side of the cottage. She took a shawl off the wardrobe door and closed it.

"Yes." He wasn't discreet as he watched her wrap it around her arms and upper body. "It's damned cold. How do you get used to it? I don't think I've felt my toes for weeks."

"You wear wool and stockings. And good boots. And still never feel warm."

"Agh. And my poor hands. I don't think it's good for their circulation."

"You should wear gloves when you're not performing. How long do I have?"

"You think I won't stay in England? You're right. A month or two. Depending on how the wind blows."

"I'll need paper and ink. I have some, but not enough."

"I thought of that. Roger North said he would supply you with what you need."

"You told him?"

"Don't worry. He seems quite generous towards you. And now I'll be forever grateful. Have you ever had so many admirers?"

"You'd better go."

"We haven't discussed payment."

Donatella went to the door of her room to try to hear any questioning of Lonati's whereabouts and saw Lidia slumped on a step halfway up or down.

"Oh, dear." Mama was in the hallway below looking worried as Lonati used his knee to nudge the weary girl out of the way.

***

Pietro Reggio's letter was written in Italian, but also in a language as foreign as English was to Donatella.

Dear Signora Cavanna,

There is an unusual ignorance in you. For it seems you do not look for victories as most woman do, dressing their attributes beyond necessity and often to the ridiculous, casting their attention around capriciously to be content with any fish they catch. I would be frustrated by your inclination to spurn rather than entice, except the choice is not yours. For your victory has, after all, been won by your eyes—not for their seeing but their being as brightly beaming as the comets are.

I should say their unintentional conquest is welcome in a world where aggressive glances often invade a man's composure, but instead express regret that I must defend myself even more hopelessly against the effect of their sudden glowing across my sky only to ruthlessly drop out of view.

For how can they be innocent of such mischief, having blinded a blameless onlooker even to the stars and moon? How can they not know how or who while others have little doubt of the heights I set my sights to?

Perhaps I am mistaken. Is it possible your avoidance is not because of who I am but am not? If there is a man who already thinks himself so high as to pretend equality with you, he deserves your esteem less than I. He will cheat for his reasons. I, on the other hand, beg with honest intentions and the hope that you will choose to give with less sorrow to an undeserving beggar than a thief.

I would rather your reluctance be modesty, or unbelief, than outright rejection of my attention that only asks for a little correspondence to promote the chance of our meeting again. That proposal may already be overthrown and I guiltless slain but still I close in faith that by some miracle my devotion will raise me from the dead.

Too patiently yours,
Pietro Reggio, Genoese
Christ Church, Oxford

Mama caught Donatella folding the letter in her lap. "May I see?"

It would have been easy for her to just pick it up and be more surprised than pleased that her spinster daughter had a suitor, but her hesitation suggested she had guessed, her walking around the room suspecting there were more important revelations there.

"Well, if you're wondering, your father didn't know Lonati was up here."

"No?"

"Maestro Lonati took advantage of the Captain's going out for some air. You know, as he always does first thing in the morning. Well, he usually eats first. And when he gets back cleans his boots. Which he's doing now."

"Good. All normal again." Donatella crumpled Reggio's letter.

"How can it be? Why should it be? You, of all, should understand. Normal is death before we die."

"No, Mama. The life we have."

"But there is more. Don't you remember? Don't you wish it turned out differently? Don't you want to feel the excitement again?" Italian suited Mama's expression as her arms began swinging, at first without aim, then at the bed to pull up its covers like clothes over a naked body. Bianchi flew from under it. "I feel different. The cottage feels different, don't you think? Not so English. Not so cold. As they left, I thought, we must remember who we are and where we are from. I'm sorry you couldn't come down. Are you feeling better? Can we practice today? We should every day. Pietro left copies of a few of his songs and said he trusted we sang like angels and could arrange for us to perform in Oxford. I know, your father won't agree. Why do we need his consent? Am I not the same prize of possibilities I was before I knew him? Nonna used to say a man was never a substitute for our dreams, just—as we wouldn't resist—an interruption to them. He might make us beautiful and happy but not to keep us so. Why didn't I listen to her? Why didn't I stay with her?"

Donatella hoped her mother didn't notice her flattening Reggio's petition under a couple of jars on her dressing table. "Nonna understood. And perhaps Papa will agree to a church or small gathering. We're tired now and I still don't feel well. But we will practice later, or tomorrow."

"Oh, my darling." her mother was relying on her fancies as much as the room's doorframe to hold her up." I know. We'll always have music, won't we? It's in our blood. And if nothing else, waiting for us in heaven."

CHAPTER SEVENTEEN

Caprice returned when Lidia did and sniffed around for her sister before she jumped on the window seat where Donatella was kneeling.

The cat let out a chilling cry. It was not a morning to open a window for any reason.

With slow strokes, Donatella calmed her while answering Lidia's unasked question: "The ivy hitting the window is unnerving, especially in the middle of the night."

Lidia was standing in the doorway. "Perhaps Tobias can trim it."

"You went to his cottage again." Donatella closed the window and watched Lidia straightening the bed better than her mother had. "You were there all night?"

Lidia fussed a long while with the pillows.

"Is he still sick?"

"He's better."

"As you take good care of him."

"It seems I should," Lidia spoke as though she had found another religious vocation. She folded her arms and put her feet together.

"What?"

The girl sat on the bed. "I want to take care of him all the time."

"You can't live with him."

"Why not?"

"He's old and you're so young."

"Like a granddaughter would be."

"But you can't talk to him."

"We understand each other."

Donatella stood up and swayed until Lidia's small strength steadied her.

The girl predictably touched Donatella's forehead and cheeks. "You're burning up, yet shivering with snow on your shawl."

"Won't you stay to care for me?"

"Of course." Lidia's eyes narrowed, acknowledging she was trapped in obligation as she helped Donatella out of yesterday's clothes, shaking and hanging her gown and folding her chemise and other underthings for laundering.

Donatella dressed again in the warmest way she could, having recently added woolen shifts and stockings to her wardrobe.

"You should go back to bed."

"See what Mama is up to."

"Listen. She sings as if no one is listening."

"But very well, all the same."

Well enough, I suppose.

The last comment, which Lidia seemed oblivious to, stalled Donatella's search for her boots.

Lidia found Bianchi laying on them.

Donatella's hands shook as she put them on and tied them up.

Wait. Lace. You're never without lace.

She went back to the dressing table for the gloves she would have forgotten the day before if it weren't for a similar reminder. They were flimsy and useless, but cuffed in expertly pointed, if slightly yellowing, lace.

***

Donatella knew what she was going to say to Tobias until she saw the smoke sputtering out of his chimney and a thrush stealing the last few berries off the holly branch nailed to his front door. She was even less determined when she heard a chesty and incessant cough and wondered if he would survive to see his garden rise from the stalks and mounds of leaves barely showing broken and brown beneath the snow.

He spit like the Captain did when he was out of doors and thought no one saw. Donatella expected to be confronted as if she was the devil. There was a silent showering of bread crusts, cabbage leaves, and chunks of potatoes.

"Liddy not with you?"

"No."

"She ain't sickened?"

"No."

"Ye need a warm, eh?"

It took a moment for Donatella to believe, let alone accept, the rough invitation.

"The fire's down. Round the back. Under a tarp. Can't lift much yet. Liddy would if she be here."

He went in and closed the door, probably expecting Donatella to go away. She took off her gloves. Everything was dripping as the sky released the sun. The hem of her dress absorbed the slush of a path that took her around the cottage. As in the front yard, there wasn't any sign of life except for birds scavenging scraps thrown out to them, tall frames, tangled stalks, and frozen grass creating eerie shapes. She wasn't afraid of anything but her own inclination to acknowledge the possibility of one season haunting the next.

She found the woodpile only partially covered, some logs spongy and easy, if filthy, to lift, others heavier than their size forewarned, a whole armful shaping her like Lonati as she tried to walk while sinking deeper into mud. She wasn't used to such labor, not since she was marooned on this island of idleness where Martha felt threatened by too much help and Lidia was there if her mother insisted she have some.

There was a lean-to at the back of the cottage that was more thrown together than constructed, with rustic poles and flapping canvas, straw strewn down for its floor. A sagging step up led to a latch-less door that opened with one push. Donatella entered a cold, unsightly room that smelled of rotting meat, a weakening flicker offering the possibility of a fireplace, while dripping suggested a leaky roof. She heard coughing again and dropped the wood when she couldn't hold it any longer.

Insistent thumping brought Tobias to stand before her, leaning on a short gnarled stick.

"Not here."

His ungratefulness should have sent her away, but she carried some firewood out of the kitchen down the curling rugs of a brief passage into the only room he could have disappeared into. It was immediately suffocating and otherwise unpleasant with greasy beams bearing down and very little light coming in, dusty curtains dropping over its empty doorway.

"That'll do, that'll do," Tobias murmured as he pounded the floor with his stick.

"Over there?" Donatella didn't wait for his answer before moving towards and almost toppling between two stools in front of the wide open hearth where a pair of boots and a blackened kettle steamed.

"That'll do. That'll do."

She crisscrossed the logs on dying embers, Tobias hardly offering the hospitality of the one seat left empty as he settled onto another.

"I think it too late," her indignation dared to comment on what wasn't happening in the heartless grate.

"Patience, m'dear. The devil will light it."

She tried to laugh, and then not to.

"I told ye afore. He be right behind ye."

He pointed to a corner left of the door and a small case Donatella remembered from her travels.

"'Tis the smile that gets ye."

"Though not you," she retorted.

"Not me."

She observed the rest of the cramped room where he not only kept company with demons but, as she assumed, also slept on a cot that would have to be cleared of clothes first. A table was cluttered with drying seeds, so he must have his meals on his lap.

"Where would she sleep?"

"Upstairs."

"One room?"

"Two."

"But you sleep here."

"Aye."

"Why not up there?"

"Don't like to. Will ye talk her out of it?"

Donatella wished she had seen the question in his eyes before he lunged forward and grabbed a poker to assault the wood that shriveled in the grate.

"No good." She meant to comfort him with the idea that he would have to start again.

He grunted, dropped the poker and turned, blood drooling from his nose. When the fire flared up behind him, the room felt even colder.

***

As soon as Donatella realized what was missing, she reluctantly retraced her steps as far as Tobias' gate. Somewhere in the cottage he was still shouting and banging, reason enough to accept that the loss of a lace glove was a price worth paying to save Lidia from her own descent into madness. It was snowing as Donatella hurried home, stooping her shoulders into carrying something under her cloak, exercising sudden strength in her legs and discretion when she left Lidia's small stained case in an unused corner of the kitchen before Martha knew she was there.

Even then, the muttering woman didn't turn around.

The Captain's study was closed, the stink of tobacco making it off limits, while the parlor was a stage offering a pretty but under-rehearsed scene of Lidia combing Mama's hair.

"Did the fresh air do you good?"

Mama's voice was tinged with irritation, Lidia tugging at a snarl.

"You just missed another caller." Mama stopped the girl's uncharacteristic assault, directing her towards two packages, the flatter opened already.

Lidia handed it to Donatella and then the other. "He said to hold this one upright."

"From Roger."

"How did you know?"

"I expected it."

"He couldn't wait."

Donatella weighed Roger's generosity before peeking into the parcel of parchment and pens, and felt the shape of the other.

"Something about the Great Seal and Sir Francis not really wanting it. Or … I don't understand these official things. I had hopes for Wroxton this Christmas, that there might be a ball, the first since Lady Frances died."

"What was her sickness?" Donatella thought of the elaborate tablet in the church.

"Probably consumption. In the end, a fit of coughing burst an important vessel."

"Poor Sir Francis. He also lost children."

"That was years ago. We can't be sorry forever." Mama motioned for Lidia to begin twisting up her hair. "We mustn't be sorry forever."

The donation in Donatella's arms seemed to disagree as it was so plainly wrapped, its hemp string dangling, its contents begging her to employ herself as though the present was tied up with blue satin ribbon and scented with jasmine.

Martha was in the room. "Look here what I found." She swung her discovery towards Lidia holding Mama's head from turning.

"What's going on?" Mama realized she was being restrained.

"How did you get it?" Lidia asked of Donatella.

"Is it yours?" Martha dropped the valise beside Lidia, who struggled between hairdressing and escaping until Donatella reluctantly took the well-worn comb out of her hand.

CHAPTER EIGHTEEN

At first it was something to do more than get done. Donatella changed the dressing table's position again and again until it was back where it started. She didn't answer her father's concern over what she was doing, but tipped the vanity mirror up and down to best reflect the brightness coming through the window; cleared off brush and hairpins, powder and lavender oil; and set a candle to the side so it cast light not shadow on her work. She investigated the packages Roger had left, smoothed out the parchment he had given her, saw she didn't need to sharpen the quills, and added water to the ink powder that spilled on her hands when she uncorked its copper container.

It wasn't the copying she delayed but going to the wardrobe for the box of music buried under a pile of books so it wasn't as dusty as they were. She fell to her knees, a little afraid of its exhumation, but finally lifted and carried it like a holy relic, put it down carefully, and opened it as if one breath would corrupt its venerated contents.

Caprice and Bianchi were shooed away more than once as she unfolded the sheets to lay them out on the bed with his and hers overlapping. There were pin-head size brownish spots here and there, the notation slightly less clear than the moment it was written. The smell of resin still encouraged her to realize an occupation.

It seemed impossible to avoid feathery strokes, a blot or two on the work to be done and a few drips on the dressing table runner.

There was, as an unkind mirror ridiculed, ink at the corner of her mouth and on a cheek. She also put her head down to draw straight lines with little movement, left to right as she was handed, thin and terse, layered evenly, filling the page as blankly as before they were there. She knew how to fill their emptiness, and yet was unable to.

She got up, sat down, got up again and went to the door to better hear Mama practicing. Her mother's voice wasn't what it used to be, reaching for breath instead of notes. Donatella paced until she collapsed on the bed, facing the weight of the beamed ceiling and eventually curling towards the window that sparkled with frosty patterns her eyes traced without breaking their continuing from one pane to another. It was an insistent exercise that moved onto the quilting stitches of the spread she sat up on, down spiraling bed posts and the folds of her skirt, into the wrinkles of her stocking feet, step by step along the dingy design of the carpet and barely creaking floor. Her mother had stopped rehearsing for what would never happen and Martha had either run out of complaints or gone home early. Lidia was always quiet, as was the Captain lost in the smoke in his study. There were only sounds of cats purring, quills scratching, and hearts quickening as Donatella rewrote the music she hardly needed to look at. She made her mark as unexpectedly as before, becoming more and more involved with its swirling and sliding and dotting, rising and falling with her shoulders and satisfaction. She was definitely possessed by a melodic hum and laughter in her head, the tease of a draft on her neck, and the surprise that she hadn't forgotten how to serve a master. She knew he was smiling as she checked her work, a mistake here and there repentantly fixed, page after page turned into another chance to show that, in theory and practice and ways she didn't need to understand, she was worthy of his presence.

Yes, it felt like he was there, pacing the room and wringing his hands as he realized he couldn't change anything. She could, with his permission. What else allowed her to hear a note held longer or twilled higher, a crescendo misplaced, or toccata written more for poetry than a harpsichordist's dexterity? What would have put such ideas in her head, except the desire of one who had touched her with his variations? Donatella was haunted by stealing a little of his genius and not enough of his heart, by leaving his death behind but not the moment of his dying, by wondering how she could go on without him after fleeing as if she meant to. She was preoccupied by a secret that hardly had anything to tell and, as a gypsy warned against, by inviting the past into the present.

"How ridiculous," she heard herself say again, while wishing such a thing was possible so the copies she was troubled to make would end up in more appreciative hands than Lonati's. There was an argument in her head, an ambiguous one like she had witnessed between two maestros who were competitors and cohorts as the dubiously majestic world that employed them also refused them. She tried not to listen to anything that might spoil her effort at keeping Alessandro alive, even as Lonati would promote himself, too.

"You will come down soon, won't you, Donata?"

Her mother's faint appeal was an almost irritating reminder that it was Christmas Eve, without a cantata or Genoese sweet bread, just the wind whining and dry little pies she had earlier tried to wash down with strong ale while Lidia plucked a couple of pullets and Martha wrapped some kind of sticky pudding for tomorrow.

"The yule log is burning brightly." This time, the Captain called up. Her cats pricked their ears at Donatella telling them she couldn't do more copying that evening.

Instead she opened a drawer into her lap and took out the letter that had mistakenly been given to her, wrinkled because she had almost thrown it away. There was something pathetic in its poetry, useless in its hopes, amusing in its declaration that proved a distraction, if nothing else. She hadn't answered it, thinking that was the best way to refute it, but holding it once more was like giving it another chance to convince her she might have one, too.

An intrusion snatched it out of her hands. Her mother sat on the bed to discover what Donatella had been keeping from her. "This is wonderful. No? What worries you?"

"That he will write more or visit again."

"We might visit him."

"No. I won't encourage him."

"But you should let me enjoy it." Mama's eyes pleaded in tears. "Do you know how I've longed to be myself again?"

"How could you not be, Mama?"

"In every way your papa demands."

"Oh, he doesn't mean to make you unhappy."

"Did Nonna never tell you?"

Donatella was startled by the mention of her grandmother, but not displeased as the room immediately filled with her books and stories, the smell of her hair and softness of her hands, even her sinewy soprano's neck and withering lips—also some confusion that their intimacy wasn't complete after all.

"No. She didn't like to talk of it, for I went against her wishes. And though you think she was liberal, she was like any mother wanting what she wanted for her daughter, and I was like any daughter assuming she didn't know as well as I did what was best for me."

"And that wasn't Papa?"

Mama didn't agree or disagree as she forgot Reggio's letter half-folded on her skirt so it slid to the floor, and stood up to stretch towards what Donatella had been doing that evening. "I can smell fresh ink. And see these aren't your compositions. No, you can write a little, so can I. But not like this."

There was coldness in her words, perhaps as involuntary as the admission Donatella made, "They are copies. For Lonati."

"He asked you to do them?"

"Yes."

"Where are the originals?"

"Here."

"Not Lonati's music."

"No, Mama."

"How did he have them?"

"He didn't. I did." Donatella took them back in an embrace that should have embarrassed her. Instead, she felt defiant.

Her mother clapped her hands, returning to the abruptness of

English. "You stole them."

"What?"

"And a little romance, too. Why did you not tell me?"

Donatella was looking for the box to put them in, feeling uncomfortable with her mother's half-comprehended discovery she hoped would be silenced by putting the evidence away.

"No wonder you scoff at Reggio, darling. When you've gazed into the eyes of ... Blessed Virgin, where did you get that?"

Mama scrambled for the cedar box, Donatella for the music half-placed into it and falling to the floor.

"Have you ...?" her mother slid her hand inside. "No. Good. You must find somewhere else. There." She looked towards the chest at the bottom of the bed.

"What's the matter?" The Captain had come upstairs.

"Oh, never mind," Mama answered him from the doorway. "It's nothing but silliness." She turned back to show Donatella the fear in her eyes.

"I'm sorry, Mama." Donatella took the blame for whatever was upsetting her.

"So am I," was an admission that seemed unrelated to what Donatella had apologized for.

As soon as her mother was gone, Donatella cleared the wardrobe's upper shelf of its mostly shabby undergarments, and wrapped the music copies old and new in a flannel pillowcase that already treasured a pair of yellowing silk stockings.

On and Off Course

CHAPTER NINETEEN

Donatella's impressions of Oxford began with the welcome clatter of a road and passing blocks of stone and timber buildings interrupted by alleyways that begged her curiosity. The public coach pulled by four linen-white horses made good time before traveling at a snail's pace down the High where pedestrians were bright and boisterous even after eight in the evening.

Their journey had advanced along an unseasonably dry rolling route from Banbury with horn-blowing stops at Deddington, Sturdy's Castle, and Woodstock. Once in the city and denied observance of his timetable by directionless people crossing the street and walking in it, the driver, George Drinkwater, expressed his frustration in a way suggested more by the blemished brass of his jacket's buttons than its stiffness. Donatella admitted only to understanding his tone.

There was yet another delay to their arrival at The Angel Inn, Drinkwater bellowing that Civil John and his four browns from Northampton had beaten them to it.

John lived up to his name, and, with a handshake that seemed to agree on more than moving his vehicle, persuaded the urgency out of Drinkwater's demeanor, encouraged a conversation between them, and prompted the Captain to take the matter of finally arriving at their lodgings into his own hands.

"I'll be dammed if we can't walk from here."

Donatella guided Mama out of the coach as no one had helped her.

"Oh, Edward, the driver will do that when he pulls nearer."

The Captain withdrew from the expertly tied and tiered trunks and baggage at the back of the coach. He looked bitterly tired, but it wasn't the first time Donatella noticed a change in his endurance.

Mama scooped up his arm. "I hope we're not too late for supper."

They even had time to see their rooms and freshen up first, the hours of The Angel for arriving, leaving, dining, drinking, playing cards, sleeping and not being able to sleep insensitive to the time of day or night. Early morning was especially disturbing with bells and whistles and shouts and whinnying, which Donatella's yawning look out a window identified as a crowd of coaches preparing to leave. She wondered how all the commotion didn't completely wake her mother, who had expanded across the entire bed in the few minutes since she had been left alone in it.

Small window panes misted with the slightest breath, so Donatella cleaned them over and over to watch the activity in the street below. Eventually, she saw the blue-hatted and red-jacketed Drinkwater climb to the height of his career and take the reins to lift his team's heads, his vehicle the last in a line of departures. He waited his turn with slumped shoulders, but sat proudly as he exerted a frosty command with cracks of a whip that persuaded the horses it would be less painful to obey.

Donatella wanted to open the window and yell after him, but the latch was stuck.

There was a knock on the door.

"Are you ready, my dears?" The Captain knocked again. "Come on, lazy-heads. Time and tide wait for none."

"I loved him better when he was at sea." Mama finally stirred without making any effort to get out of bed.

"Oh, no." Donatella saw a familiar stranger in front of The Angel. "He comes in."

"Who? Lonati? I can't imagine he'd think of us at this hour." Her mother was sitting up, her plump feet searching for slippers. She changed her mind more than once on what to wear and how to fix her hair.

Donatella was also to blame for making the Captain wait longer than he would think of things to say to someone he hardly knew and might have already decided he didn't like. As much as she didn't want to consider how she looked, she noticed her waist was too thick and her hair too flat, her eyes still darkly circled.

"Why should it matter?" Her mother was shapely in azure blue and buttery cream and spun Donatella around to pluck the strings on the back of her bodice tighter and higher. She gave a little hopeless pat on her daughter's simply styled hair and pinched her cheeks. "Maestro Stradella cannot see you now."

Mama took one more look in the mirror before intercepting Donatella, about to sit gloomily on the bed, and pushing her out of the room.

The dining area, with its low ceiling, worn wooden settles, and bare trestle tables, was still sparsely lit and pungent with candles. The difference from the night before was that they found the Captain enjoying a liquid meal on his own.

"I suppose we might order a dish of buttered eggs," he weakly welcomed them.

"Or two." Mama sat down on the bench beside him and redirected his tankard to her lips. "We thought we'd have to rescue you."

"Well, I've rescued you."

"What did you say to him, Edward?" Her lightly scolding tone spoke for Donatella's relief.

"That it was too early for such nonsense, as my daughter is bad-tempered first thing in the morning."

"Really, Papa."

"Really."

"I hope that won't stop Reggio adoring you later in the day." Mama wasn't joking.

The service was slow, the eggs watery, the accompanying bread hard, and the milk beginning to curdle for having sat too long on a shelf by the fire. Not what was expected from an establishment advertised as having accommodated princes, dukes, and most recently an ambassador from Morocco.

The Captain had his chance to complain but didn't, not even about the freezing attic room his frugality was committed to sharing and enduring one more night, when the proprietor laid a heavily ringed hand on his shoulder.

He wasn't as forbearing when they emerged from The Angel to walk down the street and someone jumped out of a doorway. Mama held the Captain back, Donatella also realizing the crime was his to commit.

Reggio stuttered his offer of a tour around the city that had already wooed them with the width of its best street and sky.

"How hospitable," Mama pretended appreciation.

"No." The Captain didn't. "It won't be necessary, as I've been to Oxford many times."

"I don't wish to assume your place, *Signore*," Reggio said, narrowing his eyes, "only to fulfill my duty as your host."

"And this other one ... Lonati ... I thought he was the reason we were here. To deliver some copies my daughter made for him before he leaves England. And see some reward for her work."

"Mama?"

"Yes, I told your papa. How else could I get him to agree to this adventure?"

"Adventure, Julianna? If that is what you think I agreed to, you'll be disappointed."

"Shall we begin and see?" Reggio swayed his raggedy head. "Let us lead the way."

He was respectful enough not to touch Donatella in any way except as his leg encountered her skirt. It almost tripped him as, dodging more footed than wheeled traffic, they crossed the street "to better view Queen's College."

They navigated back to her parents and turned into a narrow lane with cobbled trenches trickling brownish water, ramshackle housing to their left, sacred spires to their right.

"What a stench." Mama pinched her cloak up over most of her face.

"The waste of a city, my dear." The Captain nodded at Donatella attempting to look back without Reggio noticing. "Don't you remember?"

"I think only fondly of Genoa." The shifting of Mama's eyes admitted her forgetfulness. "Well, I don't recall it ever smelling like this."

"And you?" Reggio asked of Donatella.

"It was a good place, and bad," she repeated something said to her, separating from him with the excuse of staying out of the gutter.

"I think I know where you're leading, sir." The Captain took over as Donatella's escort.

"Well, you may attend me instead, *Signore*." Mama was unperturbed by her husband's maneuver that had abandoned her, even easier with her own that glibly claimed Reggio as the next best walking companion. "A father's distrust never ends," she told him with a little upstroke on his cheek. He turned his face away; it was hard not to notice how his hands trembled.

Mama refused to let the poor man sulk, her chatter in Italian and English hardly comprehensible to Donatella, let alone her father, who relished the role of protector and guide as they continued up "Cat Street," a name he thought should amuse his daughter proven by signage on the side of a house.

He stopped the procession by the vaulted entrance of a long three-storied pinnacled building and spoke of what they couldn't see of its tower tiered on the quadrangle side with columns representing the five styles of classical architecture. He couldn't remember what they were, but was clear on an effigy "Of James the first, that damned Scotsman."

His blaspheming might have resurrected a disappointment Donatella had long blamed him for, but she had lost the desire to think about it anymore. Her forgiveness obviously didn't influence him as he glared at Mama leaning against Reggio and singing softly.

"So, Papa. What is beyond?"

"The Bodleian. A magnificent library."

"Oh, can we go in?"

"It's closed to women."

She was annoyed, but soon distracted by her father's exaggeration that the building had a copy of every book published in England. However, because of the smell, it was believable that pigs were once sold in the yard at its north end.

As he added a few other points he admitted might or might not be correct, he was unusually affectionate, his arm around her. When he kissed her cheek, his face was sweaty.

"Are you all right?" The Captain asked as she should have of him, satisfied with her nod. She lagged behind him as they came to the next landmark: a strangely shaped structure, layered in wood-framed and glass-beveled windows, crowned by a simple parapet, and domed with lead dormer windows and a small cupola. Viewed rectangular from Cat Street, it protruded circular into the broader road it belonged to.

"Like the bow of a ship."

"Yes, Papa."

"He didn't think that up himself." Mama tried but could neither sever her husband's connection to the sea nor pass her daughter back to their unnecessary guide by saying, "I'm sure Maestro Reggio would rather walk with you, Donata."

Through the iron bars of a low-pillared wall, Donatella noticed a man strolling and stopping along the building's blind arcading. He touched its stone with respectful curiosity, something familiar in his flat shoulders and the tilt of his head. She almost saw his face as he looked up and down and even squatted as though to examine the structure's foundations, brushing down the skirt of his deep-blue velvet coat with annoyance for having to do so. He looked in her direction and began to walk faster, still close to the rectangular and round building until she was certain he had disappeared into it.

CHAPTER TWENTY

Donatella felt compelled to rush along the wall in hopes of finding a way through.

"Come across Broad Street to get the full nautical effect," the Captain directed. "Watch your step. Not as many coaches as the High but somehow just as much horse shit."

"It looks like a basilica to me or an opera house."

"Well, it is a theater, Julianna," the Captain seemed only vaguely interested in what he was saying, "of sorts."

"Can we go in?" Donatella was hopeful.

"Not until your papa sails back to us." Her mother lifted her face to the sky and closed her eyes. Snow was lightly falling, immediately melting wherever it landed, wetting her eyelids, cheeks, and lips.

He cleared his throat and spit. "You're wondering about those bearded busts. Locally they are called the Emperors' heads. Visitors mistake them for the apostles because there are twelve."

Reggio had gone on ahead and smirked as the women hurried towards him. He wasn't as pleased when they bypassed him up semi-circular steps, but followed them devotedly through an iron gate, its swirling crown split with each side independently elegant when it was opened. As they reached the tall paneled door, the Captain nudged Reggio out of the way and chuckled as he squeezed between Donatella and her mother.

"I doubt the building is unlocked." The Captain insisted they look above the door and appreciate armored heroes, unicorns, a festooned and crowned coat of arms, and an inscription in Latin Reggio boasted a translation of: "Charles the second, by the grace of God, King of Great Britain, France, and Scotland, Defender of the Faith."

"And long may he reign," Mama immediately explained her sudden interest in politics, "in his benefaction of Italian musicians. But will there ever be an Italian Opera House in London?"

"Oh, *Signora*." Reggio's black eyes drooped. "We shall not give up hope."

"It's open," the Captain confused the conversation until he was seen going into the Sheldonian.

The sunlit U-shaped room seemed a cross between a church and playhouse, or even an enclosed coliseum. Actually, it wasn't like anything Donatella had ever seen or read about with its painted ceiling, crystal chandeliers, elevated pipe organ, marbleized pillars, and simple woodwork offset by intricate carvings and gilding. There was wainscoting on the perimeter walls, stalls, and rising sections of seats increasingly shadowed by an upper gallery. Two pulpits and a throne suggested the place was ready for God and His pretenders. It was empty of any other visitors, but a number of women bent and polished here and there, and a workman was on his knees hammering at the floor in front of the south entrance. He stopped and looked up for the moment it took him to decide the little party of sightseers wasn't his business.

"The roof is held up by mathematics." The Captain realized Donatella's interest in the ceiling's center while Mama walked along one side of the room's seating, and Reggio, at the same leisurely pace, the other. "Not by columns or magic, but mathematics."

Donatella was amazed, as much by what she could understand of her father's knowledge as the enormous ceiling stretching miraculously like the sky.

"See how it was painted in panels," the Captain continued, "with the effect of being uninterrupted."

It was far above them, swirling with color and latticed with gold, cherubic and fiendish, no doubt allegorical, deliberately reverent and irreverent, as excellently done as any fresco Donatella had ever seen. She wasn't about to ask what it all meant, but her father wanted her to know he knew.

"Truth descending upon the Arts and Sciences to expel ignorance."

"And so it should." Reggio was close enough to Donatella to inhale the scent of her hair.

"Sir," the Captain bellowed, "can't you see my daughter doesn't welcome your attentions."

Reggio jumped, perhaps because of the Captain's verbal assault but more likely for the reason they were all startled. A burst of scales was practiced, finally to the highest note Donatella had ever heard her mother sing, held longer than was good for her.

The cleaning women applauded and the laborer whistled and raised his hammer.

"*Brava*," Reggio repeated until Mama fell against the Captain who reached her just in time, although he let her go before she could make the most of his concern.

"Roger? Is that you?"

Donatella turned to the man her father had greeted with a gentle slap on his arm. She was surprised how glad she was to see him.

"My wife had a sudden urge to sample the acoustics."

"Yes, they're excellent, Edward." As Roger stood taller he spoke clearer, "I've heard a few speeches without difficulty. It's altogether a fascinating building and I'm so glad you're showing it off to your family.

You should have let me know you were coming to Oxford. Where are you staying?"

Donatella escaped Reggio's loitering to stand beside her father.

The Captain looked pleased with her decision. "The Angel. What about you?"

"I was at the Bear last night, but plan on traveling to London later today."

"A pity. Do you have time to join us for dinner?"

Mama had overheard. "Is there somewhere nearby?"

"Of course, my friend, your time must be tightly scheduled."

"Well, I did want to go up to the roof," Roger didn't hesitate to admit, "and take some measurements. Have you seen how this extraordinary ceiling was constructed?"

"Years ago. These days I don't have the stamina to climb all those stairs. What about you, sir?"

"No, no." Reggio put up his hands as if protecting himself from a blow.

"Donatella. You must not miss this chance." Her father winked. "It's something to see, especially the views of the city."

"Oh, Papa. I get in the way."

"Not at all." Roger smiled easier than she had ever seen him do. "But I may bore you."

"Well, remember every tedious detail, my dear," the Captain said as he stepped behind her and gently pushed on her shoulders, "for I'll want to know more than I need to."

Roger went up first, taking the turning stairs slowly and encouraging her to keep to the left where they were widest. "There are approximately ... about ... one hundred." He hardly needed to make her understand when she lost count and still couldn't see the end of them. "Do you need to rest?" he asked, struggling with his own progress.

"No," she lied.

"It will ... be ... worth it," he could barely utter.

The last darkening steps narrowed and deepened. She focused on following the excellent cut of Roger's coat and the possible reason her father hadn't objected to her rise into indiscretion with this singular man. When finally she entered the loft room, she soon forgot her aching exhaustion, amazed at the stability below and construction above. There was cold light from every direction and lead-paned elliptical dormer windows all the way around. She resisted the unladylike exercise of crawling into them, even though Roger wouldn't notice once he was climbing through the timber trusses and cross beams supporting the Sheldonian's dome.

"Christopher Wren's design of this building was based on the Roman amphitheater by Marcellus," he called down.

She raised an arm across her forehead to break the glare as she looked up to him.

"It meant constructing the largest unsupported roof ever known."

She investigated the cloth-covered piles in the outer edges of the room while Roger continued balancing, stretching, measuring, and talking.

"What you can't see is how that was accomplished. Beneath the floor you walk on is an ingenious interlocking of beams, each supported at both ends, downward and upward forces making the impossible possible."

Donatella found that one dusty pile consisted of books, another of catalogs as well as single printed sheets and pictures.

Roger was obviously watching her. "There used to be a press up here, for publications by the University. Can't you smell the ink? Those are books and broadsides stored here, probably forgotten." He guessed what she was thinking. "So Wren's roof not only keeps students and speakers and honored guests dry, but also can accommodate significant weight."

"You study to build something?" She spoke louder than she was comfortable doing.

"I'm curious to a fault."

She thought she saw him slip. "Careful—"

"Look out—"

Something fell, heavily, hazardously, just missing her right foot.

"Are you all right? I'll come down for it."

She picked up the buffed brass tool. "Here."

Bunching her skirts to go halfway up a ladder, she leaned over and reached out to Roger to pass him the finely engraved sector that could hardly measure the enormity of that hemispherical roof.

"Continue up to the cupola. There's hardly room for two, anyway." He either meant what he said or wanted her out of the way.

Donatella felt there was little difference as she rose into a heavenly brilliance to be surrounded by whitewashed walls and omniscient views of a city and the sublime winter landscape beyond. Oxford was compact and compelling, softly gray with spired towers, splashed with sunshine while promising more snow, a place that accident had brought her to and another day would take her from. It was all new to her, except somewhere in its maze of streets and structures was Lonati to remind her of what had passed.

And waiting to take more than he gave.

The commissioned copies were rolled in a satchel concealed under her cloak, for she wouldn't leave them in that unsecured room at the Angel. They were more than parchment and well-powdered scratchings of music notation and Italian verse, most wordless sonatas for the violin. She was a little confused by the real intimacy of carrying them around close to her body, burdened by trying to pretend they weren't there but, at the same time, very attached to them.

She wondered if she could give them up.

Her heart pleaded for her not to. Her mind begged to differ because of the meaning those copies gave to her otherwise redundant abilities. For other reasons, too, she was on both sides of the argument. Lonati could bring them alive, while she would only hold them back from a chance to exhale again. Except she might save them from his self-interest, preservation more inherent in her loving possession that would keep them like a body entombed, a memory enshrined.

Do you really think that is what I want you to do with them when, even in death, I can sigh, sing, chill the air and warm it, stir more hearts and settle a few vendettas, too? Why should I prefer the grave to rising magnificently—and unforgettably—out of it?

Roger was, for once, wrong: there was room for two. She turned with little steps, in the sky but not of it, feeling warmer than she should have as she saw her breath and the presence that eluded her even as it was always there begging her to smile and causing her to cry, spinning her around and holding her still, encouraging her to reach up and letting her fall.

She had hit her forehead and worried there would be a bruise. Within moments, she felt a hand on her back and Roger was helping her to stand.

"It seems you fainted. It's so cold up here. Let me go down the ladder first and, if necessary, steady you after."

She had gained consciousness enough to realize how awkward, even embarrassing, that would be.

"Perhaps it was the height that made you dizzy. Even enclosed like this, it can cause lightheadedness. Not me, for I'm a bit of a monkey. Also to look at, I think."

She hoped he realized that, despite her tears, she was impressed by his self-deprecation. He bowed his head. How could he help but think he had upset her more than she already was, having nothing to offer but the felt cloth his shiny sector was wrapped in?

She was a little nauseous and weak in the ankles as she descended into the Sheldonian's loft, Roger following at a proper distance and offering annoying if well-meaning counsel of "Slowly, steady-on, nearly there, hold it" until she let the door to more than one hundred steps almost shut him out of her surprise at finding the Captain near their top.

Her father was leaning against the wall, holding his chest.

She put her arms around him and was momentarily embraced by

Roger as he helped coax the older man to sit on a stair.

"I thought you knew better, Edward," Roger tried to jest while anxiously glancing at Donatella.

"Papa?"

"I'm fine, my dear." But still her father couldn't lift his head.

Don't believe him.

She didn't doubt what she heard. "No, you are not."

The Captain rose quickly and swayed, putting out the flat of his hands to the stairwell walls, soon proving he could stand unaided, if not straight. "I'm fine. Roger, I hope you got what you needed. And, Donatella, what did you learn from this fine fellow?"

"That I'm rather more of a monkey than a man," Roger answered as Donatella considered what she should say.

The Captain seemed completely revived, laughing and advising, "Not a declaration I'd recommend if you hope to impress a woman."

Roger didn't know where to look, certainly not at Donatella, who didn't want his embarrassment to matter.

A voice that had already tested the acoustics of the Sheldonian did so again.

"Yes, Mama. We come now." Donatella realized her mother probably didn't hear her.

She went first, her father and Roger following and talking about architectural rather than amorous designs. As her descent widened, she listened to them less than the low tones of an organ like a hum that, by the time she reached the ground floor, vibrated unpleasantly in her ears, and, as if she was producing it, tickled her mouth and nose. She waited for it to burst into the full sound of towering pipes and multiple manuals including its heavily pedaled one.

It continued to murmur as though someone was determined to play it discreetly.

"Don't be shy, Maestro," her mother called up to Reggio on the edge of his seat in the shadows of the organ Roger explained was built by a German.

"He also constructed one for the Chapel Royal, and just last year became the King's official organ maker."

The Captain had already sat down, visibly sweating again, trying hard not to look as if he was distressed. "Is there ... anything ... you don't know about, my friend?"

Suddenly the sound came, large, even harsh, no longer private but demanding, Reggio lurching backwards not forwards, as surprised as everyone else and even more so when it softened again, without any decay in intensity, entreating and caressing as if without end.

CHAPTER TWENTY-ONE

Reggio's rooms weren't far from the gate tower of Christ Church, and, as their graying guide warned, its bell rang the loudest of any in the city. Donatella might have managed a smile if he hadn't touched her arm as he told them it was named Tom.

The Captain already knew that and more, including how it was recently recast to the perfect weight for hanging in Christopher Wren's latest creation and considered the nightly door closer of Oxford. "I learn more from my dear Wroxton friend, every day."

After dining at The Bear with Roger, they left him there, envying his intention of taking a nap before he traveled on to London. Reggio had told the truth about it being a short walk to his residence, but the morning had exhausted everyone's energy for the rest of the day.

Still, the mission of their Oxford trip had not yet been fulfilled. It wasn't until they reached his lodgings above the entrance of Pembroke College that Reggio admitted there was always the chance Lonati had forgotten about meeting them there.

"At best, he wants to keep us wondering."

Reggio's small sparse parlor was fireless, which might have explained why he didn't offer to take their cloaks. Donatella also assumed he was rarely required to be hospitable. The Captain immediately flopped onto a thinly cushioned chair, leaning towards the cold hearth that held nothing but charred paper and one large log.

"Is this it? No kindling? No more wood?"

Reggio shrugged. "It's difficult to carry much up here."

"Don't you have a servant?" Mama wandered into the hallway. "Oh, here he is."

"But I don't—"

Reggio stepped aside as she made certain Lonati was in no doubt he was expected, slipping her arm around his.

"I've been looking forward to seeing you again, *Signora*," Lonati said, nodded towards the Captain and then Donatella, "just across the way."

Reggio squirmed. "Oh, yes. We were to meet at Saint Aldate's."

"Saint Aldates," Lonati pronounced slowly and then pardoned them all with a sweep of his hand. "But you aren't late. We're still waiting for—"

"Oh, yes. The surprise," Reggio remembered.

"The surprise is eager to see and hear, even perform, the music of Stradella."

Mama laughed with Lonati, or perhaps it was to disguise her irritation with the Captain snoring loudly—until she decided his condition meant she might have an adventure, after all. Lonati and Reggio didn't object and soon the little conspiracy of Italians tiptoed out.

***

"Most churches in Oxford are dark, built as if sunshine wasn't expected to brighten them anyway." Reggio directed Donatella and her mother to sit in pews adjacent to an arcade before bringing out an archlute and chittare from the room beyond that appeared to be a small chapel or vestry.

Mama suggested that, as well as providing more light, additional candles would have helped to warm them. Reggio claimed he had futilely argued with the Rector about that as well as the use of the church for more than a couple of hours.

Donatella maneuvered the satchel off her shoulder and into the open. Her hands fumbled to remove the roll of copies, not sure she wanted to hand them over to Lonati. She wasn't concerned with payment as her father was, but thought Lonati might value them more for his legacy than Alessandro's.

He moved as if to take them but didn't, his stoop making him seem more defensive than aggressive. "You made them for me, didn't you?"

"Give them to him." Her mother huddled smaller and smaller in the pew and pleaded, "Please. Before I die, it is that cold in here."

"What will you do with them?" Donatella felt prompted to say.

"Bring them to life, of course."

"Not as your own compositions?" Again Donatella voiced a suspicion not altogether her own.

"Oh, is that what you're worried about?" Lonati looked over his shoulder.

Donatella spoke to the same apparition, "Please don't laugh."

Reggio squinted, as though he realized something objectionable about her.

Donatella sat and closed her eyes, wanting to withdraw from Lonati's and Reggio's ambitions, shivering, but not just because of the church's lack of heat. She wondered if anyone noticed how she struggled to hide her reactions to the restless spirit that followed her around, spoke to her, and even appeared to hold her in its hereafter. She hadn't spent weeks making those copies for any reason other than to be alone with it, no need to pretend it wasn't there watching and admiring but also admonishing her attachment to its life work, a candle flame and her hand a little unsteady and her heart still unsure.

Ah, il Gobbo.

She also heard someone tuning a violin as Alessandro had sometimes done, then saw Lonati tapping its belly and back as well as adjusting the pegs and plucking the strings. He behaved as if he didn't notice her sliding out of the pew and approaching him, her hands outstretched to finally offer what was between them.

"We still haven't decided on a price."

"Speak with my father." Donatella really couldn't discuss receiving money for the love she had put into those copies. "And promise—"

She was about to appeal to Lonati's sense of honor, if he had any, when all attention turned to a long-wigged, large-eyed, flushed young man who entered the church through its south porch. At first he reminded Donatella of Roger, mostly because he was darkly dressed with a high cravat tied so tight it gave him a double chin. Unlike Roger, he obviously relished being recognized, as he kissed Reggio on his cheeks, gently lifted Lonati's shoulders to greet him the same, and looked around hopefully.

Mama stepped towards him so slowly he thought he initiated their meeting.

"Henry Purcell, Mistress." His head nodded downwards and his hand waited for hers to offer itself. He held it for only a moment, perhaps realizing that the beautifully aged woman before him would have allowed more. He quickly found a way to remove himself from her expectation: "What's that you have, Carlo?"

Lonati understood the young man's curiosity over the roll he was holding between his right arm and side. "The magic of Stradella."

Master Purcell clapped his hands. "Originals?"

Reggio translated for Lonati.

"No, no."

"Of course not." Master Purcell moved behind Lonati, who was awkwardly flattening out the layers along the front pew's bench. "Too much to hope for. Still, good fellow, let me see."

Donatella realized the importance of the inspection, as unnerving as waiting for Alessandro's verdict while knowing nothing could ever surpass the satisfaction of that approval.

"They are very nice. Clear and fluid. No smudges, at least that I can see at a glance, and excellent placement. It's hard to find such an able copyist. At least in that, Stradella was fortunate."

This time Mama was the interpreter, Lonati shifting from foot to foot while looking at Donatella and questioning the humility in her silence.

Reggio broke his. "We now have the church for just over an hour." He sat with the archlute like a shield in front of him. "I have a new piece—"

"Oh, I must hear Stradella." Master Purcell swung out his arms as though into an embrace.

"Let me choose." Mama was irresistibly devious, lifting page after page.

"Something lighthearted and melodious, if you please." The young composer's arms dropped. "As I feel sure he would've wished to entertain us."

"It is here."

"No, Mama." Donatella realized her mother's discovery and an ache in her stomach.

Master Purcell was soon performing the selected music with his eyes and a delicate finger in the air. "Will you sing it, Mistress?"

"Yes, yes. With my daughter, Donata, as she is shy. It's her specialty."

"Really?" Master Purcell screwed his mouth, skeptical but interested.

"In fact, Maestro Stradella might've written it for her."

"Oh, no, Mama. In Rome, before—"

"You knew him?" Master Purcell motioned for Lonati, who had been listening without comprehending what should have provoked him into having his say. "I would like to hear this, Carlo. I don't see a bass viol, but Reggio can improvise. The ladies will sing. There's only one score."

"I know it by heart." Donatella blindly stepped back into her mother's arms.

"Of course you do, darling," Mama's soft voice blew into her ear.

"Ah." Purcell was watching them closely, and then turned back to Lonati, who was explaining the music to Reggio.

There was the appropriate silence before Lonati was as elegant and amiable with bow and violin as no other activity afforded him. With every stroke, nod, and faraway expression, he was an echo of Alessandro, exacting the very best from the composition and the late composer's nature, generous with his talent, uninhibited with his playing, making the music his own only as he adored it. His reminiscent virtuosity swept Donatella onto the waves of *Le donne più bella* like a ship with a steady breeze in its sails, Reggio's archlute-*continuo* encouraging the rolling sensation. Her mother's grasp of her arm and escorting vocal weakened, soon leaving Donatella alone with each poetic turn of phrase and melodic ornamentation.

Donatella listened, the sound of her own singing always a surprise. She grew more and more trusting as she interpreted the aria with good *legato*, shading and tone, her jaw relaxed and her tongue in the proper position, her chest lifted but not too proud. Lonati flourished in between her dreamy declarations, Reggio constant until the end that softened and lingered in harmony with her final passage.

She kept her eyes closed, the silence longer than before the performance, as though her singing had not only used up her breath but everyone else's, too.

"I didn't realize she could sing like that." Roger was there with her father standing just behind him.

Mama wiped her eyes, Lonati his bow while seeming uncertain how to respond.

Reggio had exchanged the archlute for the chittare. "Harry. Hear my new song."

Master Purcell put up a hand that frustrated Reggio's offer, and stepped towards Donatella with a silent clap. "Now, Mistress, I have no doubt you knew him."

CHAPTER TWENTY-TWO

Roger's decision to delay his journey to London was especially appreciated when he offered the use of his carriage for getting around the city after dark. It was also fortunate her mother had insisted they pack something more formal to wear than their original itinerary suggested they would need. As they changed, her mother noticed the bump and bruising on her daughter's forehead and powdered it heavily to affect its appearance. Donatella didn't mention her worsening headache.

Mama couldn't stop talking about how they had secured the invitation to a concert at the Cathedral.

"Master Purcell only offered because it was already open to the public." The Captain tried but couldn't spoil her excitement.

"Not how we became guests of honor." She hugged Donatella again, also ignoring the Captain's resolve that they wouldn't miss their early morning coach home.

They were no more than a few additional bodies in the crowded Cathedral, the Honorable but unassuming Roger North squeezing into the same stall next to the Captain. As usual, anonymity both suited and disappointed Donatella, but that quandary and the dismissive looks opposite were soon forgotten as white-winged choristers paraded past. Her attention was drawn up through the nave heightened by gleaming pillars alternately circular and octagonal, wide slabs atop their capitals spraying into double arcades pronouncing the pointed arches of the clerestory. She leaned forward to watch the filing of the singers into partially screened pews on one side of the aisle and the other. Boys and men quietly untied and opened their folders on slanted shelves higher than she had for kneeling with a prayer book, and smoothed the pages in a motioned harmony that boded well for the performance to come. How could they not seem angelic: shapeless and serene with tall tapers at each of their places haloing their cropped hair and blanching their faces, such fervent patience in their waiting? Donatella was glad of the time to savor the sweet scent of incense and look up towards the creamy pendant ceiling Roger was admiring so her father did, too.

The organ sounded and she thought Master Purcell was at its helm as she had heard he was recently appointed head organist for the Chapel Royal. However, he was standing in the aisle in front of and between the choir members, dressed similarly except for his long coiled wig, signaling them to rise. He closed his eyes and stiffened his lips, an intense young man, probably demanding at times, a custodian of formality with respect for those who had gone before that he expected others to have. He might have been something of a pilgrim, too, not overtly as in a religious way and less adventurous than Alessandro, but, at least when it came to music, suggesting a similar destination. It might be a question of nationality: English caution in contrast to that Mediterranean impulse Donatella had, once or twice, given in to.

It wasn't until Mama pulled her back that Donatella was aware she was leaning too far—in an unappealing way—out of the pew. Except her mother hadn't done so or said anything while sitting with her hands folded and turned towards Master Purcell who finally opened his eyes and arms to conduct, his head nodding as he counted to himself. Donatella wondered if she also imagined the cathedral taking a deep breath before it echoed with the layered sound of thin-throated youthfulness, lower harmonies, and the organ's rumbling accompaniment. It hardly mattered once she was under the spell of the canticle's long open vowels and articulate consonants, bright and clear in its upper registers with just a hint of vibrato and appropriately soulful underneath, control and sensitivity in the completeness of its sound.

A mature voice emerged into a short solo. Eventually, the youngest boys and the remainder of the singers joined in. Her mother turned to indicate something on the program card and Donatella remembered she had dropped hers. They were the last to kneel when the congregation was supposed to, the evening service and song melding into one, the choir abandoning its flair for a section of chant that was, if anything, more lyrical and affecting. It was pleasing and unsettling, the latter because of the spirits such an ancient venue and unfinished affairs entertained.

Come, come. Was there ever a moment you loved me more than my music?

Again Donatella was taken by surprise as the worshippers changed their position, this time to stand, even her mother knowing when to do so. The music rose, too, and the vocalists took advantage of their wide range. The organ's contribution was drowned in the crescendo of their final passages, Master Purcell allowing the possibility that he was steering a ship that might stay on course without him.

***

Roger insisted they walk through the cathedral. At first, he was unusually silent on what he knew about it, as if respectful of their weariness and hopeful their uneducated observations of its magnificence and anomalies would not hinder their enjoyment. Moving slowly below the intricately knotted and looped chancel ceiling that reminded Donatella of the best Genoese taped-lace, they approached the high altar to have their own thoughts on its clutter of candlesticks and statues, darkened stained glass behind and above it. She hoped no one noticed how she swayed when looking up or held onto her mother as they went back through the chancel, crossing under columns and curves between the aisles of a transept and some of the cathedral's most ancient places where more windows told stories and longed for the light of day. When in a whisper Roger announced the grave of Lady Montacute—"who gave the then priory a nearby meadow"—with little figures of children all around her tomb, the Captain decided to withdraw from further exploration. What he avoided, besides over-tiring himself and Roger's failure to keep every detail to himself, were more chapels and monuments, a shrine containing the dust of "a married nun and virgin saint", and the Watch Chamber, which was "a fine example of perpendicular workmanship."

Donatella's head began to hurt badly again. Eventually she followed her father's example, straying from the sight of a suspicious alliance between her mother and Roger as they greeted a man coming down from the organ loft.

"Ah, William Husbands. I was surprised Harry did not play."

"He also fancies himself a choir master," the man quipped. "Mistress."

"Oh, let me introduce—"

Donatella didn't hear more, leaving the cathedral to pass into its cloister, the night air that somehow breezed through it crisply comforting so her headache was slightly relieved. She walked along a little of the colonnade, easily imagined Lidia there, and considered how disappointment was the companion of expectancy. The fulfillment of that day was mostly due to dealings which had resisted planning.

Her visit to Oxford, like other things, would be remembered for how it had surprised her.

More than her head was soothed in the walkway's flickering light and vow of silence; there was a sense of healing in her heart. She was on her knees, willingly, prayerfully, feeling closer to contentment than she ever had, swooning a little again.

She almost felt prepared for Reggio's hands on her and allowed him to lift her into his arms, kiss but not revive her.

She leaned back against the inside wall of the cloister, still feeling arms around her. They weren't Reggio's. She knew she appeared a little crazy smiling at him because it didn't matter that she did. She was a passing fancy, a muse for some regretful song that would soon forget what had inspired it. He hadn't found any satisfaction with her and was already turning away. She heard voices, one she recognized as her father's, another Master Purcell's, and her mother laughing.

Even as he seemed to withdraw, Reggio stood in the way of her moving towards them.

"I must go now." She hoped her words would persuade him to step aside.

He bowed, his quivering hands reacting to his already skewed wig slipping forward. She heard her own escape echoing through the flagstone corridor.

***

It was a good-humored gathering about to disband, the Captain with his hand on Roger's shoulder, Master Purcell standing near Mama, who was more interested in an unidentified gentleman having too much fun while singing in Latin.

"Let us all know the joke," the Captain insisted.

The entertainer obliged. "'If on my theme I rightly think, there are five reasons why men drink: good wine; a friend; because I'm dry; or lest I should be by and by; or—any other reason why.'"

"Well put, Canon Aldrich." The Captain abandoned Roger to clasp the singer's hand.

"We could go now, good sir," the Canon further proved he was a convivial fellow, "and enjoy a pint and a pipe."

"Well done." Master Purcell removed his robe and revealed he was dressed the same as at St. Aldate's.

"Sounds like a plan to me," the Captain also endorsed, no doubt wishing he hadn't left his pipe at home.

"I'll pass," Roger admitted what had been assumed.

Mama grabbed the Captain's arm. "But there's a coach to catch in the morning."

He must have seen she was really expressing her frustration with being denied the distractions of his gender. Donatella also noticed his disappointment as he realized the choice he had to make to save himself the trouble, and, especially, expense of drinking too much and having to extend their time in Oxford. He barely bid the other men goodnight before quickly leading his wife and daughter into the wintery courtyard on the east side of the Cathedral while the Great Thomas tolled as if it would never stop.

Roger rushed after him. "Wait, Edward. I must fetch my driver from the Chapter House. It was too cold for him to stay so long in the carriage."

"Oh, yes, yes." The Captain's irritation indicated he had forgotten how much Roger's friendship meant to him. "But we need to leave now."

Roger was too mild a man to do more than frown and go off to get the driver.

Master Purcell seemed unaware of anything but his own interests. "I must say I was most impressed by your singing earlier. And only found out later that you did those excellent copies."

As Donatella realized he was speaking to her, she bowed a little, actually, to make less of his approach.

"I hope Carlo ... Maestro Lonati ... paid you."

"Oh, Papa took care of it."

"Of course." Maestro Purcell smiled without pleasure. "You must tell me more about the inimitable Stradella sometime. How lucky you were to know him. I was so sorry for his end." He paused and Donatella looked down to her hands, afraid he was reading her. "Death visits too often, too sudden, too soon." There was private pain concealed and revealed in those words, but he was soon curious again. "Is it true jealousy was the motive to it?"

Donatella was sorry she didn't have an answer for him.

"Well, even so, in regret of his greatness as a musician, I forgive him any injury of that kind." Master Purcell was thoughtful beyond his years. "As I'm sure you do."

CHAPTER TWENTY-THREE

Donatella's thoughts had been muddled since returning from Oxford. She remembered parts of the trip home: the pain and nausea and her mother worrying over her in verbose Italian; her father wondering if they should find a doctor in Woodstock, which would have meant changing coaches or staying away from home another night. Nothing interrupted the discomfort of the journey but her mother's hand and equally soothing sensations of sunshine, sleep, and a whisper from the past. With the jolts back to consciousness, Donatella's head pounded and the coach rolled and rattled more than her stomach could settle for.

She regretted missing the passing countryside, especially as her painter's eye might have seen it distant and intimate, its skies unsettled and gently ridged, patterned by spinneys and meadows beginning to be colored with spring, and blocked by tree-tunneled roads and cluttered villages.

She had a vague recollection of the Captain persuading the driver to detour down into Wroxton and deliver them as near to their cottage as possible. Mama described that, although it was late evening, windows and doors burst open, laughing children and growling dogs pursued the coach, and the ducks on the pond were aggressively vocal. Donatella was too desperate for her bed to be aware of that spectacle, impatient to be in the company of her cats.

She was upset with the doctor coming quickly and pushing them off the covers because they might cause her legs to stiffen.

"It's her head she hurt." Her mother was standing at the opposite side of the bed holding a candle caving into its flame.

"With a concussion, rest is important. A cool compress if her headache persists, but keep her warm. She might not want to eat. Try lemon and honey a little at a time on her tongue. And if there's vomiting, mint or fennel seeped in hot water."

"She will be all right?" Her father was in the room.

"Of course. I suggest a bath with Epsom salts, especially if she has trouble sleeping. At least, soak her feet. And don't worry her with anything."

That last of the doctor's orders was why no one told her about Lidia. Before that, there were too many other questions in Donatella's thoughts and dreams and somewhere between the two, answered by memories, voices, even sightings—especially in the dark—of what had and might have been. She thought she was going mad, even hoped she was, because then she could be as unpredictable as she liked. Once her headache and nausea eased, there was relief in her collapse, and all the tension of trying to hold up for so long gave way. It might be attributed to a bump on her head, but, like a mountain, she only appeared to be standing still, the erosion of her strength slow and sure until a landslide left little difference between what was buried and what was exposed.

Mama didn't know what to do about her daughter's distress, finally going downstairs to play the spinet and console herself. Donatella might have missed Lidia then, for the girl had cried with her before. The absence of Caprice and Bianchi was more urgent, and she quietly called them, feeling one and then the other settle across her legs. She must have fallen asleep soon after.

She awoke to a glow in the room. The candle her mother left had burned down and there couldn't be much light from the moon that was a fading sliver the early morning they left Oxford. She could hear her father knocking down the fire in the parlor grate, which he did routinely before he went to bed. The room was cold. It almost always was, and except for the muggiest nights in summer, flannel sheets and a quilted coverlet were appreciated.

She was surprised to hear a familiar hum and papers being shuffled, a busy shadow stretching up and down as it passed along the walls. She wasn't afraid, just curious and expectant. In contrast, the Captain coming upstairs was disturbing, her heart in darkness again. He opened the door a little, her mother calling, "She's sleeping soundly, my dear. So let us do the same."

Donatella didn't dare move until she was sure he had gone, wanting to get up but frustrated by exhaustion as she tried to, collapsing backwards, unable to pull her legs onto the bed and under the covers. Yet she woke to being completely tucked in, one of her cats jumping around the room as if trying to catch something. It was Caprice. Bianchi was sitting on the dressing table, looking into its little mirror, tilting her head one way and then the other, cautiously lifting a paw. Her white coat hardly explained how Donatella saw what she did.

At the hint of dawn, she realized no nails or tacks had been used to hang the sheets of music on the walls of her room. She was told to take them down, keep them in order and not doubt their existence. They were nothing but air as she picked them off and let them float to land in piles on her bed, both cats running under it.

Donatella's thoughts and actions continued obedient, but not altogether unquestioning. "How much you've done. But how is it possible?" She spread out the papers even, despite an understated protest, on the floor. She shivered and looked around for her shawl, saw it lifted from the window seat, felt her braid shift and an embrace of her shoulders, all the while the scent of jasmine intensifying. Or was it lavender?

Or another consequence of a concussion? Or the chance of love too soon and too late? Or something she would rather not think of.

What day was it? She found her journal under the pillows. Her last entry was four days ago, before going to Oxford: I am in two minds about this trip. The copies have come out well, but do I want to let them go? Still, they are promised to Lonati. But nothing is to Reggio.

So, it was Thursday, the twenty-fifth of February; a year since she hadn't expected a beginning or ending, but simply had helped with the laundry and cooking, smiled mysteriously, and painted orchids. By evening, the manner of the day had been set and it seemed nothing more could affect its history. She had planned to wash her hair and dry it dreamily by the kitchen fire.

Not weep.

She mustn't do so again. There was the music to think of, so much of it. One moment it was imagined and the next real enough to worry her, for how could she keep it all secret and safe? She picked up one page and, sitting at her dressing table, smoothed and kissed it and decided it didn't matter if anyone else believed what she did.

***

Donatella wasn't sure why she was on the floor, Mama summoning the Captain, who was gentler than he appeared as he helped her up and moved her towards the bed.

She panicked. "Take care, Papa, where you walk—"

"All right," he only agreed to humor her, "get in on the other side."

"No."

"What's this, then?"

Donatella thought her father had seen what was stopping her. He stepped aside to let her mother, who was about to pull up the covers, persuade her.

"No, Mama. I spoil them."

"Oh, dear. Are you going to be sick?"

"Look. One more." Donatella stumbled to the darkest corner, over the very floor she had prohibited her father treading on, standing on her toes and reaching to the exposed timbers.

Her mother began crying and praying until she was coughing so violently the Captain had to choose which one of his afflicted family to attend to.

"I fear she's going insane, Edward," Mama managed to speak as he led her from the room.

"Nonsense, my dear." He took a quick look back that didn't deter Donatella from searching the piles of compositions for where the stray page belonged.

It was an impossible task, the music's spirited notation disappearing as morning filled the room and she was confused about how she had spent the night. She could hear Mama spitting up and Papa calling for Martha, who usually arrived by seven. Donatella was relieved to think of something so routine. She felt a little hungry, but was unwilling to do anything about it—or just too tired, her bed nothing more than somewhere to crawl into.

She dozed on and off through the morning, at some point soothed with the warm milk Martha brought up if not by her complaining about all the extra work she had to do with Lidia gone and Mistress Hanley sick, too. Donatella considered getting up each time she woke, the cottage quiet and her thoughts tormented by what was there one moment and gone the next. She must have slept soundly until it was dark again and the sway and stretch of a flame made shapes on the ceiling and walls.

Someone offered her a spoonful of stewed broth. Just the smell of it upset her stomach.

"Mama. Is it ... yet the twenty-fifth?"

"The date? I don't know."

"We return from Oxford ... yesterday?"

"Oh, you remember. Yes. It was just yesterday."

A lemony sweetness touched Donatella's tongue as she asked what time it was, the clock downstairs answering before her mother could.

"Oh, darling," Mama sat on the bed, leaned against her daughter's shoulder and stroked her forehead, "what is it?"

Donatella, curling into her mother's arms, couldn't say.

CHAPTER TWENTY-FOUR

A letter addressed to the Captain came from London a day later. Donatella was dizzy when she stood up. There were still strange things happening around her no one else seemed to notice, but at least the headache and nausea were gone and she could understand what Roger had written as her father slowly read out loud. The gist of it was that he felt responsible for the accident that had spoiled her visit to Oxford.

Donatella was pleased Roger deemed it necessary to let her know he would have rather offered his regard in person than by pen.

Her mother seemed sad. "You should be flattered that such a highborn and high placed man takes this time and interest in you."

"There's no pretention in him. As he writes," her father recited again, "'the appointment to King's Council is just another epoch or degree of advancement in my life.'" He folded the letter. "He's a good friend." He knew enough to rationally interpret Roger's consideration.

"What more should she wish for?" Mama tantalized him.

He resisted. "Have you told her about Lidia yet?"

"I wouldn't worry her over something she can do nothing about."

"I know where she is," Donatella finally spoke.

"I will see her this afternoon," her father announced.

"To bring her back?"

"Well, Julianna, do you think I should?"

"No, Papa. Let her stay. She ... she ... has found a place."

"What?" he asked with the irritation he always showed when she couldn't find the English words.

"I don't understand it," Mama said for a different reason.

"Tobias is a decent fellow, despite his oddities." The Captain laid Roger's letter under a small stone jar on Donatella's dressing table. "My father told me his mother put the idea of demons in him. That when he was a boy he was taunted by 'Toby Nevil sees the devil!' wherever he went in the village. Now he is left alone, just a peculiar old man."

"That doesn't explain why Lidia thinks she should care for him." Mama followed the Captain out.

Donatella returned to bed and remembered her young Genoese companion as the girl had portrayed the Virgin Mary in the church of *Santa Maria Maddalena*. There was the sweetness of incense, not choking as it usually was at high mass, but lightly scenting a memory that was about more than Lidia trying not to move or blink. The accompanying music was devotional and hopeful its composer would be saved by it.

Donatella heard someone coming upstairs. Almost magically, it was Lidia bringing a bouquet of primrose buds, their lower stems wrapped in damp moss tied with blades of grass. The girl was flushed.

The flowers were fragranced with frost.

"I knew you like them." Lidia surprised Donatella again by speaking in English.

"Papa made you—"

"No."

Lidia reached over the bed to Bianchi, who anticipated a familiar stroking of her belly.

"Why?"

Lidia ignored Donatella's question for enough time to loosen a ribbon on her sleeve and tempt Caprice to swat at it. "Because you are ill."

"No. I mean, why have you abandoned us?" Donatella's hand crushed the primroses and slid them under the covers, closing her eyes so she wouldn't have to consider Lidia's reaction.

As soon as the girl was gone, Donatella placed the unfortunate posy beside Roger's letter on the dressing table. The next morning she chose Nonna's volume of sonnets by Petrarch to preserve it in, just because the book's satin cover was embroidered with silk and silver threads, its brittle interior with love's joys and wounds. As if directed by a divine hand, she found just the right pages to lose them in.

I bless the place, the time and hour of the day
that my eyes aimed their sights at such a height
and say: 'My soul, you must be very grateful
that you were found worthy of such great honour'.

It was Sunday. She was certain once she opened her bedroom window, anticipating the air would be in agreement with the sunshine warming its lead mullions. Instead, she shivered as she listened to All Saints ringing out, and approximated the hour before any villagers appeared to disappear up the lane along the Abbey wall. She expected to see Martha, who often made it known she pretended faith at least once a week and insisted her husband and children did, too. The boys' fiery hair left little doubt they were brothers, either triplets or as close in age as possible, their hopeless glances towards their father admitting they were doomed to salvation, at least for the next hour or so.

Donatella was surprised to see Lidia in the Protestant parade. The girl stood out in her Genoese cloak, walking alone and followed.

Donatella turned into her room and sulky mood. The water in the jug left next to the basin on the floor by her dressing table was yesterday's but still cleansing, especially to her eyes. Her hair also needed washing, which made it easier to hold up with the few pins she could find, the fading bruise on her forehead curious but not bothersome. As she changed out of convalescence, her nightshift chased by Caprice, who also landed on the bed and Bianchi, she stood naked longer than she ever did. Dressing required such effort; it felt awkward and unnecessary, all the pulling and twisting, lacing and bending. She should have put on her hose and boots before her corset. When she stood up again, she was spinning without moving and grabbed one of the bed posts, pressing her cheek against it until she was convinced she wasn't going down. By the time she layered herself in a fresh linen shift, woolen petticoat and skirt, and a peplum bodice whose bones had moved around in the last laundering, she was exhausted and tempted by the soft solitude of her bed again.

"*Brava.* You're up."

Her mother was in a morning gown colored like Lidia's and now Petrarch's primroses, fastened with wine-red ribbon over her bosom and spraying out to reveal the crumpled chemise she had slept in. She helped Donatella finish dressing, fumbling to tie a bow with the ends of the laces in her daughter's bodice.

"You can take breakfast with me." Her mother clapped her hands. "Your father had his and is already deep in mud."

There was a whisper of worrying over him in Donatella's head. "Is he well?"

"I suppose." Mama picked at Donatella's hair. "It's rather dirty."

"I know."

Her mother's hungry breath and gentle hand examined her forehead. "The bump has gone down. Still, you look ill, so frail, even thin, like you might float away. After noon we'll put out a chair for you to sit in the sun. Of course, not something I'd recommend if we were in Genoa."

They ate in the kitchen. When Martha wasn't there, Mama would throw off her shoes and sit on the long bench with her legs tucked under, tear at dusty bread, suck on grizzly bones, scrape at her teeth, and sing like a peasant. That morning her main activity was to make sure her daughter was eating the cold pork and stewed apples she had laid out— of course, feeding herself as well. She grew impatient with Donatella's excuse of still not having the stomach for it.

"I don't understand what happened. Roger said you fainted in the cupola."

Donatella sipped at minted barley water, prescribed by Martha as a tonic, keeping her lips on the cup's rim even when she wasn't drinking.

"He thought it was because you stood so high above the city."

All of a sudden Donatella felt clarity. "Like looking over Genoa from the esplanade of *Castelletto.*"

"Yes." Mama was delighted to be reminded. "One of those rare outings that took us nearer the sky, even more so because we were all together, your father almost content to go along with our little excursion and girlish chatter."

"I never chattered, Mama."

"Well, you giggled. Whenever you didn't know what to say, you giggled."

"Giggled?"

"You know, that silly echoing laugh you had as a child and young girl. It used to aggravate Despina. Then, what didn't?" Her mother tried to demonstrate with short repeated gasps, which just brought on a fit of coughing.

"Oh, Mama, drink."

"I'm fine. Oh, for those days again. Sometimes it's so dull around here, so provincial. Despite everything, I did enjoy our time in Oxford. If only we could go to concerts every week, and dances. And sing for maestros, again and again."

Donatella dipped a thick slice of pork into the unsweetened applesauce with its strong taste of cinnamon that burned her lips still chafed from the winds that had blown against her in Oxford.

"Perhaps if you get your strength back, we'll have better times. What's that? Sounds like a quarrel."

Donatella heard it, too: more than one person yelling outside, the Captain's voice the loudest.

"I go, Mama. You not dressed—"

"All right. But hurry. I want to know."

Donatella moved much faster than she should have, struggling with the scullery's exterior door, finally slamming it open, slipping on the step beyond that took her outside and onto a path where she stopped to look at the bleak and partially tilled garden. Even as the shouting continued, she thought they were mistaken about her father's involvement in anything but turning over cold, wet soil for another season of growing and harvesting.

She saw the spade he had just replaced the handle on laying in the mud. He was fanatical about leaving his tools stuck firmly in the ground or propped against a wall.

She walked quickly beyond the fortification of the yard towards the disturbance in the street. Villagers young and old were gathered just past the pond, no longer argumentative, but distressed. They were awkwardly silent and moved apart once Donatella was observed approaching them. A black cloak identified Lidia bending over the Captain, who had collapsed on the edge of the green.

The Music of
Friends

CHAPTER TWENTY-FIVE

Donatella didn't get out often. When she did, she was encouraged by glimpses of sun that, along with almost daily rain and even a few light frosts, persuaded sweet violets to be braver than they were. In the first week of March, she found some just inside the Abbey wall, the freshest leaves unrolled into heart shapes that were slightly downy underneath. She picked a few along with buds and blooms from a scattering of plants, holding them in a little funnel she had made out of parchment and her own inventiveness. Of course, there were primroses in clusters of pale cream and deep yellow, pin-eyed and feather-eyed, and also a few faintly pink ones.

The *bellis perennis* were like snow speckling the Abbey's ancient park as it sloped and gradually flattened towards sheep straggling out to trample and graze. Sky-singing larks, alert blackbirds, and the throaty coos of pigeons filled her head with easier thoughts than she'd had for some time. She didn't mind her mucky boots, soggy skirts, and the black under her fingernails, pushed her hood back and deliberately smeared a little mud across her cheeks.

Looking up and down she was surprised by the intense blue of the sky matched by the speedwell creeping through the daisies a month earlier than the little botanical book Roger had lent her predicted.

Soft panting caught Donatella's attention. An isolated ewe a few yards away was pawing the ground and lifting her head one side to the other. Nipping at her own bulk, the animal slowly went down to her right side and rocked like a capsized boat. Her udder was swollen, her hind legs extending apart and up with a slightly opaque bubble appearing between them.

There was the rumble of another arrival. The North's coach slowed, halted, and Roger jumped out while Sir Francis, only his head and hand emerging, instructed the driver to continue on up to the carriage house.

"Hello there." Roger ran towards Donatella. "Francis will fetch the herdsman or find someone who will. Seems this ewe wasn't expected to deliver today, else she would have been kept inside."

Except for often used phrases, Donatella was still translating English in words rather than sentences and barely understood him, especially as he wasn't thinking about her trying to.

He took off his jacket and wig and threw them at a sprawling spruce nearby, one of its low spraying branches catching them.

He rolled up his sleeves. "She'll do this on her own, if it's a normal presentation."

He sent Donatella to the front of the ewe that was upright again, instructing her to hold the head forward. She caressed the animal's nose.

He dropped to his knees. "Her water may have already burst. The head and legs are out—no, only one leg. The other might be elbowed."

The ewe butted Donatella's stomach hard and then again, the third time more of a nuzzle.

"Keep her still. I just have to push the lamb back in a bit. And ... adjust that leg."

Donatella couldn't see what he was doing, but never doubted his judgment or capability as his faceless commentary involved her in a way that avoided any unpleasantness.

"There. All being well, it's up to her now."

Roger pulled grass to wipe his hands and stood, the front of his shirt damp and sliding out from breeches that were soiled at the knees. He didn't seem to mind that Donatella continued to stroke the ewe and even whispered in Italian to her.

"How are you?"

When she didn't answer he began tucking in his shirt. "I feel responsible. I was so wrapped up in measurements."

The sheep's head abruptly twisted onto its back as the animal fell to its left side this time, her body pulsating noticeably, her tail up and back legs extending again, her lamb sliding out and down. Roger lunged forward to guide it to the ground despite the urine, blood, and bowel movement gushing along with it.

"Sir. How's it goin'?" Up the hill came a middle-aged man in a brown leather hat, coat, and side-laced leggings, his boots cleaner than Roger's fine shoes. "I see all be well. 'Specially as you are assisted."

Donatella felt uneasy because of the clipped, burring manner of his speech.

"Aye, that's it," he approved of Roger breaking the stringy membrane around the lamb's mouth and nose. Donatella wondered if it was alive. "If it nay find its breath, lift it by its back legs an' swing it. Gentle, mind."

Roger did as Donatella supposed he was told, the ewe showing the irritation he didn't. "What is it?" he asked of the other man coming close enough to investigate.

"A lassie."

Roger put the lamb down carefully, rubbing its sides before the dam shouldered him away in order to lick her baby that immediately began to wiggle.

His worker wasn't intimidated by the mother's snorting, wielding a small knife to quickly cut the umbilical cord and, soaking a rag from a bottle that also appeared from under his coat, dabbing the lamb's navel.

"Vinegar an' thyme. Like you might use to dress a chookie for roast'n." He winked at Donatella and turned to Roger. "Aw, sir. You spoilt your nice clothes."

"No matter, Cargill. Look." Roger didn't need to persuade Donatella to be enthralled with the lamb on its knees, its wagging tail hoisted when its back legs straightened and, after a few failures, its front ones did, too. The dam bleated to see it finally walking and leaping sideways, silenced when it found its way under her.

"Let the lambkin drink, then we get 'em sheltered."

"Good man." Roger patted Cargill's shoulder.

"You reek, sir."

"Thank you." Roger didn't mind such earthy teasing until he remembered Donatella. "You dropped something—"

The sassy Scotsman picked up the funnel of flowers. "Violets. For love of truth or truth of love. Primroses. For findin' the way to fairyland. Gowans to cast spells." He passed it to her.

Roger's hand on her arm diverted Donatella's attention towards the remarkably clean newborn springing around its mother.

"Ah." The confident Scotsman lifted the lamb into his arms as if making a toast with a drink, taking for granted its mother would follow him.

"I apologize if my man made you uncomfortable. We just hired him a few months ago and he's a good deal impertinent, but he knows his job and seems honest." Roger also moved away to retrieve his jacket and wig. "I must clean up."

"Yes, yes."

"I wrote to your father." He attempted to put on the wig, but just rolled it in his coat. "Did he tell you?"

"Yes, just before—" she wanted to speak quicker and more to the point than she could.

"I was caught in London, like a rabbit in a trap. No way out unless I chewed my leg off, figuratively speaking, that is."

"Well, you are here now." She didn't mean to disregard his predicament.

***

An apoplectic seizure the doctor had determined. At first the Captain seemed to know what was said around him and apologize for the tears he caused. Eventually, he didn't open his eyes, his only response a gurgling when Donatella tried to feed him gruel or broth that mostly ended up on the cloth bib she hoped he wasn't aware of.

It was strange to see him in bed all day or go so long without a smoke, hard to believe he didn't wonder if the rabbits had been in his garden again. She never expected him to be more obviously absent than when he was at sea. The whole household was paralyzed without his deep-voiced opinions and urgent step, and because Mama didn't sing and Martha dare not complain.

Her mother let Roger in, and, after a few words, come upstairs. Donatella waited for his knock on the door to her parent's room.

Unlike me, he's someone to rely on.

She knew she still wasn't thinking clearly, but Roger needn't know she was troubled by anything but her father's condition. He entered the room, bent over the Captain on the opposite side of the bed from her, squatted to be eye level with him, and touched his shoulder. Roger began to speak slowly, softly, and incessantly, about—as Donatella assumed from what little she could comprehend—finishing the carriage house and renovations in the Abbey, planting more trees, sailing, fish ponds, and even politics, which for once the Captain couldn't disagree with him on.

She hoped the monologue might stimulate her father into some sign of recovery. Instead, there was a sense of withdrawal about him that the effects of a stroke or sleep couldn't explain.

Roger's sudden silence did.

CHAPTER TWENTY-SIX

The Parson needed to know how old the Captain was and, when told, announced, "Seventy-one rings, then."

"Nine times fer a man, followed by one ring fer each year of his life," Martha explained. "Now, Mistress, what to serve was anyone to call?"

Leaving it to her mother to decide, Donatella went into the side yard for a little air but also light, the house darker than it naturally was with its windows and even mirrors draped in reams of flat black fabric sent over from the Abbey. It was ironic Donatella learned her father's age when it was of no consequence except for deciding the number of times the church bells rang for his burial. Drying mud was still imprinted with his last steps and chickweed crept over the clumps an interruption had left. While he was sick she meant to finish the digging, but every day she thought she would do it and didn't was one closer to him lying in the parlor to accommodate guests offered his unresponsiveness and favorite light meal of cider and buttered spice bread.

It was absurd to think the Captain needed company where he had loved to sink into the large chair and close his eyes to think, sleep, and prefer Mama's singing to her chatter. For a day and its evening many came to view what was lost, some mainly interested in how thoroughly the draping was done and the number of candles, why the casket was open and oak not pine, the condition of the body, and whether enough bran was put in to improve the smell. Others, especially the oldest, seemed genuinely sad, remembering the Captain's parents and siblings, all of whom were also gone, and his return from the sea with a very foreign wife he had kept secret for enough years to have a spinster daughter. Donatella knew all this, partly as she interpreted words and gestures, but mostly as Mama haltingly explained until unable to bear more memories or condolences.

Finally the parlor emptied. Donatella expected a sigh from one spirit or another, but not a visitor who still reverted to Italian when uncertain or upset. It was likely Lidia had deliberately avoided the villagers Martha had hurried out, but arrived quite by chance when Mama wasn't there to test a hasty vow to never let the girl in her house again.

Mama might have changed her mind if she had seen Lidia kneel by the open coffin, quietly weep, pray the rosary and lay it across the Captain's crisscrossed hands.

Donatella offered a sisterly embrace. Lidia appreciated it, stepped back, and looked down.

"I know so little about what happened. Won't you tell me?" Donatella lied, for she had heard why the Captain had gone to Lidia's aid. "None of those boys have bothered you again, have they?"

Lidia shook her head.

"Walk with us tomorrow."

"No. It's not my place."

Donatella only agreed with not mentioning her visit, later finding out her mother had also watched Lidia's dusky departure and noticed Roger stopping the girl for the moment it took her to refuse whatever he was offering.

It was the third time that day he had come to inquire whether they needed anything and stand by the Captain with even less acceptance in his eyes than when he first realized his friend's passing.

On the afternoon of the sad event, neither doctor nor Searcher was called for. "Not to be left to some half-witted clerk, who will scribble of sores and bloating, stoppages of the stomach or twistings of the gut," Roger explained with an indelicate tone that must be attributed to shock, before he left for the church to write the Bill of Mortality himself. Now he hardly spoke except to decline a drink, something to eat, and the chance to sit in the Captain's chair. He perched on a stool by the hearth with his shoulders slumped and his arms hugging his knees, as benign as a son and younger brother or an even safer companion to ladies adrift in waves of shock and sorrow and uncertainty. The clock striking eight, then half-past and nine should have been his cue to leave. He did get up to stir the fire, frustrated in his attempt to put on another log when Mama said it was too late.

Finally, he insisted on seeing himself out. "You mustn't worry."

Mama barely lifted her head, "Oh, I had wondered —"

"Please, be assured. You have your widow's right and this is your home, as long as you need it."

"Still, we may need to find some employment."

"Your husband put his legal affairs in my hands so you'll ... both ... be taken care of."

Donatella didn't realize Roger's hand reaching out to hers until she saw it fall to his side because he lost his nerve or changed his mind. She caught herself hoping his reservations merely reflected hers.

***

Once again death created vacancy, exhausted emotion, and refused pleasure. It caused sleeplessness, even weeping, most of the night, which was better than waking abruptly. Two men came just after ten in the morning. The coffin was closed before Donatella could have one more look or retrieve Lidia's rosary, then slid into the front hall and the way of Donatella and her mother leaving for the cemetery. It didn't matter, as they shouldn't go ahead of it. Finally a strong village lad lifted it easier than Roger and the two other bearers, all of them carrying it to the cart in the street below.

Donatella put her arm across her eyes as she walked into the unwelcomed glare of the morning. Mama leaned on her like an old woman who wasn't sure she could take another step, but Donatella expected her mother would eventually find her stride again. They were both wearing black hoods and capes, more comforted than they would admit by emerging as Genoese women, prudently if not permanently hiding what was yet hopeful even willful about them.

Donatella tried not to look at Roger walking beside them, a plain man when his eyes were downcast so she thought of how they could be full of pleasantness and ideas. He had taken just enough care with his appearance, appropriately somber and sympathetic, his chestnut brown, shoulder length periwig flattened by a small-brimmed-and-crowned hat banded by satin ribbon with two short ends hanging from an unbowed knot at the back. His long coat was sober and straight, its lapel and cuffs untrimmed, although the vest beneath hinted at swirling embroidery. His breeches barely showed; his worsted hose and low-heeled shoes were splattered with mud.

She didn't know what to expect from the languished march up to the church, her mother holding a handkerchief to her face as she coughed and meant to cry. It seemed a social occasion for some of the villagers who kept their gossiping subdued and were silent at the graveside where the service took place. The Captain would have thought the few words said about him were too many and been either amused or irritated by the Parson's use of the sea as a metaphor for his relationship with God, suggesting he had been seduced away from the sacred shore to embark on a worldly voyage with discoveries and shipwrecks possible, until ordered by the highest command to return home.

Roger wasn't particularly meditative or prayerful. If anything, he seemed distracted, shifting his hands to his back and his feet a little farther apart. He noticed the robin carrying nesting material until most of it was lost to the spindly spray of a conifer branch. Donatella had no idea how religious he was. She would love to have that discussion and others with him, to explore something of his thoughts and values and forget she must be careful not to take her father's place in his affections.

Lidia was cowering under the same broken half-blossoming crabapple tree where Tobias waited with his spade, the boy who had helped carry the coffin also watching her. Donatella should have been grateful for all the mourners there, but their clustering in between gravestones and sudden neighborliness seemed unnecessary.

It was the obvious place to meet ghosts, but not where hers wished to be seen, unless shaped in the approaching clouds or caressing like the wind giving new life to last year's leaves whirling near but not into the black hole that swallowed her father as the sea never did. She closed her eyes and wished for a sign that wouldn't be mistaken: a whisper that insisted on her listening, especially to her heart, or music that continued to be written with inspiration that required more ability and ambition than she had.

She would settle for the almost weightless touch of her arm.

She stepped forward to do what her mother wouldn't, bending down for a handful of dirt and flinging it over a precipice. Roger was beside her.

That was it. The parson closed his book and the churchyard cleared while the sky grew cloudy. A robin—whether or not the same one seen earlier—was posed atop a gravestone with nothing better to do than reprise its song.

Lidia came closer.

"What is she doing here?" Mama snarled.

Lidia's answer was a sad shrug and return to Tobias, who was too burdened by his work to notice.

"Please, Mama. She is not to fault."

"Will you come back for some of that lovely tea you gave us?" Mama sweetly baited Roger.

"Oh, no, Mistress," he all but admitted more visits with them were impossible. "I have to return to London." He didn't succeed in hiding his regret, either. "Francis hates being there alone."

Mama finally used her handkerchief to blow her nose. "Of course. I have to remind myself you're such an important fellow."

Donatella wanted to disappear.

"I'm perplexed by such a notion, too." Roger tried to relieve her embarrassment.

"Modesty becomes you, sir," her mother continued to mock him.

"I'm not being modest but sorry for myself. Taking silk might be a tonic to some but poison to me, ending life as I once enjoyed it."

Immediately, he regretted what he had said, pulling in his lips and quickly thinking how to make amends. "You must send up to the house for anything you need. We have a limited staff but it's at your disposal. Nothing could please me more than using my good fortune to in some way relieve your misfortune."

"We'll be all right," Mama sighed as she spoke.

"Yes, but," Roger solemnly argued, "not to be left to chance."

He stepped down into the street behind them as though to

accompany them back to the cottage after all. Instead, he begged their leave with a strange mutter that set him onto a path of dodging puddles in the opposite direction along the vermin-holed wall of the raised graveyard. He might have had a reason to go to the rectory until he disappeared through a not-so-secret gate to the barely greening woods high on the north side of the stately refuge his brother's marriage had afforded him.

CHAPTER TWENTY-SEVEN

Roger was constantly thoughtful, sending a copy of *The Country Housewife's Garden* with a note "respectfully" explaining a lady didn't have to be a wife to find the book useful. While it rained Donatella could heed much of its advice, English easier for her to read than speak. She wasn't so capable in the yard where her father's tools were washed and waiting. Spade and mattock were heavy and disobedient, thrown down in tears, abandoned and reclaimed with anger that was sadder than fierce. She ached with the effect of the work on her heart and body, defeated and determined in an obsession as resistant to dissuasion as Tobias' was.

"A small kitchen garden will do," Mama suggested. "We can buy what else we need."

Martha frowned, squinting and gripping her hips, probably thinking how much less there would be for thieving.

Donatella didn't easily give up her desire to make the garden her father would have been proud of: a layout of raised beds separated by narrow grassy paths, the outer borders for sprawling squash, cucumbers, broad and butter beans, and a row of tightly-tied vertical and horizontal canes to support their scarlet-flowering climbing cousins. The wall side harbored gooseberry and blackcurrant bushes, a quince and apple tree. The interior parcels were for radishes, onions, cabbage, and turnips; the coolest section for early and late plantings of spinach, burnet, black-seeded lettuce, and parsley. Against the cottage was a strip for herbs like chervil, lovage, lemon balm, rosemary, and nigella interrupted by columbine, fronted by marigolds, and back dropped with foxglove and hollyhocks.

Most of the seeds she needed were in drawstring pouches labeled and stored in the dark depths of the larder near Martha's little stashes of meat, poultry, and eggs.

On better days Donatella felt she would conquer the soil and time running out. With the barrenness of the beds before her, she could smell and even taste what was to come, and, well practiced with hearing voices lost to life but not memory, was spurred on by the Captain whistling and pretending contentment with being landlocked.

"Raised beds need be well stirred an' loosened an' loaded with dung."

She was startled, the intruder and his brogue creeping up on her.

"The honorable Roger asked me to deliver this. But I see I will be makin' a few more trips."

She didn't need to ask what was in the sack he let drop, a pungent odor released that her father could never get enough of and Mama and Martha continuously complained about, especially when it was warm enough to keep the windows open.

"This be too much for you."

She wouldn't let him know she agreed, continuing her attack on the ground.

"Allow me."

It was only as she gave him the spade that she thought to tidy herself. She straightened her cap, rolled down her sleeves, shook her skirt and used it to clean her hands before she wiped her face. There was nothing she could do about the ankle-high mud on her boots and soiled hem of her dress.

The leggy herdsman untied the bag of manure and, with strength his carrying it there had already proven, emptied it. Then he waved the sack like a flag, cursing and smiling at her without apology.

So what is his talent? Making such a stink?

"What did ya say?" The Scotsman didn't look up from turning the dark lumpy muck.

Donatella was immediately distracted from wondering why he asked. Mama was coming out of the house, looking lovely in mournful idleness, her eyes shining, her hair falling down in a way that hid the gray streaks at her temples, an effect her *la Giaconda* smile complemented.

"You have help." She didn't seem to approve.

"Cargill. Robert Cargill." He was too eager to stop working.

"Really?" Her interest softened. "Do they call you Robbie?"

"At some peril."

"Then Roberto." Mama swayed backwards and forwards as though resisting the temptation to move into the mess of the yard.

Donatella felt the need to interrupt their exchange. "Roger sent—"

"I know." Her mother wasn't altogether trying to impress Cargill. "The smell ruined what little appetite I have."

"It'll feed it when it returns." He was too clever.

"I suppose. But Donata won't manage all this on her own."

Donatella was feeling cold and weak but took up the task Cargill had abandoned.

"And if you get sick again and follow your papa to the grave?" Mama crumpled with an emotion that should have embarrassed her.

Instead she lifted up with Cargill's help as though never as grateful to anyone.

"I got her." Martha acted on the concern Donatella had, guiding her mistress into the cottage. "You come in. It looks like rain again."

***

Cargill promised to return with another delivery the next day, but it was too wet to expect him or for Donatella to further delay gathering the Captain's things for whatever her mother decided to do with them. Less than two weeks since his passing, Donatella couldn't go through his clothes, pipes, wigs, and papers without preparing an explanation of why she was doing so. The cats scratching at the door of the study didn't convince her to let them in. They were likely to disturb her determination to organize the unpaid bills, letters received, sketches of garden frames and sailing masts, rolls of maps including those her father had bought in Oxford, scraps with measurements and reminders and attempts at poetry that used English too figuratively for her to know whether it was good or bad.

His ledger had a podium of its own and was open to the day before his collapse. Donatella knew her mother would want nothing to do with the accounts and felt sure she could take them over, arithmetic not subject to language barriers and a useful skill in copying music. She slouched over the book, her face close enough to smell its ink and the final touch of the Captain's hands, the only way she could make out the rows and columns and quickly drawn figures.

"Martha is wrapping up the things you left in the hallway, but where are his boots and shoes?" Mama stood on the threshold of getting over her grief. "I'm thinking this could be our music room."

The cats ran in faster than Donatella could protect all of the piles she had made. "What?"

"Papa's boots and shoes. In the wardrobe, I think. Ask Martha. I won't go in there."

Her mother was now using Lidia's room. Necessity required Donatella to enter what had been her parent's sleeping quarters, and this time she even dared to remove the draping from the window. She thought she had emptied the wardrobe of the Captain's memory, that the clutter of footwear at its bottom was all her mother's. Most of it was, but towards the back there was a pair of sea boots and equally ancient bucket-tops, high-tongued otherwise sensible shoes and flimsier ones with red heels worn to satisfy a wife not fashion.

Donatella checked the top shelf, reached into its depths and touched something that begged to be pulled out. It was the cedar box she had borrowed for a little while, before her mother had claimed it as though taking it back.

It was empty until Donatella noticed the bottom lining slightly curled up at one corner as she was sure it wasn't when she had used it; reason enough to be curious even before she saw the parchment peeking out.

She hesitated to discover what it was, even considered pushing it into hiding again.

Why not was more convincing in her deliberation.

It was as if the once wax-sealed letter was handed to her. She took it closer to the candle and unfolded it a few inches from the tip of her nose. Dated December 1663 and addressed to My Dearest Julianna, nothing about its original location was indicated. Donatella didn't recognize the handwriting, but, following its straightforward English all the way to its ardently signed conclusion, knew who had written it.

She dropped it and any hope of believing a first love had been unrealized because her father hadn't cared for her happiness. She might even be grateful for his interference, although she couldn't be sure her mother's desires had anything to do with it. In a moment regret had become relief, her tears more for what she assumed the Captain didn't know than she now did. Her disappointment was with her mother's behavior, even if that letter, as it implied, brought an almost conscionable end to a shocking affair never more than intimate through words.

Donatella hadn't worried over her mother's flirtatiousness before. Now the harmlessness of Mama's spirited beauty was forever spoiled by a secret long kept, a hope cherished more than what had been fulfilled, and a continuing disregard not only for her husband but also her daughter.

Such a correspondence should have been destroyed the moment it was received; more importantly, cause should have never been given for it to be written.

Donatella heard the other side of the argument. She put the letter and box back and brought the footwear downstairs, glad her mother was asleep in the Captain's chair. She needed more time to get used to the idea of her as a rival, and to consider when her mother had found the opportunity to betray her family's trust as much as why she took it.

The thought of cold-blue eyes and a whiskered mouth also recalled a visit to the house near Luccoli by a young seaman older than Donatella. Robbie, as he was introduced, insisted he wouldn't stay for dinner but did so when Mama asked a second time. He was quite the center of attention interrupting the Captain's stories as often as her aunt and with more remarkable reasons. He complemented an unseen cook on the meal, Nonna on her bright eyes, Aunt Despina on her sharp mind, and the Captain on anything he thought would please him. Looking across the table at mother and daughter, his ruddy cheeks, fast talk, and false heart seduced them both.

"That Scots is here, spreading more shit." Martha began unloading the boots and shoes from Donatella's arms.

Donatella didn't want to see Cargill, let alone thank him.

CHAPTER TWENTY-EIGHT

Early April rains diluted the odor of the Captain's garden and made little lakes of its sections, a good stretch of sunny days needed to dry it enough for the first plantings that Tobias claimed were already later than everyone else's. He regularly checked it, flinging his arms around and loudly blaming Lucifer for another downpour or threat of one. Mama feared his rants and repeatedly begged her daughter to get rid of him.

Donatella wouldn't tell him to go and might even ask him to stay longer than he intended, for a cup of ale and chunk of cheese.

He crouched under the oak tree, drank, chewed, and wheezed. Now and then he pointed at the air beside or behind her, and began a new ritual of tapping the same finger on the side of his nose.

Sometimes Lidia came with him and brought a satchel of refreshments, so Donatella didn't have to give more than a nod. Tobias had fewer, shorter, and quieter tirades then, which meant Mama's constant napping wasn't disturbed. Donatella thought Lidia looked thinner even as she was becoming shapelier; also less angelic, more like a servant of man than God. She rarely spoke except to ask if Donatella was recovered, how Mama and the cats were, and when Roger was returning to Wroxton. She brushed aside any questioning of her situation with the wisps of hair blowing into her eyes.

Tobias seemed oblivious to anything but the mud, sky, food, drink, his lungs, and the demons that harassed him until he had to rise up against them once more. Lidia would shake him gently and step back as though she expected the hostility to just fall away from him. He looked dazed but not defeated.

When the Captain's garden was finally ready for sowing, Roger turned up a few hours after Lidia happily reported seeing him ride towards the Abbey gate. He was dressed as roughly as his position would allow, hatless, wigless, and walking stiffly because, as he explained more as an apology than excuse, he had just returned from London.

"I decided to make the trip on horseback now the roads are drier and we might enjoy two fine days in a row," he spoke specifically to Donatella who hoped the straw hat she wore shadowed her face and hid the strain and sweat of the morning. "I could hardly bear the thought of traveling in a carriage after another incarceration in London. My poor brother is still there, held captive by his achievements.

"I spent the night at Woodstock, where I ate too well, had a good stretch walking around, and rested adequately. I was up and on my way by dawn." He shook his head at Martha's boys who were putting more effort into pushing and punching each other than the halfpenny worth of onion sets they had been enlisted to plant. "One boy is a boy, two boys are half a boy, and three boys are no boys at all." Roger looked hopeful to amuse her, but because of her large hat was unsure he did. "How are you?"

"Hot." She was at once sorry to sound ill-tempered.

"Let me." Roger reached for the long stick she held at her hip. "I'll make the furrows and you do the sowing. Or I'll handle both."

"I want to help." She dipped a hand into the pouch attached to the hemp rope tied around her waist.

She felt indiscreet as she worked alongside him, distracted by the pleasant sensation of following the broad curve of his back to the bareness of his neck as he bent and gently opened the soil into shallow trenches for receiving spinach, lettuce, radish, and cucumber seeds.

The work inspired a recitation from him. "Their mother, the earth, will keep them in her bowels, till the sun, their father, reaches them with his heat. *The Country Housewife's Garden*. Did you like it?"

"Oh, yes."

"Well done that you could read it."

He looked back, smiled, and she was aware how, not unlike the best singers performing with more concern for their freedom than figures, her breasts and hips moved easily under her clothes without a corset to hold them.

She knew the sigh she heard wasn't entirely her own. Fortunately, Tobias wasn't looking in her direction. She wouldn't have dressed as casually if she had expected to be in Roger's company. If she appeared in any way coquettish towards him, it was purely by chance.

The flower said to the bee.

Roger swayed as he excused himself to help Tobias construct the pole-frame that would, in a few months' time, display the scarlet of the runner bean's nature. Donatella looked forward to placing a bouquet of the bonnet-shaped orange-red blooms on her father's grave, and she smiled at the thought of his often declared innovation of stringing and slicing the bean pods to serve with a little garlic and butter.

It won't be long before everyone realizes runners are a food equal to, even surpassing, their decoration. Or so he tells me.

Tobias moaned and turned towards her.

Roger stopped whistling and took the end of the twine before Lidia stepped back to unwind the ball of it, putting a hand up and down to direct her when to cut it. He was almost as tall as the two rows of whittled-down posts to be crisscrossed, tied together, and secured to the additional pole laid along the top of the frame.

"I find the A shape works best, don't you, Tobias?"

"I told ye so, sir. Don't forgit the strands to steady it in the wind 'n encourage growth."

"Good man." Roger finished the job with two more lengths of hemp cord Lidia gave him and noticed Donatella watching from where she was tidying the dooryard garden. He walked towards her. "How should good herbs prosper, when evil weeds wax so fast?"

It was there, amongst the burgeoning of useful and ornamental plants—a few already bending in gentle purples and pinks and fragrantly white, discovering new strength and lifting out of self-doubt or keeping close to the ground and insignificance—that, in what she did and didn't say, she was grateful to him for being there.

"I must admit a selfish motive." He bowed a little with the excuse of brushing himself down.

She felt herself pushed out of the border, Roger attentive enough to catch her arm when it seemed she might fall.

"Oh, I won't allow that to happen again." He let go as soon as he saw she didn't want him to. "The village is lively."

All day she had tried to ignore what was going on out of sight but not earshot, unable to deny the appeal of laughter, lively music, and singing inspired by the beribboned pole she had watched going up the day before. She didn't take part, except to secretly act out one of Martha's reminisces of being young and wanting to look her best for any possible sweetheart. "Wash in dew from the hawthorn tree, and will ever after handsome be." Martha also suggested collecting it from ivy leaves or the grass under an oak, emphasizing that it had to be done at or just before sunrise.

"Also prevents freckles, sunburn, chappin 'n wrinkles."

Donatella took a bowl outside before Martha had arrived and Mama was up. It filled a little as she shook the ivy that hung along the cottage's front door, the leaves of some kind of thorn at one end of the garden, and the grass she pulled up from under the oak tree at the other. Not sure the dampness everywhere wasn't from overnight rain, she felt silly and hoped no one saw her running around barefoot and rubbing her face and neck. She was especially glad Roger couldn't read her thoughts when later she regretted that bending and sweating had undone any benefit to her complexion.

"I might request your assistance in return." Roger put some bodily distance between them but couldn't avoid the mutual meeting of their eyes. "There are times when Francis and I miss the female touch." A grimace expressed the chance of him being misunderstood. "I mean, if we host an event, as we rarely do. All those things women organize so much better: deciding on refreshments and decorations, rearranging furniture, orchestrating servants, and ensuring everyone's enjoyment." He might have guessed she was refusing before she heard him out, with confidence to change her mind, if not her life, "In this case, a dream of mine when we entertain the divine Purcell."

Donatella tried not to react.

"You doubt he'll come. He's participated in musical evenings before, at my brother's house in Westminster. And he's even showed up at whatever tavern or rooms we've held our gentlemen's club." Roger was hardly boasting. "You were fortunate to see him in Oxford, for he rarely goes out of London. All the more would having him at Wroxton directing his work and allowing our hospitality be the highpoint of my life so far. As having known Stradella is for yours."

Would he call me divine?

"You smile." Roger couldn't know why. "Does that mean you agree?"

She knew she didn't want to disappoint him.

"He'll come if I say you'll be there."

She shrugged off the expectation Roger wasn't comfortable with either.

Yet he persisted in making her important. "He was quite taken with you."

"No—"

"He spoke highly of your singing."

"My singing teacher."

"I'll credit you, even if you don't believe it, for making my invitation irresistible to him."

You will do it, I know you will.

"I might ask Celia Fiennes to advise you. A little direction is all you need." Roger's hands surrounded hers in a more reserved petition than was soon made by the village lad not waiting to be invited onto the property, whose good looks and charm convinced him he was welcomed.

The boy made a dash to put a garland of drooping daisies and ferns on Lidia's head and he embraced her waist. "Time to play, my luv." Her gentle protest turned to a giggle when he sang, "There not be a buddin' boy or girl, this day, but be got up 'n gone to bring in May."

Lidia hesitated, but not for long, before running off with him. Roger, Donatella, and her mother, who was standing on the edge of the scullery porch with Martha just behind raising a threatening hand to quieten her sons, waited for Tobias to react. Other than wiping his arm across his eyes, there was nothing to suggest the old man had even noticed.

CHAPTER TWENTY-NINE

On the day of midsummer's eve the Great Hall gleamed with polish and high sunlight, its woolen rugs taken up and flagstones scrubbed, regal-red upholstered chairs borrowed from Broughton Castle arranged in two short-rowed sections separated by an aisle not quite wide enough for layers of skirts. The fireplace was filled with a display of larkspur, lilies, gilliflowers, ferns, and branching honeysuckle picked and presented by Tobias, and arranged by Lidia under his fussy direction. Tobias also brought sweet peas from "his most successful crop ever" to make nosegays for the ladies while single blooms would suffice for the gentlemen and their buttonholes. The flowers were kept fresh by being kept cold along with the sorbet made possible because of the ice house Roger had been experimenting with.

The dais at the north end was designated for the music of friends. Roger worried over the personalities that would perform, a program created that listed them in alphabetical order except Master Purcell was acknowledged first to perform last. The chairs and music stands were set up with the expectation they would be moved around to accommodate one complaint or other. Donatella tried to reassure Roger that musicians would always reconcile for the sake of the music, as she had seen Alessandro and Lonati do.

A month and a half earlier, they had walked through the Abbey to consider the layout of the event and how many guests could be accommodated. Some would need to stay overnight. Roger formally introduced Donatella to the kitchen and household staff who were hardly willing to take orders from her. Most of the planning took place in the garden parlor where Mama had recovered from fainting and Donatella had English lessons. It had almost completely evolved into a study and library, fitted with more shelves that still weren't enough to prevent the stacking of books on the floor and deep windowsill. Its pretty couch, once for posing and swooning and dying, was just another place for the unmanageable range of Roger's interests.

"The ... domestics must ... curse ... you," Donatella struggled to find the English words.

Roger wasn't upset or apologetic. "They know better than to disturb anything in here."

The dust that caused her fits of sneezing and Roger to open the window even though it wasn't warm enough to confirmed no one had cleaned in there for quite some time.

"This is a little madness, don't you think?" Roger was full of ideas for the concert, including a bonfire for the villagers behind the Abbey with a table set out on the terrace for sweetmeats and cider. "Cargill thinks it is. And he probably knows better than I, which is why we've promoted him to Estate Steward."

He must have noticed Donatella's frown. "He is rather wild, but he'll do the job Francis and I can no longer. We're here too infrequently."

Donatella shuffled through Roger's notes and diagrams. She had already realized his particular way of working by creating one proposal then another and another, until there was an impossible amount of papers to sift through and draw a conclusion from. Somehow Roger did, methodically, miraculously, picking and choosing, discarding and reworking, writing and drawing out the final lists and designs over and over again.

"I won't be dissuaded from making this a celebration for the entire village, too."

There were decisions made on the whats and whys if not the hows, necessitated by Roger's return to London. It was fortunate Celia Fiennes was at Broughton before her next adventure, also on horseback when she unpunctually arrived to meet with Donatella at the Abbey.

"I've only just begun my reckless travels, as my family calls them. I wish I had Roger's talent for writing about everything. I do try to regularly record the thoughts I have about the discoveries I make, and hope, before I die or am too old, to visit every county in England."

"You travel lonely?" Donatella already knew something of her unusual activities.

Lady Celia laughed. "Oh, you mean alone. Well, nearly. I'm accompanied by a maid, poor thing. The most resilient I can find who rides the bumps, endures the rain, ruins her beauty in the sun and wind, and yet still enjoys the views. Better than spending her days cleaning grates and emptying chamber pots."

"You must be in danger."

Lady Celia removed her black gloves and small feathered hat with an impatience Donatella was afraid was really with her. "Always. What woman isn't? That's why we have to be prepared." She smiled as she guessed Donatella's thought. "Yes. Even us, the plainer ones."

Donatella liked the practical and determined young woman, a godsend when it came to choosing the food, writing out invitations, and remembering those details that "for an occasion such as Roger has in mind, made the difference between being forgettable or remarkable." Lady Celia encouraged Donatella to seem in control when she wasn't, especially with Cargill and the kitchen clerk, who, from what was heard, were often at odds over the ordering and account book. Lady Celia proved her sympathy further by offering her dressmaker and to purchase the fabrics, so Donatella and her mother could have something new to wear.

The fittings happened in their own parlor, Mama shedding bereavement with an eagerness that made Donatella even angrier with her. The dressmaker suggested neither of them wear anything that showed much skin or was further from black than indigo or azure blue. Mama looked lovely in any color, a glimpse of her neck or hands or the darkness of her eyes enough to attract admiration.

For Donatella, grief was a companion, not costume. She depended on it calling on her so she would never forget it, and welcomed it quietly and almost contentedly. She saw it and heard it more distinctly than the living around her, and lay with it like a lover who was too satisfying. Time passing meant it visited less often; missing it created a new sadness allowed expression by her father's death.

"Would you have come to England if Stradella had lived?" Roger's question arose out of a gentle dispute they were having about whether and what she might sing for the midsummer's eve concert.

As she was copying over the revised program again, he sat close enough to notice a blotch on the parchment. He touched it with the tip of a finger. She was curious about his sorrowful eyes. Did they reflect the death of a favorite sister when he was a boy, or of his painter friend, Peter Lely? She didn't like to think he felt much disappointment because of the unrealized attachment to a particular young lady along one of his sailing routes, a second cousin who had mastered the lute and sang exceedingly well.

Such information had come to Donatella through Roger's conversations with the Captain, her father relating those things he assumed would be of interest to her.

Roger's most recent loss was almost as near as hers and unmentioned until he answered the housemaid's query with a confirmation that his mother had passed peacefully on the fourth of February that very year.

"She was buried in Kirtling, Cambridgeshire. You were not to know." Roger's nod appreciated her whispered apology. "She had fourteen children. My sister, Mary, died giving birth to her first. My mother's life was much longer but also much harder. The dice are tossed, over and over.

"Why are we more directed by our losses than gains? I know how it was with Francis. The family's increasing debt made him a lawyer, and other troubles sent him in a direction he otherwise might not have gone. He often confides he hasn't known a peaceful moment since he touched that cursed seal.

"Of course, it's said we're never given more than we can bear. I'm sure I will suffer worse yet and be as inconsolable as he has been. And you are."

She dared to assume what his empathy meant, putting her hand out to his arm, embarrassed and pleased that he responded with his hand on hers. "If Aless ... Maestro Stradella lived," she hesitated long enough for Roger to suspect she might not continue.

"Please, go on. It will do you good to tell me."

"If he lived I would—"

Have merely delayed the inevitable?

Roger pushed back his chair, got up and went over to close the window. "I'm sorry for how Maestro Stradella's story ended," he expressed his feelings even as he hid them, "but not for how yours has continued."

***

The North's carriage was enthusiastically noticed rumbling into the village on the Saturday before midsummer Monday. It carried the Lord Keeper and his son, along with Roger and his wards, John and Anne Lely. The girl was the older of the two and a rare enough visitor that Donatella hadn't met her before.

"She lives with my co-executor of their father's estate, Hugh May, and his good wife, and is never any trouble. John is almost never out of it." Roger pretended to box the lad's ears and made him promise to behave.

"Of course," the boy, inches taller than the last time Donatella had seen him, sneered as he spoke, "I'll behave as perfectly wicked as I am."

"He has the good looks and boldness of his father," Roger explained and excused the boy's insolence.

Anne took a liking to Lidia, who as well as working with Tobias on the grounds made herself useful in the Abbey.

At first Lidia seemed uncomfortable with Anne's attention as if not sure their friendship, even for a day or two, was acceptable. Roger saw no issue with his ward helping her sweep and dust and polish, hang laundry, gather herbs, and, with the added encouragement of the adolescently appealing John, to remember how to waste time, smile, and even giggle again.

"Oh, I wish we could be sisters," Donatella overheard Anne say.

"If your wish came true, mine would be even more sinful." Her brother knew Lidia wouldn't understand.

"Come away from the girls, Johnny," young Francis goaded him, "and help us build the bonfire. Uncle Roger wants it to be the largest the village has ever seen."

The morning of the concert the weather was warm enough to prop open the Abbey doors and windows, promising to hold with clear skies and soft breezes and realize the enlargement of the occasion outdoors as Roger hoped. Donatella was there by ten. Her anxiety was no match for his as he wondered if the audience's chairs were too close together and the performers' too far apart, the guest list too provincial and, therefore, the food choices too elaborate. He remembered how he hated entertaining and noticed the trestle tables and benches weren't set up outside. He anticipated that some or even all of the musicians would be late or not come at all, and tried to joke that, at least, Francis would be there.

"My brother is much less of an amateur on the viol than I." His eyes lifted. "And you to sing." Donatella smiled and he quickly thought how to dampen the spark between them. "Of course, Lady Celia will talk about her travels."

"I hope you finally finished your little piece," he referred to Donatella's reason for not having shared her song with him yet. "I can read by first sight quite well, but would prefer to inform my memory a little so I might play without constantly looking on the written notes. We could practice for an hour or so in the chapel."

She was very tired and in no mood to prove disagreeable, having slept only a few hours the night before because of waiting for the inspiration she needed to complete the sonnet and music she had begun over a year ago. There was none in a candle sizzling or her mother coughing. The owl vocalizing as naturally as a human voice should didn't stay around long enough for her to find anything but distraction in it. Other sounds, like the rubbing of branches or rattling of her wide open window, were merely what they were. Her head began to ache as if the madness was about to visit her again.

"Are you all right?"

"Yes, yes." She sank into Roger's arm supporting her back. "My ... composition ... is up the stairs with my clothes of later."

He let her go. "I'll get my instrument."

She wondered whether Roger chose the chapel for its close sound or because he also realized their friendship was changing and expected that under the gaze of its stained glass, before the weight of its chaliced altar, and surrounded in tapestries and oak paneling by the example of Christ, they would restrain from making anything but music. She thought he would have preferred to sit at a distance as they practiced the piece she wished wasn't so personal. With only one copy and the voice part as uncertain in her mind as if she hadn't written it, she stood beside him, lured into his embrace of the viol and holding the libretto and score for both of them to read, her hand trembling like her singing. She tried to steady one if not the other because she suspected too much vibrato would displease him.

Roger stopped playing and glanced up to the blossoming *Agnus Dei* on the ceiling above the altar until he looked at her and wondered, "Once more?"

***

When the only two female musicians had changed from travelers to recitalists, the Queen's chamber off the third floor corridor belonged to Donatella, her mother, Anne Lely, and Lady Celia, who had brought along her younger sister and a maid for attending to any if not all of them. It hardly seemed like the same room Donatella had earlier delivered Mama's and her evening clothes to: no longer silently spacious, but crowded with chatter, vanity, and expectations. The four poster bed was still imposing with its leafy paneled headboard and corbels, fluted cornice, and ring-turned end posts. Its floral-patterned draperies had, since her morning visit, been drawn up into corner bags, but the crewel-embroidered coverlet she had examined and admired was barely visible under so many dresses and petticoats, corsets, and stockings. She hadn't considered her evening footwear comfortable until she saw the lofty timber-heeled silk shoes lined up on the floor at the end of bed and feared there was a pair meant for her.

The room was made even smaller by a chest, tasseled divan, and thinly cushioned stool at a narrow table holding an embroidered hand mirror and porcelain trinket boxes and dishes. The oak and marble fireplace was, of course, unlit. The bay windows overlooking the front drive were open to a very warm breeze and the arrival of yet another carriage.

"Oh, dear. Are guests arriving?" Lady Celia, who got ready almost without assistance, reached out to wave.

Donatella felt exposed, and not just because she wasn't used to undressing and dressing with others. Her mother was giddy and easy with Lady Celia's maid bathing her feet and underarms, powdering her neck, shoulders, and face, and reddening her cheeks and lips, adjusting and tightening her corset, smoothing her hose and pushing on delicately decadent shoes. Mama expressed her opinion while her hair was fashioned this way and that until finally parted into gathered curls falling down each side of her face. Her generous body was shaped, pleated, and decorated in gray satin, beige chiffon, and an onyx breast-pin.

Donatella washed in the suggestive scent of lavender water and changed her underthings behind a screen. She emerged, as her mother commented, like someone condemned. She couldn't avoid the tight-lacing of her corset, but refused to be dusted with chalk and cerise powder and most adamantly to her lips being stained with crushed cochineal. Too much midnight-blue fabric shimmered and swept around and behind her. Her bosom was flattened, her waist elongated, and the ruffles of a new chemise, thinner than any she had worn during Genoese summers, showed flirtatiously on her lower arms and through the slashed and puffed tops of her sleeves. She might have liked how her hair was fixed—smoothly pulled off her face and through a band of pearls, cascading onto her back in a more natural curl than her mother's—if she hadn't been so distracted by the lingering embarrassment of a few hours before, when she had turned from Roger's dry kiss to Anne Lely leading Lidia into the Chapel.

Both girls had left immediately, although it was Lidia who insisted they do so, her new friend full of questions that weren't unlike those Donatella had.

"I think we're ready for life again." Her mother was standing behind Donatella, fussing with the high back pleats of her skirt and expecting her daughter to do the same with hers.

"Don't you two look lovely," Lady Celia interrupted their uncertain bond. "I hope you're pleased with your new gowns."

"Mine might fit better."

Donatella wanted to say something to Lady Celia to seem more appreciative than her mother, but Anne had come up to her.

"Don't worry," assured the honey-haired brown-eyed girl dressed as a miniature version of the woman she would soon become, "I won't tell anyone. Anyway, I think it's nice."

"What's nice?" Mama needed another interest once Lady Celia chose to ignore her.

Anne didn't hesitate. "That Donatella is to sing a piece she wrote."

"I doubt it's all her own."

There was a knocking and then again, more insistent.

"Are we all decent?" Lady Celia wondered. "I think so."

The door opened to Roger. "He's here. He's here."

"And so are we," Lady Celia enjoyed chiding him.

"I mean Master Purcell. It's important to make him feel welcomed."

"Then why aren't you welcoming him?"

Lady Celia's sister laughed.

"I'll come." Donatella couldn't deny she was pleased by Roger's surprise at seeing how she had changed.

"I feared he wasn't coming, or something had delayed him." Roger followed her as they descended the grand staircase, not noticing the trail of her gown until he stepped on it. The railing steadied her before he could.

"Again, I'm an ape."

"No." She turned to smile at him but couldn't.

"I should go in front of you."

CHAPTER THIRTY

It looked as though Master Purcell was trying to hide under the stairs. Roger inquired about his journey from London and he emerged to reveal that he had interrupted the trip with a night at Oxford and much drinking, and another at Rousham Park and even more feasting.

Donatella didn't expect him to recognize her, but when Roger moved aside she became "that most courteous copyist who had also forgiven Stradella."

"And I hope you'll pardon me, Harry, but the guests will soon arrive and you need to tidy yourself and prepare." Roger didn't know he showed concern for anything but the plan for the evening ahead.

"Well, I am a little dusty." Master Purcell winked in Donatella's direction. "I wonder if Stradella was always impeccably turned out."

They walked into the hall and Donatella wanted to tell him about the man she had known as reported but, also, in very different ways. Would Master Purcell believe Alessandro had been in need of friendship more than love, or that he had grown tired of making music for those who only listened to their own importance? Would it seem as ridiculous to say he would have rather roamed the streets, lost in the crowds and songs of Carnival, than found to be wanting in nobler society? She could describe him as flamboyant in disguise and excessive when it came to enjoying himself, yet he had the sense to be gracious in his manners, and even humble when it weighed in his favor and, especially, his purse. She might also reveal the unshaven, disheveled creature that growled with frustration and cursed the affairs that caused him more trouble than they were worth.

Surely, Master Purcell would rather hear about Alessandro's genius and even his sacred purpose: how the music came to him like the Archangel Gabriel, because he was highly chosen with or without the patronage of any prince or princess.

"It's always a dilemma, whether to please one's self most or one's audience. I make a note of the music the public dislikes, for that's often what I consider my best."

Not for the first time, Donatella noticed that, although still a young man, Master Purcell had the look of someone who had been grown up for too long.

"I expect you will please all tonight, Harry." Roger tried to turn him away from more conversation. "Now, you must long to freshen up."

"Few have patience with our suspicion of success." Master Purcell resisted Roger's direction. "Except, perhaps, a good patron and friend." He patted Roger's back. "Or wife or lover."

What Donatella wouldn't disclose was how close she had come to knowing Alessandro's heart. She could admit to copying his music but not any of those paramours who put passion before reason. She might imply there was some intimacy between them but never allow impurity in it. She could be seen to greatly admire him, to sing as his pupil and grieve like his sister, but never to tremble at the thought of him or miss him more terribly than she did her grandmother or father. She didn't want anyone to know what ridiculous hopes were dashed when she was the last to lay with him and all she could feel was his coldness.

"Are you all right, Mistress?"

It wasn't his fault. He could never be certain she would accept his way with her, for she never had the chance to convince him of her devotion no matter what took him away from her. Or perhaps she did, those whispers and touches as secret as any she had known when he was in her world, her spirit still courted by his and even more confidences passed between them.

"Mistress, what has upset you?"

Or had she missed her opportunity again, nothing heard or felt of him for some time, an absence that was hardly noticeable until she realized what couldn't take its place.

"My dear, my dear, what is it?" This time it was Roger who wondered as he shielded her from the embarrassment of Master Purcell observing her tears. "Do you need to withdraw for a while?"

Donatella was confused by Roger's question until she saw the Abbey was becoming a public place. Guests were arriving with sweeping skirts, shiny long coats, true and false ringleted hair, their shoes clicking on the bare flagstones and eager conversation filling the space and silence that had allowed her sentiments to wander.

"Are you not well?" Lady Celia asked as she and her sister were passing.

"Will you see to them?" Roger waved a hand towards the guests.

"Of course." Lady Celia puffed a little like the horse she spent so much time with, brushing Donatella's arm affectionately. "I hope you'll recover to sing, for I hear you do so quite nicely."

"I can attest to that." Master Purcell bowed a little from his distance. "Stradella's secret songbird will entertain us again. I'm sure of it."

"Rescue me, Harry." Sir Francis was finally seen to be interested in what was happening in his house, Master Purcell embracing him in greeting and then leading him into his fear with an arm across his back. "Ah. They're bringing out the food and drink. Now that's what I really long for."

Whether or not Roger heard Master Purcell, his concern for Donatella took precedence as he persuaded her to go out of the way for a little while.

Anne came along just in time to escort Donatella back into the north hallway.

"I think I saved Uncle Roger as he didn't wish to be." She was sweetly divisive, dabbing under Donatella's eyes with a soft handkerchief. "Yes, it's lovely isn't it? My mother had a talent for embroidery." The doe-eyed girl needed it herself then, so their tears mingled and they shared a smile, too. "That's better."

"Yes. Thank you." Donatella began to care about her appearance again, smoothing her skirt and sleeves, and touching the pearls in her hair to make sure they were in place.

Anne swayed in half-circles, as though hearing music she wanted to dance to, or mustering up the courage to say, "Do you love him?"

Donatella's mother was coming down the staircase.

"You look like a queen, *Signora*," Anne was quick to say.

"A disgraceful one." Despite her earlier joviality, Mama's smile was pinched, her eyes pained. "Take my arm, Donata. Let's pretend we belong in such happy moments."

***

It was Roger's decision to have all the musicians on the platform in the Great Hall, so there would be little doubt their presence was the main reason for more company than neither he nor his brother knew what to do with. It also meant the concert would be accessible to all who attended, whether by wax-sealed or word-of-mouth invitation, the hall's entryway clear for a standing audience behind the seated one. Roger's plans, thought and written out over and over again, were all about "making a society of music" like he had known as a boy, when even "the steward and kitchen clerk played" as his sisters sang.

By six o'clock sunshine defined the high heraldic windows at the west end of the dais and streamed down upon it. The crowd was steeped in musky fragrance, clashing colors, watchful flirtation, conversational anticipation, and consuming more drink than food, seemingly oblivious to the performers as they tuned up. Outside behind the house, after a rowdy parade, villagers enjoyed the chance to feast at the Norths' expense. They danced to their own fiddlers and waited for the sun to set and flames to rise up from the mountain of logs and brash so high a ladder had been needed to put the last bundles on top. Sir Francis wondered where his son and John Lely were, Anne's shoulders rising and falling with either disapproval or envy for her brother's ease of escape. Donatella could only imagine the boys preferring to play according to their age rather than privilege by rolling down banks, climbing trees, throwing stones, and even wading in the fish pond, which Roger should not know about. Fortunately, he was preoccupied with Master Purcell setting the stage with an eye and ego for making sure he was positioned front and center.

"If this is where the musicians play, who's up there?" Mama's observation caused Roger and Donatella to turn and also notice shadowy movement and the light of a candle in the gallery.

"Ah. Wraiths might be among us," Cargill suggested.

Master Purcell opened his arms in hopes of settling the performers.

Roger extended a hand not only to greet each of the men, but also to assist in positioning stands and the music on them. His concentration was investigative and appreciative as he examined the variety of instruments, his curiosity finally satisfied by a question put to a long-faced, small-shouldered man in a burnt-red coat who sat at the harpsichord, his long pale fingers offering a succession of pitch notes.

"Here, Drago. All. You must meet—"

Donatella had already realized Reggio wasn't there. At that inconvenient moment her mother wondered why.

"Reggio hasn't ventured out of Oxford since February, due to congestion in his chest," Master Albrici, recognized from the Christmas celebration at Broughton, offered. "Then he often suffers from love's sickness."

Obviously, Roger thought there was nothing else to say about the man in question, a little frantically inviting Donatella up on the dais and announcing her as "Stradella's best kept secret".

"Stradella? The composer and libertine?" Leonora, the middle-aged singer Donatella had met upstairs, seemed as insensitively curious as her mother.

"He had lodgings in the house in Genoa where I lived."

"Ah, that explains your accent." Leonora's loosening ringlets fell like fingers pointing to her barely covered breast. "And the secret."

"Sister," Maestro Albrici scolded, "we're not here for gossip."

"You'll be lucky to silence her in that respect," another of the Italian men said.

"What would we do without brothers and husbands?" Leonora laughed and soothed the one she called Matteo with a kiss on his mouth.

Donatella felt a touch on her arm and saw it was Roger entreating her to move to a seat in the front row that Lady Celia and Anne had kept for her, her mother on the other side pulling in her skirt and acting unaware that Robert Cargill was standing nearby.

"I wish Lidia could sit with us." Anne turned, so Donatella did, too.

Lidia was obviously burdened by the width and weight of the platter she carried in for the buffet table.

"Yes, why not?" Donatella meant to stand and even go to her.

Cargill crossed his arms. "She has work to do."

Anne's shoulders slouched. "If I could take her home with me, she'd be a companion not servant."

Donatella remembered how she had failed Lidia and tried to think of something to say.

However, silence was called for, first by Roger clearing his throat and lifting his hands and then by Lady Celia who stood and clapped, Anne immediately imitating her. Without any show of impatience, Master Purcell motioned for a quick run up and down the harpsichord keys and soon realized it might take the command of a violin or two. That was enough to get the audience settled and quieted, except for a little persistent whispering.

Master Purcell nodded to Sir Francis, who wasn't quite invisible in the shadows under the gallery, and then to Roger, who was much closer to him.

"To my hosts, benefactors, and dear friends, I thank you for opening your doors and purses to my music and self, and especially for giving me a reason to escape the tyranny of London."

There were gasps and murmurings that Master Purcell enjoyed for a few moments. "I refer only to the courtly chains of service I put upon myself."

It was as if his shocking and relieving confession was rehearsed when there was a playful burst on the recorder from "James Peasable" as Master Purcell announced him.

"Jacques Paisible," the young Frenchman corrected, without a hint of hostility.

"How's Moll, Jack? Did she have another engagement? Perhaps, at Whitehall?" The theorbo player mocked him.

Plaisible's face tightened. "No. She's at home."

"On Suffolk Street?"

"Yes."

"Well, within reach of ... Whitehall."

With a little stamp of his right foot, Master Purcell allowed nothing more to be said except as he introduced "the conspirators in making music worth listening to."

Thomas Eccles and Thomas Farmer stood to attention with their violins in position to be played at a moment's notice, but Matteo Battaglia hadn't yet picked up his. Robert Carr and William Gregory straddled their viols. With the theorbo resting against his chest and reaching off to one side with his arm, Charles Coleman also sat, as did John Abell encircling his lute. Jacques Plaisable answered his second introduction with another seeming impossible flourish on the recorder, while Bartolomeo Albrici and Giovanni Battista Draghi exchanged vulgarities in the Italian style at the announcement that they would take turns on the harpsichord.

Master Purcell waved the singers forward and kissed the hand of Leonora, "an angel who could not leave England again, even if Matteo must go without her." He showed more reserve with Henrietta Bannister, the wife of the late John and mother of the younger, and called William Turner an accomplished composer himself, a fine countertenor, and true gentleman of the Chapel Royal.

Master Purcell bowed to them all, the back of his wig matted and his coat creased, the ribbons undone on the bottom of his breeches, evidence of a mend here and there in his hose, and his ankles leaning out due to the wear on his shoes. As he straightened, his arms lifted up until his hands were close together above his head, reminding Donatella of a priest celebrating the Eucharist, his congregation silent in preparation for the miracle they were about to receive.

His arms fell and the strings began with a pavan in G minor that was reflective and hesitant but gradually rose to the occasion and opened the mood for what came next. A chacony did, in the same key, pulsating with bowing stokes up and down and brief pauses in slowly intensifying obstinato. The bass dropped out and came back in, its rhythm processional and melody clear with fleeting variations, its development quickening and relieving while weaving possibilities into a conclusion that couldn't be more simple.

Plaisable was willing to share his recorders for a fantasia on a ground for three and continuo with Gregory and also Draghi, who was hesitant to leave the harpsichord to Albrici. There could be no doubt Batholomeo enjoyed his victory and the power it gave him, swaying to and fro as he moved the music along, his smile widening while the breath-taking of the other men shortened and their playing became increasingly wild. There was so much music in so little, the hall echoing with its joy, the audience moving in their seats while handmade pipes joined in as the standing room under the gallery belonged to anyone who wanted to be there, just as Roger had hoped it would.

Yet, with the villagers shoulder to shoulder, their children lifted up and swayed like bunting, their laughter and chatter and then clapping before Master Purcell gave the signal for it turning those seated from delight to disgust, he might have wished he had heeded Cargill's warning.

Oohs and aahs made Master Purcell's cheeks pinker as he took the hand of Leonora and brought her forward. Unfortunately, cheers and even whistles greeted the prospect of her singing "She Loves and She Confesses, Too" accompanied by a self-directed Charles Coleman on the theorbo. Her bright eyes and voice, swelling chest and gestures were unashamed and confident that honor was no match for love—a meaning Donatella's mother helped her understand. No clarification was necessary when a long-faced Henrietta stepped up to insist on concealment of the heart's desire, a nobler course than pleading for or forcing love, so it was lost to silence in the grave. Despondency sighed out with her breath, Leonora only agreeing as her echoing part required. The divergence and blend of their crying vocals was joined in a dramatic and richly harmonic final section by Master Purcell singing bass, all three voices slowing and softening until they culminated in a single sound of grief.

Stillness inescapably filled the room like smoke overcoming its occupants, only broken by fits of throats clearing and coughing. Donatella squeezed her mother's hand or her mother squeezed hers, as aware as everyone else there was more despair to come. Draghi, who had claimed the harpsichord again, followed William Turner's sudden falsetto into "A Dark and Melancholy Grove". The countertenor's head and chest voice mixed on waves of low and high emotions, his consonants clear and vowels open, nothing about his singing pushed and yet such force in its exhibition, creating a pain in Donatella so deep and beautiful pleasure could never again be preferable.

"A swelling grief siezes on ev'ry string,

"And I weep when I should sing."

Her trembling was also fear. She looked around for Roger to speak to about withdrawing herself from the concert, but he was already on stage seated behind Gregory and Carr. He seemed awkward with his viol as he tried to mirror how they were positioned with theirs to perform another of Master Purcell's purely instrumental inventions. Roger had mentioned practicing a collection of sonatas, yet he appeared surprised when, at a moment's notice, the gentle opening changed into a highly spirited tempo. Such erratic pacing continued, but he soon found his stride in keeping up with the constantly changing moods of the music: strolling and scuttling, wandering and dancing, whispering and proclaiming and pausing with the best of them.

There wasn't any doubt he could move beyond the mere handling of harmonic progression, contrapuntal conversation, daring dissonance, and cooperative interchange to the engagement of his whole being in every stroke and sound, thought and sensation.

Watching him embrace his viol and the extremely physical yet almost ethereal experience of the musical performer, and realizing how he could lose and find himself with such creative passion, Donatella feared her future in love was as alive as it was dead.

Setting the Watch

CHAPTER THIRTY-ONE

Donatella stood on the dais wondering where to look that wouldn't make her more anxious. She was glad the hall was darkening and the villagers were more interested in John Lely shouting that the bonfire was about to be lit. Some of the seated spectators were restless. A few were getting up, including her mother.

Others turned side to side as Roger positioned his chair beside her and Master Purcell announced she was going to sing her own composition.

"Although," he added, with a glance upwards and then towards the gallery where a candle still flickered in its emptiness, "I suspect her much missed mentor had something to do with it."

She wouldn't disagree, if only because he had put attention on what rather than how she would perform.

"Who was that?" someone asked.

"Alessandro Stradella."

"Wasn't he a scoundrel?"

"Only as you'd rather listen to slander than magnificent music."

Donatella felt increasingly grateful to the young maestro whose loose ribbons, mended stockings, well-worn shoes, and pink cheeks belied the richness of his character.

"Are you ready?" Roger asked.

She lifted her shoulders and chin. It was a long few minutes before he began playing and then did too soon for her to concentrate on the inhalation of sound rather than drawing adequate air from her lungs. Once she caught up her voice came out of a yawn relaxing her throat and opening her mouth, her tongue moving up and down, higher notes just below the cheekbones, mid-range behind the teeth, lower focused in front of the lips. Visualizing the lyrics meant less chance she would forget them, and closing her eyes might also overcome her nerves. It helped that she was familiar with Roger's playing, although not even a kiss in the chapel had prepared her for the softening and filling of each sound between them that might arouse suspicion. Her words, written and now vocalized out of her longing for what was lost, were too obviously underscored by his wish to be more than a temporary companion to her regrets. She wasn't sure how to let him know she felt the same, except by allowing his performance to embrace hers like the viol held between his legs and the bow underhandedly while sliding across the strings almost without touching them. The nature of the instrument and of Roger himself meant there weren't any impassioned declarations, but perfect for accompanying the solo heart, every stroke was constant and clear without the need for much embellishment. Eventually, empathetically, she sang to the same effect, repeating the sonnet's sestet in English as Roger had suggested, fully sharing the music and meaning of her escape to a strange somewhere between endings and beginnings.

She held the final note beyond Roger's attachment to it, letting it hollow out and disappear into disbelief that she had come so far.

The applause Master Purcell insisted on might have been convincing if he hadn't stopped it abruptly and taken Roger's seat and viol instead of introducing the keyboard suite listed next on the program.

Roger shook his head at Albrici, who sat expressionless at the harpsichord while Draghi leaned on it sleepily. The other musicians also seemed unperturbed by the change or just too weary to worry about it. Leonora and Henrietta exchanged looks that put them among the majority in the hall who didn't know what to expect.

Donatella was about to take her seat when Albrici made a gentle entreaty on the keyboard. It didn't prepare anyone for a violin's declaration turning the room towards it and then back to Master Purcell, creating a musical dialogue that grew argumentative if more and more playfully so. Donatella recognized the unencumbered movement, risky improvisation and colorful continuo, as well as the sultry slowing down. There were even a few plaintive phases, but ultimately a sense of being carefree and all in a rush to finish.

What doubt could she have when she heard "Stradella. Sinfonia in d minor" followed by a mixture of astonishment and appreciation, "Matteis. He's here. You didn't tell me. What a treat."

***

Donatella felt cold despite the very warm evening and bonfire that, kindled with conifer brash, eagerly blazed up through the center of its structure of precisely piled hazel, oak, alder, holly, willow, and ash logs as Roger had recommended for steady burning and tradition. By the time she was abandoned to the crowding on the terrace, the inferno was collapsing inwards to grow higher and higher. It was unapproachable by those with trailing silk and satin, flounces of lace and dangling ribbons, and anything else about their appearances to consider. A beacon to the village revelers, it illuminated their sense, superstitions, and faith as their children played too close to it. Old and young alike joined in its leaping twirling dance, their voices also crackling, fiddlers and drummers and pipers making music that had never been written down. Some carried cressets lit from the fire and ran close to the ladies and gentlemen on the terrace to terrify or tempt them. A few of the visiting musicians were more adventurous than intimidated or offended, including John Abell who had already discovered Cargill's hypocrisy and drinking prowess.

Mama caressed a sweaty strand of hair off Donatella's forehead, which led them to speak of the heat and the appeal of getting out of their dresses and corsets.

It was too late. Roger and Masters Purcell and Matteis found them before they could devise—or were certain they wanted to—a plan of escape.

"Ah, this is the *signora* I made swoon." Matteis lifted the fingertips of Mama's right hand to slide his lips across them. She wasn't tempted to let him know his mistake.

So Master Purcell did. "No, Nicola. Here's your victim. But it wasn't your fault. I think she's inclined to look for ghosts." Purcell's teasing did not lessen Donatella's awkwardness when the extravagantly dressed Matteis laughed and kissed her hand more formally than he had her mother's.

"Stradella haunts all who play him for he cannot leave us to improvise too much." If anything, Matteis was a taller and larger-bodied shadow of Alessandro with his long darkly defined face and an air that was querulous and yet very agreeable.

"Well, I don't blame her either," Roger finally spoke, standing as close to Donatella as he dared without letting anything but his words defend her, "for when the raptures came anyone might've thought it impossible a mere mortal could've created such music or be performing it."

"And so I've done Stradella justice. But does that mean he'll now be content in his grave? I suspect that is up to others." Matteis stepped back, bowed to Donatella, took her mother's hand again and let it slip away, but couldn't disappear into the crowd because he loomed above it.

"Seems the rabble is having more fun than the rest of us." Master Purcell folded his arms.

He must have noticed Jacques Plaisable, George Coleman, and Matteo Battaglia with John Abell down by the bonfire. Even Leonora had succumbed to her husband's entreaty—or her own sense of adventure—and joined them.

"Shall we?" Roger couldn't have surprised Donatella more if he had kissed her again in view of so many.

She turned to her mother who didn't notice because Cargill was coming up the hill.

"But ... my gown." Donatella wouldn't, however, refuse the admiration in Roger's eyes.

"Yes." Roger accepted too easily. "It is rather fine and cumbersome."

Donatella felt someone gathering up the back of her skirt and was a little hostile until she saw it was Lady Celia.

"Just twist the train to the side and tuck it around your arm. And don't get too near the fire." Lady Celia helped Donatella achieve an effect that encouraged Roger to be attentive, if only because he realized the instability of her shoes for walking down the sloping field.

"I'll come with you." Anne relieved his dilemma by hooking Donatella's arm and leaning against her. "What's it all about, Uncle?"

"Setting the watch on St. John's Eve," Roger explained, "in case evil spirits are among us."

"I'm sure they are." The girl laughed at her brother leaping over the red-hot perimeters of the fire as a few village boys dared him and young Francis looked on.

"Wait here," Roger insisted. "I must see to this."

"I wish to dance, don't you?" Anne wondered, still holding onto Donatella's arm so as she swayed and even jumped her captive did, too.

Donatella wiped a palm up and down her neck.

"Yes, it's awfully warm." Anne's eyes sparkled with the mischief her brother didn't hesitate to act out. "Who's that?"

Tobias had reached the boys before Roger did, brandishing a fist at them and shouting.

Roger's hand on Tobias' shoulder calmed him a little, but not for long when a great rush of air caused Anne and Donatella to cling to each other and flames to flare outwards and then upwards to a new height. There were screams as the dancing circle disassembled, shouts as musicians of all kinds and even fearless boys also scrambled to safety, and a sacred silence Nicola Matteis' booming observation broke.

"Look."

On the terrace, his entourage, mostly ladies, questioned without doubting him, "What? Where?"

"Can you not see it, that unmistakable shape?"

Certainly, Donatella acknowledged the figure in the flames, and, as few could understand or even hear her, described his back arching, shoulders soft, neck extended, head tilted, and elbow extended.

Roger was coming up the hill with young Francis and John Lely in tow. "That's the fire burning itself out."

"Perhaps." Matteis laughed like a bass singer over-breathing. "Or how a devilish musician might still amuse us."

"Your performance roused him, Nicola," Master Purcell spoke before going back inside the Abbey.

"Out. Get out," Tobias yelled and was about to put his arms into the fire, a couple of village men pulling him away from it.

"Oh, no." Lidia ran from her duties, pleading with Roger as she didn't need to.

"Of course. John help get him home. No, Francis, you stay here. In fact go inside and see if your father needs you. No, Anne. It's late. Stay with Mistress ... Donatella."

Some of the villagers were already gone, but the rest looked on as Lidia, John, and another lad who had loved her longer led Tobias away from his watch of the bonfire that, as soon as they disappeared, disintegrated into a heap of sparking embers and swirling smoke.

***

Donatella had no idea where her mother was. It was half past ten by the time carriages set out to take neighbors back to Balscott, Broughton, Banbury, and destinations not farther than an hour or so on the road. Sir Francis only needed to see them go to believe it was time to flee to his slumbers, taking his son with him. The musicians wouldn't leave until the next day, Leonora and Henrietta withdrawing with Anne upstairs, Donatella following them to change her shoes and pack up the clothes she had left in the Queen's room. Meanwhile, the men turned the Great Hall into a tavern that would eventually serve for a few hours' sleep as well.

They raised their glasses and voices to support Henry Purcell in catching Roger off guard as he greeted Donatella coming down the south stairs.

"As Roger last night to Jenny lay close
"he pulled out his Budget and gave her a dose,
"the tickling no sooner kind Jenny did find..."

One booming voice after another joined in and, when that round concluded, there was another:

"I gave her cakes and I gave her ale,
"and I gave her sack and sherry,
"I kist her once and I kist her twice
"and we were wondrous merry."

Roger made great strides to get away quicker than Donatella could struggle down the front steps in lower heels that lengthened her skirts.

She might, of course, go on without him. Little torches lined the way back to the village, the breeze since sundown cooling and bringing in the scent of rain to explain the absence of stars.

She heard her name as she longed to be missed. "There you are." She appeared to Roger as he did to her.

"It seems the stable boy has gone to bed," Roger also announced his whereabouts as she stepped into the courtyard still cluttered with construction. "I won't disturb him."

"No." She propped herself against the great stone slab of steps she had seen Lady Celia use to mount and dismount her horse.

"Where's your mother?" He came closer but stopped at arm's length.

She wouldn't say what she suspected.

"I could hitch up one of the horses."

"Let horses sleep, also." She was glad to make him smile. "I change my shoes. See." She lifted her skirt to just above her ankles.

Once more he kissed her for the first time, only his hands and lips touching her, only his hesitation tempting her, only his belief in her innocence allowing her to believe in his. A parasol pine sprinkled them with needle dust, which he carefully brushed off her hair. She did the same with his wig. Silently and separately they walked towards the new carriage and stabling house, through the central entrance, its classical gable finally completed. Roger took her hand as they walked into its dark, humid interior. She heard and even felt the questioning snorts of horses kept there for ploughing, riding, and pulling, stepping as carefully as Roger did between the two rows of stalls she knew were gated with gracefully wrought iron.

"Didn't want to spook them." He dropped her hand.

He reappeared with the sound of scraping and a flash that lit the candle he placed in a wall sconce, but not before it dripped on his hand. Bridles, halters, reins, bits, harnesses, and saddles were hung on the walls, a small bench, table, and bed also in the room she assumed was for cleaning tack and spending the night when a horse was sick or in foal.

"Boyle's phosphorous and sulphur trick." Roger put down the coarse paper and splinter of wood.

She reached out to examine them as she thought might please him.

Instead, he would have her do so in his arms, the bench almost tipping before he centered them on it, his mouth frustrating her attempt to say something better left unsaid. He untied his cravat and unbuttoned his coat.

She couldn't resist the touch of the fine warm linen beneath it.

He stood up and took it off to hang on a hook on the back of the room's door, which he closed. She looked away and when she saw him again his shirt was hanging over his breeches. She might resist his intent, but not his concern as he examined the bed's flimsy frame and lifted its slim mattress to place on the floor. After positioning and smoothing it, he seemed more grateful than she was when she needed his help to step out of her dress.

His bringing her down was awkward and even a little comical because his wig slipped. He pulled it off, his own hair not cropped as close as she had seen it before, curling rather girlishly over his forehead and ears. He realized the pearl circlet in hers was uncomfortable to lie back on and slipped it around her neck instead, fingering it and wondering if it was a family heirloom.

"You must ask Lady Celia," she whispered and wished he was someone else.

He was too principled and English, looking on her like a treasure he should have left buried, allowing her to breathe through his kisses and think too much about how he was handling her, respectful of her modesty and considerate of her consent. There weren't any tricks or urgency or pain, all she knew of love absent except as she could make it appear with her eyes closed.

They lay in the stifling, barely lit room for an hour or more. Roger slept on and off while she watched for any sign that he was sorry to take another man's secret to make his own. When he got up he busied himself through any sense of shame—evident in the lowering of his eyes and high color of his cheeks that might have been caused by the heat. He placed the mattress back on the bed, quickly tucked in his shirt and put on his wig while she dressed in her regular clothes and twisted up her hair with pins he picked off the floor.

He took down the required harness and lit the candle in a tin holder on the table from the one barely flickering on the wall. She followed him to a stall where he spoke softly to the horse he chose, promising he wouldn't keep her from her dreams for too long.

***

The fragrance of dewy pines and linden and evening stock flowers made the early morning ride almost pleasant. So did sitting necessarily close to Roger on the makeshift box seat of the tipsy two-wheeled conveyance he made sure was balanced in the back with a couple of lumpy sacks. Her beautiful gown was wrapped in his elegant jacket, a tarpaulin covering all the cargo. She thought the bonfire was the cause of a slight smell of burning, but then they neared the estate gates where the odor became stronger and the sky to the south brightened even though it was beginning to drizzle. Roger's hope of discreetly taking her home was dashed even before they were seen, raised voices alerting them to some trouble. He supposed it was the result of too much drinking before he saw hastily-dressed women and even girls with leather buckets and satchels, wooden bowls, and stone jugs they plunged into the pond and handed over to a sober team of men and boys who ran up the village's darkest lane with them.

"Hey. Look. Stop."

The horse obeyed sooner than Roger did.

Donatella inhaled and Roger squeezed her hand to guide her down.

"Anyone hurt?"

"Don't know. Looks like that crazy Tobias set it on purpose."

***

Donatella looked in every room, but her mother wasn't there. Feeling lightheaded, she changed into her boots and put on a cloak before rushing back to the pond, an unknown man driving the cart as it returned. There was a continued if slowing effort to fill the containers as they were returned, Donatella not walking as fast as she could to discover why someone shouted that the devil had won.

It seemed very possible she was on the road to hell. She didn't know how she could identify the smell of burning flesh, but it was undoubtedly ahead of her, mingled with a slightly sweet scent that reminded her of dried lavender and another with a hint of bitterness like overcooked spinach or turnip greens. At the last narrowing curve, the heat was more intense than a mid-summer's night could account for, soon enough explained by the sizzling wreckage of a cottage.

Lidia, parts of her clothes blackened, was holding up Mama looking uselessly lovely in limp silk and chiffon.

There was a body on the ground John Lely and Roger were trying to shield them from, but Donatella saw it was Cargill, his hair and eyebrows gone, his jacket melted, his right hand bloodied, and his left foot bootless.

"He went in, then Lidia. The lad," John pointed out the tall handsome boy who only cared that Lidia saw him as a hero, "got her out."

Roger pulled up Donatella's hood, the rain steadier than his hand.

***

Donatella remembered Martha's suggestion of Valerian root seeped in hot water for at least ten minutes to calm Mama and ease her cough. She expected Lidia to be too distraught to take care of it, but the girl dazedly insisted, and, while the drink brewed, even fed Caprice and Bianchi the chicken livers she found in the pantry that were probably meant for a pie. Donatella also brought her mother a cold sage and rosemary sausage left over from breakfast the day before.

Mama refused to eat or drink. Her soft crying curled her sideways into sleep and persuaded her daughter to care for her again.

Tired as she was, Donatella only went to her own room to hang up the gown saved from ruin by Roger's jacket that suffered some damage, but, knowing his resourcefulness, not irreparably. Before she closed the wardrobe she put the few sheets of her song in with the many more pages of Alessandro's music than she had brought from Genoa. She felt enveloped by them, forever in their possession.

A little while later she noticed another day had begun. It was a dreary one as long as the rain continued and Martha couldn't stop talking about what had happened, but brightened a little when spritely Caprice beat Bianchi's hobbling down the stairs, Lidia took a basket out into the garden, and Roger bowed through the hedged gateway, swatting at midges.

Donatella opened the front door just as he reached it. He was sweaty and dirty, his chin bristled, his wig held under his arm, his eyes wide and red with exhaustion.

"They found the old chap, what was left of him." He knew he had told her too much. "I have to get back to Harry and the others, although I doubt they're awake yet. Francis won't want to deal with them."

Roger smiled when he saw the coat laid across her arms, his hand slipping under it to touch her hip and keep her wondering. He tried to stop her cats escaping for he couldn't know, until she told him, that they wouldn't wander far.

His shoulders expressed his relief, his soothing voice that he would call on her again soon.

She didn't watch him walk away. Not only had the rain stopped and the clouds lifted and lightened into angel shapes, but the sun composed her outlook as birds took their music to the sky.

Donatella's Song
A Petrarchan Sonnet—English Translation

The Secret
Why is there little to say of a time
when courtesy cost me your devotion?
So much of my life, so much detention,
modesty in love the cause of my crime.
Yet, I was nearly foolish in my prime,
but saved for your Orphean persuasion
and, alas, the chance of imitation
that would only make your memory mine.

To speak of the heart's secrets is to give
away their endurance, and so concede
they might be fabricated out of need
more than truth. No, it's better that they live
on covertly in poetical creed,
kept as constantly joyful as plaintive.

Wroxton, England, June 1683

Historical Perspectives
Of To A Strange Somewhere Fled

"(The) history of private men's lives (is) more profitable than state history."

~ Roger North, from his *General Preface & Life of Dr. John North*

Roger North (Sept. 3, 1651–March 1, 1734) and **Sir Francis North** (October 22, 1637–September 5, 1685):

I didn't have to imagine a male protagonist for the sequel to *A House Near Luccoli* to contrast the temperament and lifestyle of the charismatic and roguish composer, Alessandro Stradella. English biographer and lawyer Roger North well suited that role, especially as Donatella landed on his doorstep.

Rather timid, even unsociable, Honorable was Roger's title and the core of his character. He lived slowly, carefully, with a firm sense of belonging to his family, country, and the reaches of his intellect and interests—"practical diversions" that included writing, philosophy, architecture, mathematics, horticulture, sailing, and music.

Roger was born at Tostock, Suffock, the sixth son of the Fourth Baron Dudley North and Anne Montagu. Despite a fifteen year age difference he was very attached to his eldest brother, Francis (great-grandfather to Lord North, Prime Minister of Great Britain during most of the American Revolution), and benefited from Francis' professional and personal connections that took them both to the heights of Charles II's court. In 1682 Sir Francis was appointed Lord Keeper of the Great Seal and Roger began his service as King's Counsel. Although staunch royalists, neither was comfortable with the cutthroat political environment of Restoration England.

Thanks to Sir Francis' marriage to Frances Pope, who died in 1678, Wroxton Abbey became his and Roger's retreat from London. The Popes had been leaseholders of the Abbey since the middle of the 16th century, transforming it into the Jacobean manor house still evident in its present structure. Sir Francis bought out his sister-in-laws' inheritance and his descendants continued their tenancy of the Abbey well into the twentieth century.

"As to musick," Roger and Francis carried on the North tradition of pursuing its appreciation, study, and performance for familial and social pleasure, and solitary distraction. Their grandfather had traveled in Italy and took a great liking to the music he found there. Roger received instruction from the English composer, John Jenkins, and possibly other masters including the spirited Italian violinist, Nicola Matteis. It is likely that Roger played the viol, theorbo, harpsichord, organ, and even the violin. He observed and participated in the musical scene of London, his thoughts on theory and performance leading him to eventually publish *The Musicall Grammarian* (1728). *The Seventeenth Century* volume of *Blackwell's History of Music in Britain* references Roger at least twenty-eight times.

Roger penned biographies of his brothers, a wandering autobiography titled *Notes of Me*, and even a *Discourse on Fish and Fish Ponds*, continually and painstakingly recording his reflections and findings on countless subjects. He was one of the executors of the estate of the famous portraitist Peter Lely, and guardian to the painter's son, John, and daughter, Anne. His architectural talents came into play with improvements made to the north wing of the Abbey and the addition of a coach house and stabling, and he also managed extensive tree planting on the estate. Beyond the scope of *To A Strange Somewhere Fled*, the untimely passing of Sir Francis in 1685 was an oppressive blow to Roger personally, but also professionally, for he had lost a true companion and ally at Court. After Sir Francis' death, he spent a little more time at Wroxton with his brother Dudley and, while winding up Sir Francis' affairs, they found some distraction in setting up a laboratory and forge there. Charles II died the same year as Sir Francis, and the next Roger was appointed Attorney-General to Queen Mary of Modena, but by 1687 he had turned his back on Royal and Parliamentary conflicts and uncertainties and devoted himself to writing and the improvement and self-sufficiency of the estate he had purchased at Rougham in Norfolk.

Roger attained a good fortune when at the age of forty-three he married the daughter of Sir Robert Gayer. His wife, Mary, received little mention in any of his writings or surviving correspondences. Evidently, she put up with the "plaine" living at Rougham and was otherwise dutiful, as their union produced seven children.

Roger was a quieter, plainer, more cautious, modest, and moralistic figure than Alessandro Stradella, but no less singular, creative, or complex, which made him as interesting to write about. He exhibited a similar if less reckless compulsion to engage himself in the possibilities of the gifts he had been given and to scoff —less openly and, as it turned out, less perilously than Stradella—at a society that expected him to behave as if he was compliant with it.

Henry Purcell (10 September 1659–21 November 1695)
It was during my research for *A House Near Luccoli* that I came upon

the claim, noted in the introduction to *Purcell Studies* edited by Curtis Price, that Henry Purcell had openly regretted Alessandro Stradella's death and, because of the Italian's "great merit as a musician," forgiven his fatal indiscretions. True or not, it stirred me to somehow bring the celebrated English composer into Donatella's continuing story, and, on reading Roger North's assertion that the high point of his musical experience was entertaining the 'divine' Purcell, I was even more inspired to do so.

Henry Purcell was as obscure a figure as Stradella in terms of how little about his personal life was recorded. Despite his legacy of being a uniquely English composer, he enjoyed and sometimes emulated the Italian style. He met his end at a younger age than Stradella and in a way that left as much conjecture as to why. Was it chocolate poisoning, the result of pneumonia brought on by being locked out of his house by his wife after a night of drinking, or 'just' tuberculosis?

He came from a very musical family. His father, who died when Henry was a small child, and his uncle, who became his guardian, were members of the Chapel Royal. His brother Daniel was also a composer. Henry had been a child chorister; his earliest known work was probably completed when he was ten or eleven.

The English maestro enters the pages of *To A Strange Somewhere Fled* at age twenty-four, already appreciated for his celebratory, church, theatrical, instrumental, and incidental music, and overcoming the constraints of the English language to write songs that perfectly complemented the poetry they were inspired by. In 1683 he was an organist for Westminster Abbey and the Chapel Royal, and about to publish his first collection and be appointed royal instrument keeper.

He was a man of sorrows as well as joy—of six children born to him and his wife, only two survived to adulthood—his copious creations defining him as the scarce accounts of his life never could. I found him fascinating as much because of his mystery as mastery.

Celia Fiennes (June 7, 1662–April 10, 1741)

Never to marry, this daughter of an English Civil War Parliamentarian and granddaughter of 'Old Subtlety', the 8th Baron and 1st Viscount Saye and Sele, Celia was unlike most young ladies of her time and situation. In her twenties, she began her horseback journeys around England when it was mostly wilderness, doing so, she claimed, to improve her health. She continued her adventures for many years, visiting every county, on the road with only one or two servants, keeping a diary, published as *Through England on a Side Saddle*, to note places, people, great houses and gardens, drains and quarries, innovations and annoyances. No one studying England in the 17th century can be sorry she exhibited such resilience and daring and left such a vivacious account of what she encountered. Although native to Wiltshire and living mostly in London, in the course of her travels it seemed natural that Celia would stop at her grandfather's old haunts to visit the relations she had at Broughton Castle as well as friends in the surrounding area, such as nearby Wroxton Abbey, describing its alterations as "all in the new fashion way."

It's not proven but often assumed that she is represented by the 'Fine Lady on a White Horse' in the famous nursery rhyme, *Ride a-Cock Horse to Banbury Cross*, the medieval market town of Banbury being near Broughton and Wroxton.

I find it impossible to resist noting that present day actors Ralph and Joseph Fiennes' family line is linked to Celia's.

The Italians

After the restoration of the British monarchy in 1660, Italian composers and performers arrived in England to find a welcome and work, some in the court of Charles II where lively, lavish, and constantly evolving entertainment was encouraged, while others visited for brief or extended periods or settled into being employed in or outside of London in churches and theaters and for private concerts.

Carlo Ambrogio Lonati (c.1645–c.1712)

Il Gobbo della Regina, the hunchback composer, violinist, and singer who initially made an appearance in *A House Near Luccoli* was probably born in Milan but little is known of his early life. Lonati first made friends, music, and trouble with Alessandro Stradella while both were in Rome under the patronage of Queen Christina of Sweden, and went to Genoa ahead of Stradella where he also preceded him as impresario of the Falconi Theater.

There is evidence that Lonati was in London—seen with a famous female singer—sometime between 1686 and 1688. Ordered out of Genoa after Stradella's murder in February, 1682, and with gaps in his activities and whereabouts for some time afterwards, it's conceivable he traveled to England before the visit made notable because of the company he kept. His abrupt intrusion on Donatella's new life was, in the course of writing *To A Strange Somewhere Fled,* as much of a surprise to me as it was to her.

Pietro Reggio (1632–1685)

There is much mystery surrounding the life of the "slovenly and ugly," to quote diarist Samuel Pepys, composer, lutenist, and singer, Pietro Reggio, who was probably from Genoa, as he was referred to as Pietro Reggio *Genovese*. He was employed in Stockholm by Queen

Christina before her abdication and subsequent move to Rome where Stradella and Lonati encountered her. Eventually, Pietro traveled to France, and, if the inscription on his tombstone is accurate, to Spain and Germany. He had moved to England by 1664, where Pepys and another writer, John Evelyn, were entertained in very different ways by him. Whereas Pepys wasn't overly impressed by "Seignor Pedro" who played the theorbo and sang Italian songs, Evelyn included Reggio's singing in his description of the "rare music" he enjoyed after dinner one evening.

Reggio made his living in London for a time, performing and teaching, and also had associations in Oxford where he may have resided. His claim to fame is a collection of songs he published in 1680, mostly based on the verse of Abraham Cowley (1618 -1667) who was among the leading metaphysical poets of the 17th century.

Nicola Matteis (?–after 1714)

Roger North couldn't hold back his high opinion of Matteis' virtuosity, grace, and genuineness as a violinist, awe at the Neapolitan's imposing physical presence, or regret that such an admirable musician went from refusing to perform in public to being drawn to the need for wealth and recognition that, as Roger saw it, sent him into decadence and disease, and, ultimately, proved his downfall.

Nicola arrived in England after 1670, apparently not interested in royal service or public appearances, because, as Roger North also indicated, he might have to perform with amateurs. Despite his resistance, his popularity grew in the 1670s and 1680s. He is given credit for having changed the manner of violin playing from the French to Italian style, publishing *Ayres for the Violin* that provided detailed bowing instructions and directions for tempo and ornamentation. Still, his compositions were difficult and many were discouraged in their efforts to play them. John Evelyn was among those who praised Matteis' vigorous style that made his performances so memorable.

Various Italian, English, Scottish and French Musicians

Bartholomeo Albrici (1634–?), a composer native to the seaport of Senigallia in the province of Ancona in central Italy, taught and played the harpsichord. He spent time in Sweden with his brother Vincenzo in service to Queen Christina, and traveled with him and their singer sister **Leonora** (1640's–1700?) to London in 1662 where they all were involved in the King's Musick. Leonora was married to **Matthew Battaglia** (1640–1687), a musician to the Duke of York, later James II. **Giovanni Battista Draghi** (ca. 1640–1708) was an Anglo-Italian composer and organist invited to London by Charles II to help establish an opera house. That project was unsuccessful, but Draghi, nicknamed "Drago", found other ways to contribute to the music of the court and remained in England for the rest of his life.

Besides Henry Purcell, other English musicians make themselves known in *To A Strange Somewhere Fled*, including **Henry Aldrich**, church musician, Canon of Christ Church and eventually Vice-Chancellor of Oxford University; **Henrietta Bannister**, wife of John Bannister "the elder" and music tutor to Princess Anne, daughter of James II; **Robert Carr**, viol player; **Charles Coleman** "the younger", possibly a lutenist and theorbist; **Thomas Eccles**, a violinist who was said to have played in taverns; **Thomas Farmer**, violinist at the Duke's theater in London and in service to Charles II and James II; **William Gregory** "the younger", lyra viol player, composer and member of the King's Musick and the Chapel Royal; **William Husbands**, organist at Christ Church, Oxford; and **William Turner**, composer and singer who served at Lincoln and St. Paul's Cathedrals, the Chapel Royal and with the King's Private Musick.

Also helping to add a flourish to the midsummer concert in *To A Strange Somewhere Fled* were Scottish composer and singer **John Abell**, Gentleman of the Chapel Royal, whose English songs showed Italian influence; and French composer and recorder player **Jacques Plaisable**, or "Pleasable" as he was mockingly referred to, who performed at the Drury Lane Theater and married actress and singer Mary "Moll" Davis after she was dismissed as Charles II's mistress—with a lavish pension and house as a parting gift—when the nubile Nell Gwyn came on the scene.

The Setting

I hardly expected my 17th century Genoese journey through the writing of *A House Near Luccoli* to direct me back to Oxfordshire, England, where I lived from 1974 to 1990. Then I began to consider a sequel that would require a destination for Donatella beyond Genoa. Her flight from grief returned me to a first view of "Wroces Stan"—old English meaning buzzards' stone— a village mentioned in the Doomsday book grown out of ancient crossroads, valley slopes, ochre stone, straw thatch, Augustinian principles, and aristocratic privilege. It was a place small enough to comfort and stately enough to unsettle, reclusive and inviting, its character formed as much by its lower as upper class—as is seen in the character of demon-obsessed Tobias, who is based on a real village resident I had known— a world as wild as it was well-designed, its seasons defined by flowers, fungi, berries, and trees, ever increasing clouds, fog and frost, rain and more rain so sunny banks and deep shadows were always noticed.

Wroxton Abbey, situated in a secluded parkland to the southeast of the village, was documented as a manor in the 11th century. One hundred and twenty-eight years later, a tenant, Guy de Reinbeudcurt, founded an Augustinian priory there. Due to the dissolution of the monasteries under Henry VIII, much of it was destroyed. What was left of its buildings and demesne was leased to the treasurer of Henry's Court of Augmentations, responsible for the dissolved monasteries, Sir Thomas Pope, who was the founder of Trinity College, Oxford. In 1551, Sir Thomas granted his brother, John, a ninety-nine year tenancy, and in 1556 endowed the manor and lands to Trinity College that subsequently renewed the lease for John's heirs. Construction on the manor surviving as the central portion of its present structure was begun around the turn of the 17th century by John Pope's son, William, the 3rd Earl of Downe. A lack of male descendants eventually passed the leasehold to the 3rd Earl's daughters, and one of them, Frances, married Sir Francis North, the lawyer involved with the settlement of the Pope estate. Sir Francis was succeeded as 2nd baron by his son Francis; his great-grandson Frederick, the most famous North, 2nd Earl of Guilford, titled Lord, and serving as Prime Minister to George III, made extensive alterations to the grounds and some to the house. A library and chapel were most likely added by the famous architect and landscape designer Sanderson Miller in the mid-18th century, but a shortage of funds limited further enhancements. The current interior decoration and windows owe much to Prime Minister North's granddaughter Baroness Susan, who also oversaw the completion of a south wing that finally gave the house symmetry as viewed from its west-facing front and fulfilled the North family motto: *Animo et Fide Perage.* Carry through to completion in courage and faith.

Baroness Susan's Irish husband took her surname, and their son, William, managed the estate until his death in 1932 at the age of ninety-six, marking the end of over two hundred and fifty years of the Norths' occupancy. All the family's effects were sold off and the Abbey was turned into a warehouse during WWII. In 1948, Trinity College of Oxford leased it to Lady Pearson, who rented out large portions, which caused extensive damage. Farleigh Dickinson University of New Jersey purchased it in 1963 and undertook an enormous effort to repair and modernize the building as well as restore and enhance the gardens and pleasure grounds, creating the splendid campus celebrating its fifty year anniversary in 2015.

I was a junior in college, accepted into the program at Wroxton College to study English history, literature, and theater, when my life-changing connection to Wroxton Abbey and village was initiated. A three-month semester spanning the last chilly damp weeks of an Oxfordshire winter and the muddy beginnings and eventual warming and burgeoning of its spring turned into sixteen simple and complicated years of my calling Wroxton home.

As I began writing *To A Strange Somewhere Fled*, what I thought would come out of my memories and feared would be limited by my experience and prejudice slowly emerged from a more informed and imaginative perspective, a past long before mine that not only furthered Donatella's exploration into life and love, but made me more understanding and appreciative of the unique opportunity I'd had once and then again: to linger and live in Wroxton and even the Abbey itself, and make a little private history of my own there.

About the Author

 Writer and artist D.M. (Diane) Denton, a native of Western New York, is inspired by music, art, nature, and the contradictions of the human and creative spirit. Through observation and study, truth and imagination, she loves to wander into the past to discover stories of interest and meaning for the present, writing from her love of language, the nuances of story-telling, and the belief that what is left unsaid is the most affecting of all.

Her educational journey took her to a dream-fulfilling semester at Wroxton College, England, and she remained in the UK for sixteen years surrounded by the quaint villages, beautiful hills, woods and fields of the Oxfordshire countryside, and all kinds of colorful characters. This turned out to be a life-changing experience that continues to resonate in her life to this day.

She returned to the US and Western New York in 1990, and has since resided in a cozy log cabin with her mother and a multitude of cats. Her day jobs have been in retail, manufacturing, media and career consulting, and as a volunteer coordinator for Western New York Public Broadcasting. She is currently secretary for the Zoning and Codes administration in the town where she lives. In addition to writing, music and art, she is passionate about nurturing nature and a consciousness for a more compassionate, inclusive and peaceful world.

Please visit her website, http://www.dmdenton-author-artist.com, and blog, https://bardessdmdenton.wordpress.com where you can contact her. Also, find her on Facebook, Twitter, Goodreads, LinkedIn, Pinterest and Google Plus.